To Pat:
Enjoy!

Somewhere in Between

Suzanne Glidewell

ISBN: 978-1-54395-578-1 (print)
ISBN: 978-1-54395-579-8 (ebook)

ACKNOWLEDGEMENTS

Thank you to Ben for his unending love and encouragement. Thank you to Jim Mains for over ten years of friendship, collaboration, and just plain knowing how to make things happen. Thank you to Erica Jolly for being a brilliant and excellent editor.

THOMAS

I WASN'T SURPRISED IT WAS RAINING. AFTER ALL, THIS was Seattle. I gazed out the window of my childhood bedroom watching the pattern of the raindrops fall onto the sidewalk that grey January morning. It was a soft rain, nothing substantial, but enough to prevent anyone from hoping the sun would come out. Appropriate weather for my father's funeral.

The closet was empty except for the one suit I had packed; I hadn't worn it since my sister's rehearsal dinner four years earlier. After getting dressed, I turned toward the mirror on the wall.

Staring at the reflection, I wondered was this how I was supposed to look? Did I fit the part of someone whose father had just died? Unshaven, I ran my hands through my dark, scruffy stubble. It seemed appropriate. Not only did I fit the role of a son whose father had just died, I was also the Prodigal son returning from his misguided attempt to live amongst the creative snobs of New York. I looked broken, and what better way to pay homage to the dad who had never supported my dreams in the first place? He won. Here I was again, now sentenced to work at the family business. Reluctantly, I headed downstairs.

My older brother and sister had already arrived with their own families crowding the kitchen and living room. There were five grandchildren running around and my older sister, Margaret, was holding the sixth and youngest one. I went over to hug her.

"Hey, Tommy," she said softly, embracing me. Her eyes were bloodshot. Grief had overcome her since our father's heart attack six days ago. She'd lost the man who had always considered her a princess.

"You didn't shave?" My brother's voice cut through the quiet moment. The note of disapproval in his voice was clear, but I had come to expect that from Michael. It had been a constant in my life since I was fifteen. That was the same year I'd surpassed him in height, despite being five years younger. I took after our mother's Italian side, while Michael got all my dad's stout Irish genes. His temperament, too.

"Will you leave him alone, Michael?" snapped Margaret. "He's in a suit. He's here. That's all that matters." Since childhood, Margaret had been my protector. Her unconditional regard for me was one of the few things I liked about my family. Margaret saw the best in everyone, no matter what. Her tone and facial expression were enough to silence Michael.

"Where's mom?" I asked, changing the subject while I turned to pour myself a cup of coffee.

"She's upstairs. She's changed her outfit three times," Margaret responded, concerned.

"She probably doesn't want to come down to everybody running around," said Michael, before turning to scowl at to his oldest child. "Jesus! Hunter! I told you to turn that damn thing off!"

Hunter, who was playing with some annoying electronic toy, froze and his face began to break. He ran towards his mother, Colleen, who scooped him up and consoled him while walking out of the room.

"It's surprising she hasn't come down, seeing as how you're so cuddly this morning," I commented, taking my first drink of coffee. As expected, this drew a cold stare from Michael.

"Margaret," he said, ignoring me, "just go and get her. I don't want to be late." He turned his back to me, joining Colleen and his four children in the living room.

2

"Tommy, please," Margaret turned to me, "just try to get along with him today."

"Me? I'm the disagreeable one?" I said, knowing she would take my side.

"No, but you're the more easy-going one. Here," Margaret handed me her seven-month-old daughter and headed upstairs to find my mother. I tried my best not to look awkward while I held my niece, who I'd met only four days earlier. Thankfully, my brother-in-law Chris came over to take the baby when she started to fuss, communicating the uneasiness we both felt in the situation.

I've always been the black sheep of my family. Traditionally this title goes to the middle child. However, with Margaret being the people pleaser that she was, the role was deflected to me. Michael embodied everything my parents – particularly my father – ever wanted in a son.

He thrived on order and responsibility, embracing our family's Catholic faith; he even joined Knights of Columbus at eighteen, the youngest age possible. Perhaps more importantly, before he could even talk, everyone could already tell that Michael loved cars. Since our family had owned O'Hollaren Auto for sixty years, this only further endeared him to my father. Michael had started working there at fifteen. Now he ran the place.

I, on the other hand, never wanted anything to do with cars. I preferred drawing and painting to everything else. That did not stop my father from insisting that I learn the business and skill of auto mechanics as a teenager. Admittedly, it was a handy tool to have in high school and college. Earning extra money by working at the shop allowed me to pay my way through college and eventually move to New York. That was the one thing I could appreciate about my father now that he was gone.

The second strike against me was that I never took to Catholicism. I routinely took bathroom breaks to get out of mass. In my first confession at age seven, I denied I had anything to confess, and by the time I was teenager I refused mass altogether. This was my worst offense in my mother's eyes, even in adulthood. She had pointedly reminded me of this shortcoming when she instructed me within three hours of arriving back in Seattle that I was not to receive communion at the funeral because I was obviously not in "a state of grace." She was sure to include the invitation to go to confession prior to the funeral to correct this matter, and had even offered to drive. I didn't make it, though. No surprise there. Luckily, my mother had enough going on to distract her from worrying too much about it.

Despite her misgivings about my lack of religion, or any spirituality for that matter, my mother deserves credit for not discouraging me from pursuing my love of art. That brings us to my third and final strike. While my mom always seemed to enjoy my drawings and even bought me my first set of professional paints in sixth grade, my father was completely ill prepared for having an artist – a sissy – for a son.

My father, like a true Irishman, preferred to pretend the problem didn't exist instead of trying to deal with it at all. He hoped he could just change me in my sophomore year of high school, when he forced me into an apprenticeship at the shop. But, yet again, I disappointed him when he discovered I'd taken a large box of spark plugs and a quart of oil to use for one of my paintings. It was from that point on that our conversations were limited to basic greetings and the occasional parental instructions, always given when my mom was not around to act as a mediator.

By merely being myself, I caused a rift in my parents otherwise perfect marriage. I overheard many of their late-night arguments, my mother pleading with my father to make an effort to understand me, my father countering that she babied me and was doing me a disservice by not demanding I be manlier. My father truly believed it was frivolous to spend time and waste money making art when I had an obvious opportunity to engage in a real profession, like being a mechanic. My mom would always use Michelangelo painting the Sistine Chapel as her defense. My father would argue I was not and never would be as good or as important as Michelangelo, no matter how much my misguided mother supported my efforts. To him it was most important that I find a skill that could ultimately lead to supporting a wife and kids. And canvases, no matter how pretty, were not a way to pay the bills. As much as I hated to admit it, I couldn't argue with him on that point when I considered the current state of my bank account. My mother had to pay for my plane ticket home.

When I'd finally decided to move to New York three and a half years ago, my mother had acted like I'd broken her heart. But I think there was a relief that I – the catalyst of tension between her and my father – would no longer be around.

That hadn't kept her from delivering ceaseless guilt trips over the years. She once said that she didn't know if she would recognize me if she ever saw me again. Perhaps that was the silver lining she found in my father's death. It brought me back home to her. Regardless of my lifelong disinterest in the family business, my father had left me half ownership of the shop. He had always been a fair, traditional man, so it wasn't too surprising that he would leave the business to both of his sons. Part of me wondered if it was just a scheme – his final attempt to force me into embracing our family's trade. My brother would move into the head manager position while I filled in the open mechanic position. God forbid he hire someone who actually wanted to work in an auto shop, but I guess financial stability isn't the worst thing he could have left his son, the struggling sissy artist.

So there I was, sitting in Blessed Sacrament, a church I had not been to since my sister's wedding four years earlier. I would never have predicted that the next time I'd be sitting in that drafty, ominous chapel would be for my father's funeral. But there really would have been no other reason. I sat through the funeral mass, going through the motions I had committed to memory like any cradle Catholic. I tried my best to comfort my mother, my brother was already comforting his wife, and my sister was burying her face in her husband's arms.

I tried to find comfort in the priest's words, but they didn't take. Oddly, going through the motions helped a bit. It gave me something to do, something to focus on. Acting like a son who was consoled by the ceremony and tradition, rather than the reality of it all; a son who didn't know if he would really miss his father all that much and felt intensely guilty for acknowledging that. I couldn't wait for the ceremony to end. If I was going to mourn at all over the man, I preferred to do it in private.

Throughout the service, I could feel everyone's eyes on me. There was immense pressure to live up to the expectations of how I was supposed to act. I found myself holding out hope that God – or whatever higher power – may be at work that day. Despite my best efforts to be reverent and open, the content of service left me with little comfort. I hoped the rest of my family had had a different experience.

As I took my place as a pallbearer alongside Michael and two of my cousins, I stared ahead stoically, hoping, even possibly praying, that I wouldn't screw up. I avoided eye contact with my mother, because I knew seeing the look in her eyes as she watched the love of her life be carried away for good would finally cause me to break down. I had misgivings about my relationship with my father, but I never questioned the love and devotion he and my mother had for one another. Theirs was one of those old school, traditional relationships my generation romanticized.

Even though I was avoiding eye contact with everyone, a young woman with wavy sandy hair wearing a black pea coat caught my attention. I thought she would look away, since most people were staring down at the ground, lost in their own emotions. Instead she locked her bright blue eyes with mine, exchanging a look of understanding and compassion that I wouldn't expected from a stranger.

After setting the casket into the hearse, I moved toward the bottom of the stairs outside the church, where the church coordinator had ordered the immediate family to stand. My thoughts wandered to the woman who had just locked eyes with me. Aside from myself, she may have been the youngest adult there. I kept my attention on the entryway of the church, waiting for her to come out.

Finally, I saw her step outside, talking with an older couple I didn't know. Then they left and another middle-aged couple approached her. She seemed to know way more people than I did at my own father's funeral.

"Who is that?" I leaned over and asked Margaret, between receiving condolences. Beyond general attraction, I also felt some sense that I knew her from my past.

"That's Maura McCormick," she whispered to me. "Her parents have known Mom and Daddy for years. Don't you remember? She was in your Confirmation class."

I tried to remember her and couldn't stop staring while I greeted people who'd come to pay respects to my father. She had a memorable demeanor, a girl next door quality – she wasn't overly made up, but still attractive with her petite frame and large blue eyes. But I had no memory of her. Most likely because I was never very involved in church and ultimately didn't follow through with receiving the sacrament of Confirmation, much to my mother and father's dismay. Of course, I'd been high during the few prep classes I had attended, so most of the experience was a blur. As I stood there in that moment, I was disappointed that I hadn't made a point to get to know her back then. Something about her made me think she would understand what I was going through.

MAURA

I PROBABLY SHOULDN'T HAVE STARED AT HIM AS LONG as I did. Thomas O'Hollaren probably didn't remember me from our teen years, and no doubt having a stranger stare you down at your father's funeral would creep a person out. It's just that he looked unbelievably sad and lost when I looked into his hazel eyes. It took just about everything I had to stay in that pew and not run over to hug him. Once again, probably an unwanted gesture from a stranger, but being a bleeding heart social worker, this was not the first time I'd felt compelled to break social norms and hug someone I didn't know. Luckily for Thomas and everyone else there, I've learned to control this urge over the years.

I found my way out of the church and greeted my parents' friends Bill and Judy Buckley with a smile.

"We didn't expect to see you here," Judy smiled back, holding Bill's arm.

"My parents weren't able to make it because they're in Olympia looking in on my grandma, so my mom asked that I come," I replied.

"Oh, I hope nothing's wrong," Judy said, her tone switching to concern.

"No – I mean, well, Grandma's eighty-six, so you know, just your usual stuff with getting older," I dove in. "She had knee surgery, so they just want to make sure everything is fine. She's in a great retirement community. I think she may even have a boyfriend."

I paused, realizing that in my babbling I'd given the Buckleys more information than they'd probably wanted. An urge which, unlike random hugging, I unfortunately had not learned to control over the years.

"It was a lovely service," I said, backtracking.

"Yes, yes it was," Bill agreed. "It's just a shame how suddenly it happened."

I nodded with a concerned face.

"Have you had a chance to talk to Mrs. O'Hollaren?" I asked. "When my mom talked to her, she said she was so focused on planning the service that she really hadn't had time to grieve. We wondered how she would be doing after there wasn't anything left to plan."

Judy nodded. "The Altar Society has arranged a meal delivery schedule already. Annabelle Proctor is going to invite her to join the widow's group after a little time has passed. And I'm sure between your mother and me, we'll keep her busy. Plus, she has all those grandchildren, thank God. And did you see that Thomas finally came home?"

I nodded, knowing now that Judy Buckley had started talking, I would get very little opportunity to speak.

"Thank the Lord," she went on. "I know how much she has prayed over that. He's going to be living with her, which I think will help a lot. She also said he's going to be working at the shop with Michael. Maybe this is the way it was supposed to happen all along. I mean, it's definitely unfortunate, and so sad that David had to die, but I know it's such a comfort to Jackie to have all her children back home. Who knows? Maybe Michael will be a good influence on Thomas and he'll finally settle down."

Judy cast me a knowing smile. Her hint was not lost on me. I was twenty-five, and whenever any single, young, male came on the radar of my mother and her friends, they felt the need to point out his eligibility. I decided to ignore the hint, given that it seemed inappropriate for Judy to play matchmaker with David O'Hollaren's grieving son at his funeral.

"Mrs. O'Holleran is lucky to have caring friends like you guys," I said, smiling. "I'll be sure to let my mom know that people are holding down the fort right now."

The Buckleys nodded and made their way down the stairs. I said a quick hello to the Connors, another set of my parents' friends, before heading down the stairs to see the O'Hollaren family. My mother expected me to send my apologies for her absence.

Even though I felt like I should have left Jackie alone, I waited my turn in the small line that had formed. I could tell she had been crying earlier, but she'd pulled herself together to receive condolences. She had a nice flush on her face without any mascara marks.

That's impressive. At least she's not an ugly crier, I thought. Then I reprimanded myself. *Way to be superficial, Maura. The woman is in mourning!*

Jackie immediately enveloped me in a hug when I came to the front of the line, thankfully saving me from my internal lecture.

"Oh Maura, thank you so much for coming," she said, radiating genuine warmth.

I nodded, thinking she didn't need to thank me, given her current life situation.

"My mom wanted to apologize for not being able to make it," I told her. "I was supposed to give you a hug from her and a reminder to eat, or drink wine. Whichever is easier."

Jackie smiled and I was proud of myself for being able to break her sorrow if only for a moment.

"Of course, I know. Your mother called me and told me about your grandma. I hope she's doing all right," Jackie said. "Will you be joining us at the wake? It's at the house. The church wasn't going to allow alcohol and I just knew that would've disappointed David."

I felt touched that she was being so familiar with me despite her troubles.

"No, unfortunately, I can't, I just came on my lunch break and have to head back to work," I told her.

"Of course, the youth shelter," she said, grabbing my hand and patting the back of it. "Your mom is so proud of you and the work you do."

Feeling awkward that the conversation had turned to me rather than Jackie, I wondered if this whole experience had led Mrs. O'Hollaren to make a point of saying affirmations to everyone she encountered.

She hugged me again, but continued as she pulled away, "Make sure you say hi to Thomas. I'm sure he would be glad to see you again."

Another person stepped forward to offer condolences and I was removed from Jackie's focus. I looked a few feet over to see that Thomas was no longer standing next to his sister, Margaret. He must have gone off somewhere. I couldn't blame him. I would be avoiding people, too, if my father had died and I hadn't gotten to say goodbye.

———

A few weeks after David O'Hollaren's funeral, I sat next to my parents in their usual pew at Blessed Sacrament during Sunday mass. We were in the middle of the second reading, but my mind was wandering. I spotted Jackie O'Hollaren sitting in her usual spot with her family. Thomas, I noticed, was missing.

I had been thinking a lot about Jackie and her family. Thinking about their loss of course led to me worrying about my own family. Well, worrying about my parents.

I was an only child. It had always been just the three of us. This had always made me feel like we didn't have enough numbers to use the term 'family.' I was comfortable using the term when you threw in relatives; there were nineteen relatives on my dad's side, and twenty-seven on my mom's. Growing up with thirty-three cousins always made me feel like we were the weird ones to only have three of us.

My parents didn't plan on having only one child. In fact, being the traditional Catholics that they are, they had always wanted a large family of their own. Well, probably like four or five kids, so "medium-large" as my dad liked to call it. It took them six years to get pregnant with me and then after my mom gave birth there were complications that led to an emergency hysterectomy that nearly killed her. This event was one of her favorite things to bring up whenever she felt the need to treat me to a guilt trip. She would usually let out a heavy sigh, followed by, "Okay, Maura, it's not like I almost died trying to bring you into this world or anything." As far as dispensing guilt goes, I've always firmly believed my mother could put any Jewish mother to shame. Yet I digress.

My parents considered adopting, but ultimately decided not to. I have always been curious about the exact reason why they didn't, but whenever I pressed, my mom's standard answer was to say that while God's plans were different than her own, she had to trust that His were better. I was impressed by her ability to be open to other possibilities, even when it meant letting go of something she'd dreamt about for most of her life. Even though it was sometimes overwhelming, I couldn't deny that it was pretty great having two parents who wanted nothing more than to parent multiple children, but who ended up putting all of that love and energy into just me.

I, too, have a fondness for large families. Growing up, I always loved the chaos that inevitably unfolded with every holiday or major birthday. It is impossible to truly know what's going on at our family gatherings, since there are usually five or more people talking at once, and it seems like someone is always crying because with a family that big, there are perpetually babies present. Perhaps I enjoyed the chaos because at the end of day I got to go back to my quiet, orderly life and didn't have to learn how to function successfully in the continual activity. As a child, my cousins would constantly tell me I was lucky to be an only child, mostly because I had my own room and didn't have to share anything.

But that's the thing – if you don't have to share anything, that usually means you don't have anyone to play with either. Don't get me wrong, my parents did their best to see to it that I did not develop into the negative stereotype of an only child. That meant hosting many slumber parties, frequently having to donate toys and participate in community service activities, and many, many years of Girl Scouts.

Personally, I think they did a relatively good job, because every roommate since my freshman year of college made a point to say that they couldn't believe how easy it was to live with me, even with my unfortunate tendency to fill silence with rambling. (Of course, the verdict was still out whether any man would be able to tolerate it enough to ever marry me.) That being said, I was never naive enough to think that any of these relationships actually replicated the unconditional bond that happens between siblings. How comforting to know you wouldn't have to face the death of your parents alone.

When I thought about what the O'Hollarens were going through, I couldn't help but consider what it would be like if one of my parents were to die. To go down to a two-person family seemed unthinkable and tragic. In response, I had been calling and checking in on my parents more regularly ever since David's death. I had even made a point to attend the earlier nine a.m. mass with them that morning instead of my usual eleven a.m. The O'Hollaren family also always came to the earlier service.

From my place in our pew, I looked across the aisle and saw Michael O'Hollaren rest his hand on Jackie's back as she held his youngest son in her lap. While Jackie was experiencing such immense grief, it must have been a relief to have three adult children to rely on. I had no doubt that her daughter, Margaret, was frequently coming by the house, and that Michael, ever the responsible one, was making sure that all financial concerns were in order. From what I knew of their spouses, they were also doing their part to help support the family structure.

As we moved onto the Gospel reading, I was still not paying as much attention to the readings as I should have been, but that was typical for me. The adorable youngest toddler from the Anderson family caught my attention, distracting me from my initial distraction of thinking about the O'Hollarens. I noticed that Melissa Anderson appeared to be showing.

Pregnant? Again? How can someone I went to high school with have five kids already? What's the rush? Okay, so that sounds bitchy. Someone could ask you, 'What's the hold up, Maura?' And how would you like that?

Just then, Margaret O'Hollaren's baby started to fuss, bringing my attention back to the O'Hollaren's pew. Again, I wondered why Thomas wasn't with them. Now that he was back in town, I had assumed that he would attend mass with the rest of his family, especially in light of his father's passing. Maybe it was silly of me to think that he would be as comforted by religion and family as I would be. And normally someone not going to church wouldn't concern me that much – to each their own – but I couldn't seem to shake Thomas from my thoughts after I noticed he was missing, even after spotting Melissa Anderson's two-year-old shoving too many Cheerios in his mouth.

How sad would it be to have your dad die and feel completely alone? I wondered. *Oh, don't be dramatic, Maura, you don't know if that's true...*

I had no real evidence that he was feeling alone...but I remembered what his eyes looked like at the funeral and knew I wasn't wrong.

———

Time was moving particularly slowly the next morning. I had a progress note open on my computer screen and had only managed to get two sentences completed in fifteen minutes. I kept glancing at the clock, then looking at the list of progress notes and treatment plans I had to complete, followed by the list of people I had to call, and then finally back at the clock. I let out a heavy sigh and contemplated taking a break to go get a latte down the street.

"Good morning," Sydney, my office mate, greeted cheerfully as she entered. "You know there's no sighing allowed until after two."

She handed me a latte before moving over to her desk and setting her own cup down to take off her jacket.

"You read my mind," I smiled taking the first sip, loving that she knew my exact order of double shot of espresso, vanilla, and fat-free milk.

"What are work wives for?" She sat down, turned on her computer and started checking emails.

Sydney Gregg and I had known each other since the eighth grade when we were in the same homeroom. She was known as the class clown and a tomboy. She always chose basketball or football with the boys over talking about Hollywood crushes with the girls. We were friendly to one another but didn't become friends until senior year of high school when we worked on student class council together. We were always in our own little world, presenting random ideas to increase school spirit like an interpretive dance team or "Rome-coming," a toga themed Homecoming dance. Our ideas usually got vetoed, but it didn't stop us from amusing ourselves.

I had been ecstatic when Sydney decided to stay local for college and attend the University of Washington where I was going too. We clung to one another the first few months of our freshman year, making a point to have lunch and dinner together several times a week, but we saw less of each other over time as we got more into our studies and found ourselves more involved in campus groups – the Catholic Newman Center for me, and the Queer Center for her. Sydney came out in the second quarter of freshman year. No one who really knew her was surprised.

It crossed my mind at the time that perhaps Sydney didn't feel comfortable being my friend in light of the Church's stance on homosexuality. I even asked her about it one time after a few too many beers. She told me, in true Sydney fashion, that she understood being Catholic wasn't a choice for me and that I was born that way. That settled the matter.

We reunited junior year when we were both accepted to the UW School of Social Work, where we completed our bachelor's and eventually our master's degrees. Last year, I emphatically encouraged

Sydney to apply when a case manager position opened up at to the University District Youth Center, where I had been since my first internship. I like to think that the idea of sharing an office with me for the better part of the day was why she applied, but I knew more than likely it was because she was extremely gifted when it came to working with homeless teens.

Sydney just looks like someone a teenager would open up to and trust. She wears her dark brown hair cropped in a pixie cut and several piercings decorate her ears. Her work attire usually consists of khakis, a button-up shirt with a vest, and Chuck Taylors. When she rolls up her sleeves, part of a beautifully intricate floral tattoo is revealed on her right forearm. Teens are naturally drawn to her.

I, on the other hand, look like a square. I have long, dark blonde hair. It's wavy on a good day, but usually ends up frizzy or in a sloppy bun. I have no tattoos. That isn't because I think it's bad to have tattoos, I just have a low pain tolerance. Besides, I don't think I could pull off the look. I could see myself not taking the commitment seriously and ending up with something I would ultimately regret like a cat with sunglasses or Jabba the Hutt.

Don't get me wrong, I eventually develop a good working relationship with all the teens, but it just seems to take me a little longer to get there than Sydney. I can't really blame the kids. Ever since I've been friends with Sydney, she's always been the one I go to to spill my guts and seek advice.

"So did you do anything fun this weekend?" I asked after giving her a couple minutes to settle in. I still hadn't finished the progress note I'd started almost twenty minutes earlier.

"Nah," she answered with her back to me, not looking away from her computer. "Went out to dinner with Julie's parents for her dad's birthday."

Julie was Sydney's girlfriend. They'd been dating for three years and living together for one. I'd been pestering her about marrying Julie ever since they'd moved in together. Sydney insisted she was not dragging her feet, and it was just because I was Catholic and a virgin that I thought it was acceptable to get married at twenty-five.

To disprove her point, I usually responded by naming several people we knew from high school who had gotten married before twenty-five and weren't religious. Thank goodness for Facebook stalking; otherwise I'd have nothing to challenge her point. My goading hadn't made an impact on their major life decisions so far. Sydney has never been one to cave to peer pressure.

Catholic or not, I couldn't understand why someone would hold back on getting married after dating someone for three years, regardless of whether they were having sex. Maybe I read one too many fairy tales as a child, but I love the idea of making an official commitment to someone and vowing to be there for better or worse. I decided not to pester Sydney about marriage for the time being; it seemed too annoying to go there on a Monday morning, even for me.

Instead I asked, "Where'd you go?"

"Uh, Toulouse Petit in Queen Anne. It was pretty good. What about you?"

"Not much, I hung out with my parents, saw Ethan on Saturday."

At that, Sydney turned around with a grin.

"Oh, you saw Ethan? Was it a date?"

"I guess. I don't know. Maybe…he probably thought it was."

Many of the men I – and other young Blessed Sacrament women – end up dating very rarely ask us out on official dates. Instead, they rely on a series of social events to replace what a normal person would call *dating*. The pattern I've observed for the past three years is as follows: A man goes to several Blessed Sacrament Young Adult events and talks mostly to the woman who interests him. Next, they informally hang out with a smaller group of the same young Catholics, and then if he deems her a good fit, they may attend church together.

I've spent a lot of time trying to analyze and understand why these men, or rather boys, seem to oppose taking women out one-on-one. The Church does not have a courtship policy or demand that young single people use chaperones. Sydney believes the reason is simple. They're all pussies and scared of rejection, or they didn't like vaginas – which she has bluntly declared on more than one occasion when listening to me analyze past interactions.

"So what did you guys do?" she asked.

"A group of us went to the basketball game. They had a deal on tickets for alumni."

"Ethan went to UW?"

"No," I shook my head, "he went to Gonzaga and moved over here to work at Microsoft a year ago."

"So did you have fun?"

"It was okay," I shrugged. "He didn't know a lot about basketball but he kept talking trash about Gonzaga being better. I think he thought he was funny, but it kind of annoyed me."

"God forbid anyone talk trash about your Huskies," Sydney rolled her eyes. She had enjoyed her time in college, but I was more of a diehard fan when it came to Husky sports. "You should give him a break," she continued. "You are kind of cute when you get worked up about your Dawgs. He was probably trying to flirt."

I thought back and realized he had been laughing at my retorts, and there had been more than a couple of times when I'd playfully shoved his arm. Maybe Sydney was right. Her voice interrupted my thoughts.

"So, has he invited you to sit in his pew yet?" she asked. It was her turn to tease me, apparently.

I rolled my eyes.

"No, not yet, but he texted to make sure I'm going to Wednesday night mass this week."

"Well, sounds serious. We'll have you married off by spring," she winked and turned back to her computer. I decided to follow her lead and focus on my work.

Eventually, it was eleven thirty. I'd made a large dent in my paperwork. An alarm went off on my phone and I looked down to see a thirty-minute reminder flashing "Change Oil." I'd forgotten about the appointment. My dad had been nagging me about getting my oil changed for the past two months. Ever the helicopter parent, he had finally just made the appointment for me. Luckily, I had programmed it into my phone when he told me, otherwise I would have given him further proof that I couldn't survive on my own and needed to move back home.

Despite the fact that I was twenty-five, had two degrees, and a full-time job, my parents still thought it was in my best interest to live with them. I don't think they thought I was totally incompetent. They just had empty-nest syndrome. It didn't help that I wasn't producing any grandchildren to fill the void. So for the time being, I accepted their over-involvement. It was always nice when I didn't feel like having to cook dinner and when it came to routine car maintenance.

"I gotta head out to get my oil changed," I told Sydney, standing up to grab my coat.

"You want me to get anything while I'm out?"

"Nah, I'm good, I brought leftovers."

"I'll text if it ends up taking longer than lunch." I gathered my things and made my way to my car. I glanced in the rearview mirror to make sure my hair was smooth, and I wondered if I was going to see him.

THOMAS

I PULLED UP TO THE SHOP IN MY FATHER'S OLD CHEVY truck. I had just finished my second cup of coffee and was already thinking about my third as I walked into the shop. In the three weeks I'd been working there I hadn't gotten used to waking up at five a.m. and I was sure I never would. My father had always been adamant about opening at six a.m. so people could drop off their cars before heading to work. He was incredibly proud to own one of the few shops that operated before eight a.m. Occasionally I'd worked the early shift in college, but never the full twelve-hour shift, six days a week. This had been my reality for the past month.

Michael insisted we both be there 'round the clock, just like Dad. I couldn't help but wonder if my father's early heart attack had stemmed from overworking, but no one else seemed to have made that connection. I could've sworn Michael had said something about the two of us splitting time at the shop once I'd been re-trained and acclimated, but there had been no mention of it since we'd read the will.

I didn't say much around the shop. Michael had been in bad mood ever since I'd started. I could see the disappointment in his eyes each day when I got out of dad's truck. I knew it was because it was me coming to work instead of our father. I could empathize. I had never wanted to spend my days working with Michael, let alone trying to run a business with him. So I let Michael continue to handle the business side of things. He obviously knew more than I did, having been there full time since he was eighteen. I decided the best way I could get him to ease up on my work hours was to delve into becoming a competent mechanic.

I was actually surprised how quickly it all came back to me. I had Frank DeAngelo to thank for that. Frank had worked at the shop since I was ten. He was one of my father's most trusted mechanics, and he helped my dad train both Michael and me when we started. Frank had graciously taken me under his wing again, reminding me how to work on everything from realignments to transmission replacements.

My dad hadn't really had friends, but I think he'd considered Frank more than an employee. Frank looked the part of a mechanic, even when he wasn't wearing his coveralls. He had a dark complexion and dark hair with silver threaded throughout. I had never seen him without stubble. I particularly enjoyed Frank's frequent use of the word "fuck." I had found out just the week before that some of the other mechanics had started taking a tally of how many times he said it. They kept a weekly pool unbeknownst to Frank, and more importantly, to Michael.

I had to admit, I didn't hate working there as much as I'd anticipated, with the exception of the early wake up time. I even felt a little sentimental on my first day back, when my brother handed me the coveralls my dad had kept after I swore I was never coming back. I'd spent nearly four years in New York trying so hard to convince everyone around me that I belonged in their world; that my art was substantial. The constant rejection was exhausting. When I finished a canvas, I no longer felt like I'd accomplished anything. Instead, I questioned whether I was wasting my time. The one passion I'd carried with me since I was six years old turned into something I dreaded even attempting. At the shop, though, my name on my coveralls was all that I needed to belong.

Being there was simple. Show up, find the problem with the car, fix the car, go home. I could now see how this appealed to my father and brother. I was still certain I couldn't do it for forty years, but for the time being, it was a welcomed change to have a new routine and nothing more than my mechanical work scrutinized.

"Morning," Michael muttered gruffly. He handed me the day's schedule of appointments, giving me a non-verbal order to post them in their assigned locations. I walked over to the coffee pot and poured myself a cup.

"You wanna get going on that?" Michael snapped. "We got people getting here in ten."

Too tired to snap back with a clever quip, I tucked the schedules under my arm and followed through on his order. I glanced at it while I hung the first schedule. Obviously, I hadn't convinced Michael of my ability as a mechanic yet, since he'd put me on the mundane task of oil changes for most of the day. However, it was the first time he had me working independently. This was progress, I decided, taking a sip of my coffee and preparing myself for a slow day.

I had just finished my lunch when I saw her drive in. I'd be lying if I said I hadn't noticed her name on my schedule, and I wondered if it would be the same Maura McCormick from my dad's funeral. She was wearing the same black pea coat, this time with a scarf. Her hair was down again, but it looked more golden than before, most likely because the shop had better lighting than that old musty church. I watched Michael wave her further into the garage while I walked over.

Michael approached her when she stepped out of her car, smiling as he greeted her. "Hey, Maura. It's good to see you. Your old man said you would be coming in today."

"Yeah, he wanted to make sure I got my oil changed. Said I've been putting it off too long, and obviously that would get me stranded on the freeway in the middle of the night and murdered," she said sarcastically, then paused, realizing she'd just brought death to mind for a man who'd just lost his father.

"Oh, crap. Michael, I'm sorry! I shouldn't have said that," she said. "I'm such an idiot. I had this whole thing in my head I was going to say about your dad and I just blew it; damn it."

"No, no don't worry about it," he assured her. "We really appreciated you coming to the funeral. Dad would've gotten a kick out of you making an ass out of yourself just now." He let out the first real smile I'd seen in weeks and patted her on the shoulder.

"Well, good, I'm glad I could do that for you." She turned her gaze to me and I suddenly felt awkward.

"This is my brother, Thomas," Michael motioned toward me. She reached out and shook my hand.

"Hi. Yeah, we've actually met," she told Michael, smiling.

"Oh?" he asked, looking over to me. I tried to remember any interaction I had with her in high school, but nothing came to mind.

"Yeah," she continued, "we were in the same confirmation class, but that was forever ago, like nine years. You probably wouldn't remember."

I stayed silent, not knowing if I should lie about remembering her.

"Yeah, Tommy was never one to pay attention during church-related things," Michael explained, his disapproval evident, at least to me. "Anyway, he's the one who's going to be taking care of you today. I just wanted to come over and say hi."

"Before you go I wanted to tell you, if you and Colleen ever need to get out and want me to babysit, just let me know," she offered.

"You sure about that, Maura? You know there are four of them now," he warned with a smile. I was having trouble recognizing who he became around her, and I started to wonder if Michael was just nicer to people from church.

"Four doesn't scare me," she laughed, nonchalantly waving her hand. "I'll just bring over lots of candy and Disney movies."

"Thanks, I'll let Colleen know," Michael nodded to her and then to me before going back to supervising work on another car.

I turned back to her and looked briefly at her blue eyes before looking back at the clipboard in my hand. "So, oil change today?" I glanced up to see her nod. "I'll go ahead and check your air filter and all the fluids, too. Anything else?"

"Nope," she shook her head. "That's it."

"Okay, well, it should take about twenty minutes. You can have a seat in the lobby," I held my arm up and directed her. It must have looked like this was my first time working with a customer. "I'll come get you when I'm done."

"Kay, thanks," she smiled and pulled out her phone while she walked to the lobby. I watched her walk away, then realized what I was doing.

While I worked on the car, I went back and forth between wondering if I should've acknowledged being in the damn confirmation class together and wondering why I should even care. Changing oil was easy, and I was thankful for that. But I almost wished I had something harder to focus on so my mind wouldn't keep wandering and planning how my next interaction with that woman should go.

It wasn't like I was inexperienced when it came to women. I could actually be quite charming with them when I wanted to get laid. She was attractive enough, but the fact that I first laid eyes on her in a church in the middle of my father's funeral detracted from the over-all effect – and she wasn't hot enough for the forbidden aspect of it to be a turn on. Also, there was something that weirded me out about a woman who made a point to go to a middle-aged man's funeral on a Tuesday afternoon when she wasn't even related to the guy. Who did shit like that? I guess someone who freely offered to babysit my brother's four feral children.

I finished the job and walked into the lobby, where Maura was sitting in a chair with her legs crossed. She had taken her coat off. I noticed her black boots and slender legs accentuated by her well fitted jeans. Okay, so maybe she was hot enough to picture fooling around with in one of those church pews. I tried to find a physical flaw that could be a turn-off, but failed. Then I realized I was staring at her. Now I was the creepy one. Luckily, I don't think she noticed.

I tore my eyes away from her legs. "Maura," I said, and my voice came out hoarse. So much so that she didn't even look up from her phone. "Maura McCormick," I said in a louder, normal tone. She looked up and smiled, then turned to fetch her coat. She walked up to the counter.

I was thankful that I had both the counter and computer monitor between us; the physical boundary seemed to help me from becoming even more awkward. Admittedly, I had never really graduated past the sixth-grade maturity level of women providing me with the three main emotions of fear, confusion, and excitement. And here I thought I would have gotten over all that shit by now. How many aspiring models did a guy have to sleep with to move past that? *Good, think about those girls*, I told myself. They were all way hotter than her anyway.

"So, I changed your oil, replaced the air filter, and topped off all the fluids. Everything looks good."

She nodded.

"Did you have any questions?" I asked.

"Yeah, actually, I did."

I looked up from the screen, trying my best not to look captivated by the color of her eyes. Fuck, when did I become such a little bitch?

"So, I know that it's still kind of soon, but I was just thinking, you've come back into town, and maybe don't know anyone and maybe you're bored, but there's this thing…"

The barrier between us didn't seem to protect Maura from awkwardness, but for some reason, it worked for her. "There's a group of us from Blessed Sacrament; we go to mass on Wednesday night and then we go to Latona Pub in Green Lake afterwards. And I just wanted to invite you."

I didn't know what to say. She sensed my hesitation. "I mean, you don't even have to go to mass if you don't want to. Sometimes people just meet us at the bar afterwards. I get it, most normal people don't like to go to church on a weeknight," she laughed.

"What do you guys like to do at the bar?" I asked, picturing totally different activities from what I considered normal bar behavior.

She raised an eyebrow, clearly thinking my question was weird. "Uh, drink beer and talk? It's not like we hold a Bible study or anything if that's what you're asking," she laughed. She must have seen the relief on my face. "C'mon Thomas," she leaned on the counter to pat my arm, "You know Catholics don't read the Bible. Obviously, it would take away from the fun of drinking."

I couldn't help but smile back at her. Now I understood her effect on my brother. "Anyway, no pressure; I know you probably have a lot going on and maybe aren't ready to go out, but I just thought it wouldn't hurt to invite you."

"Thanks, I appreciate the invite," I said.

I didn't commit to going since I didn't want to spend my few hours away from work with religious people—maybe if it led to sex with her, but I could already tell she was the type that required more work than I was willing to put into it.

"So, what do I owe you?" She pointed at the computer screen.

"Actually, it says here that your dad already paid for it."

"Oh God," she let out a heavy sigh. "How embarrassing."

"Look at it this way: it's more money for beer," I said.

She smiled back at me. I was just glad I'd managed to say at least one cool thing before she left.

———

Wednesday night rolled around and I arrived home at six thirty. The smell of lasagna greeted me when I walked into my parents' house. Delicious. It reminded me once again of the benefits of living with my Italian mother, but if she kept feeding me like this, none of my clothes would fit within the next month.

Even though it seemed like I was the one reaping all the benefits of our living situation – free food, free rent, the occasional load of laundry being done for me – my mom also benefited. Having me around kept her busy and gave her something to fill the time so she could grieve at her own pace. She wasn't ready to be a widow living alone in the house she and my dad had shared for thirty years. All of us knew she didn't want to go a whole evening on her own in the house. I didn't mind it. I would have been stupid to try to pay rent I couldn't afford just so I could have my own place. Also, it was nice to know that for once, I was living up to my family's expectations and doing something that no one else could because of their own commitments.

I walked into the kitchen, set my keys down on the counter, and was surprised to see my mother standing there with her coat on and her purse around her arm.

"Oh good, Tommy, you're home. I was afraid you were going to be later and I was going to have to leave a note."

For some reason, my mom didn't think to call me on my cell phone anymore. It was like she thought the number only worked when I was in New York.

"You going out?"

"Yes. Judy finally convinced me to go out and have dinner with her. I hope that's okay."

It seemed like she had used all her energy to convince herself that she wanted to go and now she was unsure if she wanted to follow through.

"Of course, you should go." I knew it was the best thing for her, even if she was reluctant in that moment.

"I made lasagna for you." She pointed at the casserole dish on the counter. Only my mother would make an entire lasagna just for me to have for dinner by myself.

"Thanks," I poured myself a glass of water.

"You sure you'll be okay? I know I sprang this on you last minute."

"Mom," I told her as I had so many times since moving back, "I'm twenty-six. I'm good. Maybe I'll even go out and meet up with some people, too," I mentioned, trying to calm her guilt; probably not the best decision, since it also piqued her curiosity.

"Oh? Who?" she asked, her tone sounding overly interested.

I smiled, appreciating that she was trying to stall.

"I don't know, maybe some of the guys from college who are still in the area," I threw out the first thing I thought sounded believable. But I didn't really want or intend to go out on a weeknight when I had to be up so early the next day.

"Oh, good. I think it's good for you to get out there and start socializing. You're too young to be cooped up in this house," It sounded like she was talking about me but I assumed she was projecting. She was ready for a night out. "Well, have a good night whatever you decide to do, and remember to lock the door." She leaned in and kissed me on the cheek before heading out the door.

After a long shower, I went back downstairs, cut myself a piece of lasagna, and sat down in front of the TV. After a few moments, I realized that I, too, felt uncomfortable being alone in the house, especially when it hit me that I was sitting in my father's chair. I realized that no one had sat there since he had died.

He's dead.

The thought just kept surfacing in my mind while I ate my dinner. I turned on the TV to try and drown it out.

It didn't work.

I ate more quickly than usual, thinking that maybe stuffing myself would be a better distraction from all the memories that were starting to surface.

He's dead.

I aimlessly flipped through the channels – making it at least three times through the rotation.

He's dead.

It was another unsuccessful attempt at distraction.

I was caught off guard by how unsettled I felt, especially since I didn't particularly care for the man and he had been dead for over a month. I glanced at the clock and saw it was 7:42. I considered going to bed, but knew I was too restless to sleep, and the memories would probably just become more vivid in the quiet darkness of my bedroom.

Then I remembered Maura's invite. Honestly, it had been in the back of mind all day, because, well, Maura was good looking, but I had disregarded it given my opinion of church goers in general. But since I desperately wanted to avoid sitting at home unwillingly replaying memories of my dysfunctional relationship with my father all night, I would have accepted any invitation I got at that point.

Latona Pub was only a few blocks away – about a fifteen minute walk – and the best way to distract myself from all the unresolved shit going on in my head. So I headed upstairs to get ready for my first night out since returning home…my first trip to a bar since my dad had died. As I put on my hoodie before walking out the door, I thought about how my dad's death was going to be a permanent marker of time for me. Events would be labeled as things that happened before he died and things that happened after he died. It seemed like such a weird thought to have.

I glanced at my watch before I walked into the bar. I wanted to make sure I wasn't too early. It was eight thirty. I took a deep breath and walked in. The bar was pretty open so I immediately spotted Maura in the far corner. I scanned the group she was with, grateful it looked to be only six other people. I had a brief moment of hesitation, wondering if avoiding being alone in my father's house was worth hanging out with a bunch of Catholics who actually went to church. Before I could turn around and ditch the plan, Maura looked over to the door and saw me standing there. She quickly made her way to me.

"Hey!" she exclaimed with a big smile. "You made it!"

Maura's enthusiasm was contagious, and I couldn't help but smile back, which confirmed to me that I would much rather be there than at home. It seemed I could actually meet a woman at a bar without planning to sleep with her, at least for one night.

"I'm glad you came out!"

I nodded. "So that's your group?" I asked, motioning to the corner table.

"Yeah, I'll introduce you, but let's get some beer first." She started walking over to the bar.

"I can't argue with that," I followed her.

She rested her arms on the counter as she waited for the bartender. "It's my turn to buy the pitchers," she explained.

"Are you sure your dad didn't call in early and buy them for you?" I joked.

"Very funny," Maura smiled, rolling her eyes. "But," she sighed, "you would be surprised at the actual probability of that happening."

The bartender approached her and she turned to order. "Hey, can I get two pitchers of the pilsner and eight glasses?"

"Actually, just seven glasses." I leaned in to ask the bartender, "Can I get a pint of Mac & Jack's?" I looked over to Maura and explained, "They don't have it on the East Coast. I haven't had it in over three years."

"That'll be thirty-seven dollars," he said, setting the pitchers and my pint down in front of us. Maura handed him her card. I reached for my wallet, but Maura grabbed my wrist and shook her head.

"It's okay, I got it," she told me. "You can buy the next round. Or who knows? Maybe I'll call my dad and he'll come down here and buy us all shots," she winked and handed me the pint glasses to carry while she took the pitchers.

I followed her back to the table, hoping everyone there was as cool as Maura.

"Hey guys," she announced, placing the pitchers on the table, "This is Thomas; he recently moved back to the area."

I set the glasses down next to the pitcher, and Maura started pointing at people. "That's Jessica, Tessa, Mary, Jacob, Ethan, and"– she got to the final young guy at the end of the table–"Father Sean."

I noticed he was wearing a white collar with a black button-up shirt just as she said his title and name. Apart from the collar, he didn't fit the model of what I expected a priest to look like. He looked more like a frat boy than someone responsible for delivering mass every Sunday. Maura walked over to the end of the table where he was sitting and set the second pitcher down before pointing to the open chair. I headed over, not completely wild about the idea of sitting next to a priest all night, but I sat down and quickly took a sip of my beer, enjoying the fact that at least I have been reunited with Mac & Jack's.

"So, what're you drinking?" Father Sean asked, pouring the pilsner into his glass, which surprised me. I hadn't expected a priest to drink beer.

"Mac & Jack's," I said, not quite comfortable making eye contact yet.

"Nice. Now that's a good beer. Maura, why didn't you get a pitcher of Mac & Jack's?" he hassled her.

"Because more people like a pilsner than an amber," she explained, as if it were obvious. I was surprised to hear her using a tone like that when addressing a priest.

"Ever the people pleaser, this one," he motioned toward her. "So, how do you know our Maura?" he asked, taking his first drink.

I hesitated, trying to think of a way to explain without having to bring up my father.

"Our mothers know each other," Maura intervened before I had to figure it out. "Thomas just moved back from New York for work," she explained, giving Father Sean a look that seemed to communicate something to him.

"So, Thomas," he started, and I was suddenly worried about what exactly he was going to ask me. I thought surely it was going to be something about death and Jesus and I would be forced to give some bullshit answer to save face. Or worse, he was going to invite me to pray with him. "Do you think the Mariners have a shot this year?" he finished, looking up at a TV that was running a story about Spring Training.

I blinked, relieved that the question had nothing to do with anything spiritual.

"I don't know," I said calmly. "I mean, it looks like it's going to be good with Felix every five, but we can't expect him to do everything on his own."

While I may prefer painting to cars, Mariners baseball was something my dad managed to get both his sons interested in when we were growing up. Of course, it helped that Ken Griffey Jr. was on the team when he'd started teaching us about the game. My love for the Mariners remained steady over the years, especially when I was living in Yankee territory. This was a conversation I could handle without Maura's help.

"What do you think about Cano?" Father Sean asked, sounding more knowledgeable about the topic than I had first anticipated.

"I think it's a good start. I mean, that's the thing, we're fine if everyone stays healthy, but that's never guaranteed. Seager and Cano should be able to deliver on offense."

"It's unfortunate how much focus shifts to offense in the American League."

"What they need is for the American League to get rid of the designated hitter altogether," I said matter-of-factly, amazed that I was talking baseball with a priest, while in a bar, drinking beer.

"Exactly!" he yelled, putting his pint down and holding up his arms. His enthusiasm caught the attention of the table. I assumed this was a challenge he faced as a priest, people always thinking he had something important to say.

"Oh, Thomas and I are just fixing all the problems in the Mariners' organization and the American League," he explained, nonchalantly lifting his pint to clink glasses with mine.

"So, Thomas, what do you do for work?" asked Ethan, the guy sitting across from Maura. He was wearing an Oxford shirt with slacks – pretty formal compared to my Weezer shirt from six years ago and my zip-up hoodie and jeans.

"I'm a mechanic."

It was the first time I'd said that. It felt weird, but a lot more comfortable than calling myself an artist. When people had asked me what I did for work in New York, I'd have to tell them about whatever restaurant or temp office job I was filling at the time, and then explain that I was really an artist, hoping to maintain some semblance of dignity.

"Oh." I could see he wasn't sure what else to say. He didn't look like the type who knew much – or anything at all – about cars. "So, like cars?" he asked, proving my point. I had to remind myself not to be an asshole.

"Yep," I kept it simple.

"Hey, that's awesome," Father Sean interjected. "You'll have to give me the name of your shop. I've got an old car that I want to give to my nephew, but I want to make sure it's running all right."

"Actually, here," I grabbed my wallet, pulled out a business card, and handed it to him. "Just call and we'll set you up with an appointment."

My first thought was how excited Michael was going to be to work on a priest's car. Then I realized that Father Sean was about to notice the name O'Hollaren and bring up my dad. He would probably offer condolences, which I would clumsily accept like I had been repeatedly doing for the past month. I was tired of it. It seemed like my dad's death had bothered everyone more than me and anytime it was brought up I was left to analyze my lack of emotions that went against all societal norms.

"Great, thanks" he said. To my relief, he left it at that and put the card in his pocket. I wondered if Maura had warned him not to say anything.

"So…" I began, trying to get the attention off of myself, "I'm guessing you guys all know Maura from Blessed Sacrament?" I was horrible at small talk and went with the only connection to these people that I could think of.

"For the most part," Maura shared, putting her glass down. "I met Jessica, Mary, and Jacob at Blessed Sacrament after undergrad, and then we met Ethan just this past year when he moved out here from Spokane to work at Microsoft."

"So, like computers?" I asked, wondering if he would catch my smart-ass remark.

"Yeah, I'm a programmer. They've got some very interesting stuff going on there. I'm really glad I moved out here."

He hadn't noticed.

Out of the corner of my eye, I saw Maura try to conceal a smile and I knew she had picked up on the joke. She started talking before Ethan could bore me more.

"And I actually know Tessa from when we were undergrads together at UW. Thomas went to the University of Washington too," Maura shared with our half of the table.

That caught me off guard, but before I could find out how she knew that about me, Father Sean interrupted.

"Oh, you're really going to skip over me like that?" he said, smiling at her.

She let out a sigh, looking annoyed.

"No, no, it's fine if you want to play it like that, Maura."

Ethan and I both looked at Father Sean, confused by this exchange.

"What she's failing to tell you is that she also met me when she was in undergrad and I was a grad student, before I rocked the collar," he explained.

"I was not skipping over it. I just didn't see the point in getting into it tonight with new people around," she defended herself.

He was shaking his head, feigning hurt feelings.

"You're a cold woman, Maura Ann McCormick."

"I am not!" she said, smiling but still looking uncomfortable. "Most people would be happy if I kept our past to myself."

It was starting to come together for me, but I could tell Ethan was having trouble arriving at the same conclusion.

"Secrets are not a holy way to live, my dear Maura" Father Sean said condescendingly.

"Fine!" she blurted.

Father Sean seemed to enjoy the rise he got out of her.

"We dated! A looooong time ago. For some reason, Father Sean wants you guys to know that." She choked down a gulp of her beer, most likely to calm down.

"I feel it's my duty to warn young, single men about the consequences that may occur, should they someday decide to date you. Most importantly, one of them being: a vocation to the priesthood."

"Oh my God, really?" she sighed.

"Maura, we shouldn't call upon God when we're not praying," he corrected, still enjoying the reaction he was getting from her.

"I was," she fired backed. "As in, 'Oh my God, what did I do to deserve the torture of having Sean Finley in my life?" she finished, dropping his title.

"Anyway," Father Sean looked at Ethan and me as he leaned in, acting as if he had important information to share, "Maura is what we in the business like to call 'a priest-maker.'"

Maura shook her head, staring up at the ceiling. I had to admit, I found her dynamic with Father Sean entertaining. He sat back and took a swig of his beer, proud of the information he'd just shared.

"That's not even true," she had her hands up in the air and looked at him pointedly.

"Oh, it's not?" he smiled. "Maura, how many guys have you dated who ended up becoming priests?"

She sighed before answering. "Three."

"Three! Now, I'm not a math guy, but I'd say that's a pretty high average compared to your standard Catholic girl, especially given the current shortage of vocations. I mean, if the Archdiocese got a hold of those numbers they might end up hiring you specifically for their vocations department."

She was still shaking her head, but also smiling at him.

"So gentlemen, be warned: you spend too much time with her, and you may end up like me."

"And no one wants that," Maura said, preparing for a toast. "To making sure we save the world from more Father Seans."

Father Sean was the first to raise his glass. I took a sip, then locked in on Maura's blue eyes, and found myself once again wanting to know more about her.

After that entertaining discussion, the conversation gradually became dry thanks to Ethan, who couldn't stop bringing up church-related things. I've never met anyone more into papal history. It didn't even look like Father Sean was enjoying the conversation. Maura must have noticed the glaze over my eyes, because she nudged my arm.

"Hey," she whispered.

I raised my eyebrows in question.

"You want to go grab another pint at the bar?" she motioned with a mischievous look, like a kid pressuring me to skip school with her.

I nodded and followed her lead.

"Hey, does anybody want another?" she questioned the table as Ethan continued droning on to Father Sean.

They declined. They'd be heading out soon anyway.

I followed Maura to the bar, where she ordered two pints for us.

"Sorry," she said, turning to me. "I didn't think Ethan was going to spend the whole night recapping Pope Francis' latest soundbites."

"It's fine," I shrugged.

"Actually, that's a lie," she confessed. "I kind of knew it would happen, because it usually does."

I was just glad to get a break from Ethan. Our drinks arrived at the bar.

"So yeah," she stalled awkwardly, "I hope you don't regret coming out."

I slowly shook my head and stared at my glass. "No, no, Wednesday night, out with strangers, drinking beer with a priest, hearing about the Pope. What's to regret?"

She smiled at my sarcasm. "I know; I guess it wasn't the best thing to invite you to. I just, I don't know; I mean, I know I don't really know you, but I just felt like you might want a distraction...from everything..." she trailed off, trying not to mention my father's death.

"This seemed like a better thing to invite you to than the Stations of the Cross and soup supper I'm going to this Friday."

I didn't say anything, wondering whether I should tell her she was right. My silence made her nervous.

"Which, now that I say it out loud, sounds kind of pathetic, even to me, that this and that are my main social events for the week," she reflected.

"Can I ask you something?" I interrupted before she got a chance to become more neurotic, cute as it may have been.

"Sure."

"Should I know you better than I do?"

She looked quizzically at me and I clarified.

"Because I've tried to remember you and I just don't, but I feel like I should know you because you know several things about me."

"Yeah, kind of creepy, huh?" she admitted. "Well, we did sit next to each other in the few confirmation classes you went to because they put us in alphabetical order, but we never spoke. We went to different high schools. When my mom met your mom earlier that year through some church thing and she found out that your mom had a son my age, she felt it was very important that I not only know about you, but also your whereabouts: confirmation class, college, New York, where you sleep. You know, just regular stuff like that."

"So you're not my stalker, but your mom is?"

"Precisely. She's the creepy one you've got to worry about. Just be glad she's not on Facebook, because she would be all over your shit."

I was amused at how clever and dry she could be, and a little surprised to hear her curse.

"So then, to be fair, you have to tell me about yourself."

"What do you want to know?"

"What do you do when you're not at church or at bars talking about church with people you go to church with?"

"I work. I'm a social worker at the University Youth Center. We work with homeless teens and young adults."

"Well, shit," I laughed. "Of course."

I tilted my head back. I wasn't expecting her to have a virtuous profession in addition to regularly attending church and offering to babysit my brother's kids. Maura had just confirmed that she was officially a better person than me, and most everyone else, for that matter.

"What?" She looked a little confused, but not offended.

"You work with homeless kids for a living? And go to church all the time? Are you for real?" I shook my head and leaned into the bar. "I'm starting to feel pretty shitty about myself right now."

"It's not like that," she started to downplay.

"I bet you volunteer somewhere in your free time, too."

She took a breath and looked down at her glass, not saying anything. I knew I'd proven my point. Maura tried to hide the smile creeping up on her face.

"Occasionally, I may go to the food bank to help with donations, but it's not a big deal," she said, trying to sound nonchalant.

"And how occasionally would that be?"

She shrugged, still trying to be modest. "Like once, maybe twice a month."

"I think that's considered regular, not occasional," I laughed.

It was fun to give her a hard time. I imagined it was the opposite reaction from what Maura usually got when people found out what she did with her time.

"See, I was expecting to go out with some Catholics tonight and feel a little weird about my lack of religion, but I wasn't expecting I'd be hanging out with the next Mother Teresa. Now I'm feeling a little self-conscious. Do you rescue kittens in your free time as well?"

"You know, I've gotten a lot of responses to what I do for work, but I think you're the first to make fun of me."

"And what do people normally say?"

"I get a lot of, 'Good for you; someone's got to do that job, I'm just glad it's not me.'

And then sometimes I get questions like, 'Why do you think people end up like that?' or 'Isn't it really them just choosing to be homeless?' Which is usually followed by some sort of justification for why they don't give panhandlers money, and for some reason, who they voted for. I should just start to tell people I work at Target. People love Target. Right? They rarely ever have a problem with Target."

"Virtuous people are sometimes hard for us selfish assholes to be around. But, you know, Maura, sometimes you just gotta let the haters hate."

"You know, I do normal stuff too," she stated defensively. "I watch TV. Sometimes I like to run."

"Ugh! You exercise too? Can I just say on behalf of the majority of us who don't have our shit together, Maura, can you just stop while you're ahead? You're really making the rest of us look bad. I mean, there's a reason Ethan can't shut up about the Pope and it's because he's just grasping to stay on your level."

I finally had her laughing and before I knew it I started laughing too, for the first time in a long time. I was remembering what a good time felt like.

"I mean, really, it's just not fair."

"I had no idea I was upsetting everybody so much," she joked.

"You know, maybe that's why I was sent here tonight," I touched my chest and looked at her with mock virtue. "God wanted me to tell you that while He appreciates you taking His teachings seriously, like taking care of the poor and loving the downtrodden, you're really pissing some people off and you need to cut that shit out, 'cause this is America; we shouldn't have to feel uncomfortable when we don't want to. Maybe I could help you learn how to function more superficially."

"Oh, and how long would that take?"

"You know, mastering the art of not giving a shit about actual important things takes some time. I mean, I've been working on it all my life. It's not to be taken lightly. And I've got to say," I paused for effect, "unfortunately, I don't know if I have a whole lot of hope for you. You seem pretty entrenched in this whole *caring about people* thing."

"Ah, man," she said with defeat.

"I know. It's a shame, too, because I think if I had gotten to you earlier, you would've had potential," I sighed.

"So does that mean we can't hang out anymore?" she asked, playing along.

"I don't know, I feel like if I don't keep tabs on you, you may start rescuing those kittens or donating too much blood; and we, the slackers of the world, definitely don't want that."

I paused and tried to think of something I could do with her that wasn't too much like a date but didn't involve church. "You know, I do like to run too, so maybe that's something we could do together. You won't make me feel insecure about being a bad person and I can keep you from yelling at other people about how great you are at saving homeless kids and praying to Jesus."

"So that's why I've been getting flipped off in the park when I run," she said with feigned revelation.

I nodded.

"See, you need me," I looked over to see her smiling. I finished my beer and turned to see that half of Maura's group had dispersed and the rest were clearing the table. I saw she was finished with her drink, too, so I stood up. I wanted to make my exit before having to exchange awkward goodbyes with her friends.

"I think I'm going to head out."

She stood up after my announcement. "Well, thank you for coming out.

"Yeah, thank you for the distraction. I appreciate it."

"Anytime," she said softly. Before I could determine the appropriate way to say goodbye, she leaned in a gave me a brief hug.

"Take care." I headed out the door.

The cold air hit my face as I walked outside, and I felt more awake and alert than I had in a month. It was like being around her had breathed life into me again. I kept thinking about her as I walked home. Her sense of humor. The fact that she was so easy to be around even though she was almost a complete stranger. And of course, those damn eyes. Before I knew it, I had made it home, not caring that I had to get up in five and a half hours.

MAURA

AS PLANNED, I ATTENDED STATIONS OF THE CROSS AND the soup supper at Blessed Sacrament on Friday. Call me weird, but I love the season of Lent. Admittedly, I didn't when I was little. Obviously, it's super depressing compared to Advent, and what kid really looks forward to having to give up something they like for forty days in addition to hearing about Jesus getting ready to die? Most grown-ups don't really enjoy it either.

But as an adult I thought it was one of the more interesting parts of the Catholic tradition. I'm always trying to wrap my brain around the idea that there was someone who cared for humanity so much that he was willing to die in the most painful, humiliating way to save it. It makes sense to me that we would spend forty days contemplating the complexity of it all. Yes, call me cheesy, but to me it is one of the greatest love stories I know.

I showed up right before Stations started. Getting there earlier would have increased the likelihood that people I knew would invite me to sit with them. My tardiness ensured that I could sit in a middle pew alone near my favorite statue of Saint Jude. Lately, I had been feeling kind of alone when I spent time with the young adult group, so I took it as a sign to take a little space that evening. It was the same give-and-take I had been struggling with for the past year with the young adult group. I wasn't really enjoying my time with them as much as I had in the past, yet I didn't have many other options when it came to socializing.

Normally, I was a self-described social-butterfly. It had always been that way; it probably came from being an only child and feeling like I had my fill of alone time growing up. I had the benefit of staying in Seattle after I graduated, so I was able to maintain most of the relationships I had built during college, and even lived in a house with four other girls who I had met from the Blessed Sacrament young adult group...until one by one they all got married and moved out.

About a year ago, I realized I was living in the same house with four different people who I didn't really know and who were all four years younger than me. Everyone else had moved on and I was literally still in the same spot I had been when I was twenty-one. So I made the decision to move out and get my own apartment, and for the first time ever live completely on my own.

There were days when I loved it, and there were days when it seemed too quiet. But when I thought about trying to live in a house with the people in the young adult group again, it was less appealing than having to deal with my neurotic train of thought that could sometimes become magnified in all that quiet time. And that's saying something. Over the past four years, the group had become more and more traditional and I had not. It's not like I thought we should get crazy and have a rock concert for Jesus in the sanctuary, but a consistent topic of conversation at young adult events was a desire to get back to some pre-Vatican II practices, like having mass in Latin. And for some reason, the latest trend for the young adults was praying the Liturgy of the Hours, which for the life of me, I just didn't get.

I told myself that I just lived a different life than them. I liked to think that if they had met half as many homeless teenagers as I had who had turned to sex work to survive, maybe they would change their opinion on giving kids condoms. Or maybe even voting to raise taxes to allow for more preventive programs for at-risk kids and families, instead of getting so stuck on how handouts shouldn't be given to people on drugs or whatever it was they thought was a sin. I would even be okay if they didn't change their minds, but if at the very least they were able to recognize just how complicated some things are instead of seeing everything as black and white and easily solved by saying a rosary.

I could have church shopped. It wouldn't have been too hard to find a more left-leaning church in the Seattle area, but that just seemed like a cop out. I would be no better than those I was critiquing by seeking out people who thought just like me. Anyway, I had gone to Blessed Sacrament since my family moved to Seattle when I was in middle school, and as everyone knows, we Catholics are never huge fans of change. When I went to mass and the whole parish was there, young and old, it still felt like home and that was what was important to me.

As I sat and reflected quietly on the way of the cross, I silently expressed my gratitude to Jesus for sacrificing his life for me. I asked for strength to be as selfless as him. I found my mind focusing on how lonely he probably felt during his execution. I admitted that I, too, felt lonely at that point in my life. I validated, as most Catholics do during prayer, that others were definitely worse off than me and that I should've been more appreciative of the relationships that I had...but I went back to admitting that I was lonely. I was not sure what I should ask for, or if I should even ask for anything, but it felt like a big step for me to admit to myself, and to God, that I was lonely and didn't want to be anymore.

The Stations of the Cross came to a close and some of the people remained sitting quietly in the pews. Others began gathering their coats to head towards the hall. I genuflected, exited my empty pew and walked up the side aisle. Ethan, who was with a group of other young people, saw me and waited for me. He whispered hello. I nodded. We walked into the hallway. I noticed that he was wearing his glasses and concluded that he looked better with them than without them.

Ethan Linden was considered one of the more eligible young men in our group. He was twenty-nine and a computer programmer for Microsoft. It was kind of ridiculous how much female attention he'd gotten when he first came to Blessed Sacrament; not that the regular men of the group didn't do the same thing when a new girl showed up. It seemed like people in the group were constantly assessing whether the others were good marriage material, which I couldn't really fault them for. I mean, I wanted to get married too, someday, but after getting burned in the past, my primary focus was just finding people to socialize with who had the same cultural background as myself.

Ethan had dated a couple of the women in the group, but I don't think any of them developed into anything serious. The gossip I'd heard was that he just stopped talking to each of those girls without really giving a reason. For the time being, he seemed to be somewhat interested in me, texting me, talking to me at events, sitting next to me. Surprisingly, I hadn't allowed myself the opportunity to over-analyze his behavior. I regarded this as actual growth on my part, because in the past, all it seemed to take was a good-looking guy smiling at me before I had our entire wedding planned. I had decided that until he declared he liked me or asked me out on an actual date, I wouldn't really waste time trying to determine whether I liked him or not.

Ethan was as clean-cut as they come. His light brown hair was cut close to the sides with a slight tuft at the top, usually styled in place by gel. I had never seen him in anything but a button-up shirt, and he wore jeans very rarely. From what I'd gathered from conversations with him, he was very traditional when it came to Catholicism, with a high devotion to mother Mary. The thing that I found most interesting about him was that he had gone on over twenty mission trips to Mexico and various parts of Central America, even using his paid vacation time to participate in them. I had trouble picturing him doing this, mostly because I would think you'd have to dress down on a mission trip building houses or working in an orphanage.

"Why don't you go grab a seat?" Ethan snapped me out of my daze. "I'll go grab us some soup."

I didn't turn him down. I always appreciated chivalry. I prepared myself for the more-than-likely fact that the rest of the single young women would find their way to sit at Ethan's table. I didn't really feel jealous or territorial, but over the last couple of weeks of Ethan's perceived interest in me, other women seemed to have responded with increased interest in him. Many of the group activities turned into Ethan holding court while I sat there and witnessed the other women try to impress him with how Catholic they were.

While Ethan was in line, the Dominican priests walked in and I was surprised to see all five of them from the priory, including Sean. I was slowly getting used to seeing him in his friar's robe, but still couldn't bring myself to call him Father Sean in my head. Father Jack, the director of Blessed Sacrament, greeted the group and then led us in grace.

Ethan approached the table where I was sitting with two bowls of lentil soup.

"Thank you," I smiled, and before I knew it, our table was filled with four other young women. For the moment, they were engaged in conversations amongst themselves.

"So how was the rest of your week at work?" he asked once we had settled.

I realized that he was just being friendly, but I wasn't sure how to answer because I knew my work week was drastically different than his own. I contemplated the reaction I would get if I said that I had an intake puke on my desk from drinking too much, and that I'd had to make multiple police reports for rape, but it was all good because we got someone enrolled in school and a couple people qualified for housing. I knew all too well not to share stuff like that with him, or anyone I hung out with besides Sydney, so I simply responded, "Pretty busy; I'm glad it's Friday. What about you?"

"Yes, definitely. So, your friend Thomas isn't joining us tonight?" he maintained eye contact, almost as if he was trying to gage my reaction to Thomas being brought up.

"No, I don't think this is really his thing."

"Oh, he's not Catholic?"

"Not practicing, I don't think." I didn't offer any more information. He stared at me for a couple seconds, trying to read me.

"That's too bad." He passed me a roll.

.   "So," I changed the subject, "what are your thoughts on lentil soup? Personally, I think it's way too healthy. I like my soups cream-based and full of fat." I made him smile and got the attention off Thomas.

"Oh, so like a nice chowder or a lobster bisque?" he joked.

"Oh my gosh, bisque is my jam."

"I'll have to remember that. Personally, I like the predictability of a good chicken noodle soup."

"Ethan," Jessica chimed in from across the table, "I make the most amazing chicken noodle soup. I'll have to give you the recipe, or better yet, I could make it for you sometime."

"Oh, that would be good. I don't think I would trust myself to make it. You know, I am a guy."

The four women laughed. I thought to myself that Ethan should have been able to follow a recipe; he was a grown-ass man. This was a classic example of how traditional roles for men and women had been so played up in the young adult group over the past few years.

Being a young adult group, the topic of vocation got talked about a lot. Catholics believe that everyone is called to a specific commitment; single, married, or religious life. The majority of the women currently involved in the Blessed Sacrament young adult group had discerned that their vocation was to be married and become a mom. It was almost as if what they were doing for a living was simply a time-filler until the guy showed up. Maybe it was because I'd spent so much money on grad school, but I currently saw my vocation as being that of a social worker, whether I got married or not.

"You know what would be great is if our house could host its own soup supper night," Marie, who was actually my replacement in my old house, suggested to the table.

"That sounds like a great idea, Marie. We could also pray the Liturgy of the Hours to give it even more substance," Ethan suggested, and the four of them thought it was a fantastic idea. I thought it sounded horribly boring.

"I'll put together a Facebook invite and send it to the group," Jessica said enthusiastically. "I really think we need to look into doing more events with substance as a young adult group. It seems like the majority of things we do are purely social."

"Like the blanket drive for the homeless last month," I said.

Jessica caught on to my snarkiness. "Well, no, I know that had substance, but you know, really if we aren't prayerful and mindful of God when we're doing these things, then I don't think we're really doing as much as we could for them. What I'm talking about is how a lot of our events involve going to bars."

"I find the alcohol makes some of us more interesting," I said with a smile. Luckily, my comment was taken as good natured, judging by the smile I got from Ethan. Jessica, however, did not smile.

I sat through the rest of dinner listening to everyone else talk about their week and upcoming plans to go skiing and snowboarding as a group in two weeks. Apparently that event had enough substance for Jessica. She shared that she was so excited to go but nervous because she was a beginner and would of course need Ethan to help guide her through the slopes.

Ethan was disappointed to hear that I had decided not to go, and even further disappointed to hear that I was not a fan of skiing or even snowboarding. He insisted that I probably didn't like it because I'd never had the right teacher, and stated boldly that I would like it if I ever went with him. I politely said that maybe I would go next year and give him the opportunity then, knowing I would most likely not. It was just another instance where I was in the minority of the group.

I felt it unnecessary to go off on a rant about how the activity was way too expensive for someone who didn't do it regularly and that I simply hated being cold unless I was at the coast and there was an ocean to look at. Also, the first and last time I ever went skiing was when I was ten and I spent the entire weekend repeatedly falling and getting made fun of by two other girls in my Girls Scout Troop. I don't even think there was a badge associated with the trip, so why the hell we were even there in the first place was beyond me.

When I got up to clear my dish, I managed to sneak back into the church away from everyone. I wandered over to the small Eucharistic chapel area in front of the tabernacle. I sat there, quietly wondering why I was in such a negative mood. I hadn't been there by myself for very long when I heard a familiar voice.

"Has He told you how to fix all the world's problems yet?"

I didn't even bother to turn around. I knew it was Sean.

"Maybe I'm telling Him how I would fix them," I commented smartly.

"Wouldn't surprise me." He sat down one row behind me, three chairs over. "So, how have you been?"

"Fine," I answered simply. "You know you shouldn't be here."

"Yeah, probably," he sighed, "But I just have this feeling that I'm supposed to check in on you."

"Could it be guilt surfacing from the fact that you dumped me four years ago so you could run away and become a priest?" I was still not looking at him but stared straight ahead at the tabernacle.

"No, I already processed that a long time ago," he stated honestly.

It dawned on me that we had been in a similar position when he broke up with me, except it had been in front of the tabernacle at the University's Newman Center chapel a few miles down the road. When I thought back on it, I was embarrassed by how much I had cried. I knew now that it would never have worked with Sean, but at the time it had seemed like my heart and several other vital organs had been ripped out.

"Well I'm sorry you have that gut feeling. It doesn't change the fact that having a conversation alone with me could lead to perceived scandal, and I'm sure Father Jack and the others have already strongly advised you against doing something like this, or probably ordered you not to do it."

"Yeah," he said simply. "So I should ignore the fact that I feel like God is telling me that I need to talk to you?"

"You know, what God tells you – or what you feel like God is telling you – never seems to work out in my favor," I said with a slight laugh.

Sean didn't say anything but continued to sit there, because he knew me well enough to know that if he waited in silence long enough I would blurt something out. He was not wrong.

"I can't believe you had to announce to everyone on Wednesday that we dated. I have done you a huge courtesy for the past six months by not bringing it up to anyone, not even my mother, and believe me, she's tried to get me to talk about it. I just smile and say I don't think much about it. I've done a superb job of only talking to you when you talk to me. I don't joke around with you; I call you by your title, even though that's extremely weird to me. And you repay me by announcing to everyone something that happened over four years ago, which has probably spread like wildfire by now to everyone else. And now I don't even want to be around you because I think people are going to be watching and analyzing every interaction."

"You're right," he said when I finally paused, "I shouldn't have announced it to the table like that, but Maura, the past six months have been so strange with you being so formal. I guess I selfishly wanted the interaction we used to have when we were friends, and I know what buttons to push to get you to react that way. At the same time, I think that allowing some of the people to see a slightly human side to a priest isn't such a bad thing. I like my story of how I came to find my vocation, and you're a part of it and I'm not ashamed of that, nor do I think I should be."

"You know, some would have misconstrued it as flirting. You keep it up you're putting your reputation on the line," I said firmly, wanting to protect him even though he was five years older than me.

"I know," he said seriously. "But Maura, I am serious when I say that I get the sense that something's amiss with you."

"Everything's fine. You know, it's what you always complained about; silly Maura and her touchy-feely, hippy-dippy theology wanting to just hug everybody all the time and sing Lead Me Lord, while everybody else my age wants to explore Latin and read encyclicals and talk about GK Chesterton."

I was finally facing him and saw him smile at my description. Sean knew full well that we were complete opposites in how we chose to express our faith.

"And after you left, I tried really hard to get into all that, thinking that my lack of knowledge in that area was why you left, but I just don't connect to it...and I'm starting to think there's something wrong with me because I don't feel as passionate as everybody else here does about those things."

Sean stared at me for a moment before speaking again.

"Look, Maura, it's like running. You remember how much I hated running? And you always loved it. There are other ways to exercise besides running, but that doesn't make either superior. It's the same thing with faith; we all chose to express it in different ways outside of mass; it doesn't make one way holier than any other... unless you turn into one of those people who actually think the trees and rocks are talking to them and telling them the secrets of the universe; that's just weird. I can't get behind that."

I rolled my eyes.

"So seriously, *you* read Chesterton?" he asked in disbelief. "I'm just reminded of how many times I tried to get you to read it and how stubborn you were about it."

I shrugged, "I said I gave it a try. I thought my Dorothy Day books were far more interesting."

"Socialist," he teased.

I turned away from him and I went back to looking at the tabernacle, knowing that conversations like this with him were rare now. I tried to just appreciate it in the moment.

"So, what's the deal with that Thomas guy?"

"I told you before we went out on Wednesday, his dad, David O'Hollaren, died a month ago, and I invited him out because I figured he probably didn't know a whole lot of people around here anymore.

"What did Ethan think about it?"

I raised an eyebrow and turned to look at him.

"I don't know what he thought about it. I didn't ask him. Why?"

"No reason," he said innocently. "I just thought there was a thing with Ethan and I was confused when you spent the night talking and laughing with Thomas."

"You sound like a middle school girl right now."

"Four years ago, I promised you that someone better would come along. I want to make sure I do my part to support you in that quest and that may mean sounding like a middle school girl from time to time."

"Well, there's nothing to talk about," I said simply. I turned my attention away from him again. "Ethan has never asked me out on a date so I don't know what he's thinking, and Thomas doesn't go to church and may not even believe in God. I don't think either of them is the person you were referring to."

"People can surprise you. I never thought a spitfire college junior would be the one to get me to get my act together and start living up to my potential."

I knew without looking at Sean that I meant a lot to him and it transcended any sort of romantic love.

"Well, potential agnosticism aside, I like Thomas," he shared. "Sometimes it's nice to just be around someone my own age who can talk sports and doesn't want to know how to pray the Liturgy of the Hours."

"Oh, the burdens of a young priest," I said flatly.

"You don't know the half of it," he responded with equal sarcasm as he stood up. He touched my shoulder. "You are the best person I know at loving people just as they are...you need to know that God is able to do exactly the same for you."

He quickly genuflected before heading over to the priory.

———

I was finishing straightening my hair when I heard a text notification. It was from a 206 number not programmed into my phone. I pulled up the text.

Hey Maura, this is Thomas. You up for a run this morning?

There I was standing in a skirt and sweater, just about ready to leave for Sunday morning mass. The last thing I had planned on doing that morning was going for a run. I was about to text my apologies that I would have to take a raincheck. Then I stopped and remembered Thomas' expression at his dad's funeral. I considered the possibility that he was looking for someone to talk to. There was a mass at five forty-five that night; it wouldn't be that big of a deal to change plans; it wasn't like I was meeting anyone there this morning.

Sure. You want to meet up at Green Lake and 65th in twenty minutes?

I felt myself exhale after I pushed send. I had butterflies in my stomach and didn't know why. It was probably because of the small rush from the semi-exciting event of switching up my mass time unexpectedly. Pathetic, but I was a creature of habit. I stared at my phone, waiting for a confirmation before committing to changing my clothes.

See you then.

I returned to my room and pulled out my sports bra and black running pants with the lavender band around the waist.

Where is that matching shirt? I wondered. Then I caught myself. *Since when do you care whether your running clothes match?*

But I told myself there was a good reason for it. *I am merely being functional. It's a long-sleeved shirt and it's cold outside. Oh! There it is!*

I assembled myself and looked in the mirror.

Well, I do look pretty cute in this outfit, I complimented myself in my head.

Stop it. How vain do you have to be to be this concerned about how you look when you're going to meet up with someone's whose dad just died?

Since we would probably be jogging at only a moderate pace, a simple braid would do for holding my hair in place.

Maybe a sloppy bun would balance out the over-effort of the coordinating outfit? I considered.

You're being ridiculous. Shit. I left my straightener on!

After saving myself from accidentally setting my apartment on fire, for probably the fourth time that month, I strapped my phone to my arm and headed out the door. My apartment building was just off Roosevelt and Sixty-fifth, which was a little over a half mile away from where I was meeting Thomas. I had ample time to meet him, but I found myself jogging when I walked out onto the street. It was like I was trying to expel nervous energy. Thank goodness he was standing at the street corner waiting for me instead of the other way around. The last thing I needed was more time to become more neurotic. He was wearing a navy long-sleeved t-shirt and some basketball shorts, looking far from a serious runner. I wondered if he ran at all or if he'd just made it up as an excuse to see me.

You're certainly full of yourself this morning, Maura.

"Hey," I smiled hello.

"Hey, you look like you're ready for this," he commented on my outfit.

The light turned and we started to walk across the street.

"Oh, I am," I confirmed confidently. "Are you?"

"I don't know. I mean, I don't have the matching outfit and I don't have one of the cool arm band thingies for my phone like you," he teased me.

I felt a little self-conscious but decided to roll with it.

"I brought the phone so I could call the ambulance when you pass out."

He gave me a small smile.

"Good call, but I will have you know that I used to run in a little place called Central Park," he feigned a cocky voice and I gave him an exaggerated look of shock. "So yeah, this isn't my first rodeo."

He stretched his arms and twisted his waist as we made our way to the pathway around the lake.

"Are we going to do this? Or are you just going to stretch the whole time?"

"Set the pace, m'lady," he held out his hand in front of me. I started a slow jog to warm up.

"How do you feel about talking when you run?" I always asked that when I ran with someone for the first time. I had a hard time not talking when running with a partner, but some people liked to focus on their pace and hated to be slowed down.

"I try to avoid it when I'm by myself, because people tend to think I'm crazy, but I won't judge you."

"Thanks, you're too kind." I was quiet for minute. "It's about three miles to run the whole thing around. Sound good?"

"Yep."

"So, how'd you get my number?" I knew I hadn't given it to him and I could not picture him asking his mom to get it from my mom.

"I was inspired by your mom and tapped into my inner stalker. I got it from the database at the shop. I know your address now too."

"Creepy. My mom would be proud."

"Yeah, but I'm a step behind because I'm guessing you already know where my mom lives since you suggested meeting up here."

I felt my cheeks get a little more flushed, knowing it was more from being called out than from the run. I decided to be nonchalant. We had already established on Wednesday that it was weird how much I knew about him without really knowing him. I tested the waters to see if he wanted to talk about what he and his family were going through.

"And how is your mom?"

Social worker 101: people are usually more comfortable sharing with you when you're both in the middle of an activity they can't stop and when you're not staring directly at them. Sydney and I joke that the quickest way to get a kid to tell you their full life story is to take them on a long car ride. I tested this theory as I continued to look forward and run alongside Thomas.

"She's okay," he said honestly.

I wondered if he was going to stop there.

"She actually went out to dinner with one of her friends Wednesday night. It was the first time she's gone out for something other than church or groceries," he continued.

"Did she have fun?"

"I think so. She was more interested in how I spent my night when she found out I met up with a bunch people from Blessed Sacrament – specifically Father Sean." He did a higher pitched voice, "'Tommy, what's he like? He seems like such a nice young man. You should hang out with him more.' I think it made her a little too hopeful I would go to mass with her this morning and introduce her."

"You didn't want to?"

"Go to mass? Nah. I think once every four years for a wedding or a funeral is enough for me. Besides, I'm pretty sure you're filling my quota for me."

I didn't say anything and waited to see if he'd say more.

"Speaking of which, why aren't you at mass?"

"I'm going tonight at five forty-five," I said simply.

"Oh, for a second there I thought maybe I had given you too hard of a time on Wednesday and you had turned to the dark side."

"Nope. How's it going at the shop?" I turned the attention back to him. He stayed quiet for a few moments as we navigated our way around some walkers.

"It's all right. It's kind of weird stepping into it after being away so long. Although, technically I own half. I never thought I'd own half of an auto shop. I just figured he'd give it all to Michael."

"Would you have wanted that?"

"When I'm waking up at five in the morning to go to work, yes," he joked. "I don't know, it's not like I was doing anything better with my time and I know, despite Michael never being willing to admit it, it's helpful for him to have me there. Now if he would just let us each work a forty-hour week instead of both of us doing a sixty-five."

"Sixty-five hours a week?" I confirmed, surprised.

"Yep. Six a.m. to six p.m. Monday through Friday and eight a.m. to one p.m. on Saturday. If the shop is open, we're both there."

"You guys must be exhausted. That must be hard on Michael and his family." I thought about Colleen taking care of four kids by herself and Michael being too tired to help.

"Yes, poor Michael," he said flatly.

"Sorry, I mean poor Michael AND Thomas. Better?"

"Much. You know, he's the one who decided to do it this way."

"Then why not ask him to change it up?"

I guess I was being naive because he let out a laugh.

"That would require him to be comfortable having me there on my own."

"Well, when do you think he'll be comfortable?"

"I don't know. We're talking about a five foot eight inch angry Irishman; when are they ever comfortable?" he joked.

"You don't consider yourself Irish?"

"As you can see by my rich Mediterranean olive complexion," he held out his arm as we jogged. "I take after my mother's Italian side."

"Yes, and Italians are never stereotyped as overly emotional. Well, you won't ever get it to change without talking to him," I said simply. "Maybe you can get Colleen on your side."

"Is this what you do for a living? Encourage people to create divisions in their family in order to get what they want?"

"No, most of my kids are estranged from their families. I do this for free."

I decided to keep quiet for a few minutes. Then I asked, "So if you weren't fixing cars in New York, what were you doing?"

"Wasting time," he said quickly with a smile.

I wondered if he would give me more of the story.

"I moved out there after I graduated to stupidly pursue being a painter."

"You must have liked it a little bit to stay for almost four years." "I think I liked trying to prove my dad wrong...but when I wasn't able to, it stopped being fun."

I was surprised by his frankness.

"Your dad didn't want you to go?"

"No, he wanted me to stay and work at the shop. I barely got him to agree to let me go to college, and that was under the pretense that I would get a degree in business to help at the shop. When I turned business into my minor and art into my major, he wasn't too happy about that, either."

"I didn't know you were an artist."

He didn't respond. I could tell he didn't want to talk about art.

"So that must be helpful to Michael that you have a little bit of background in business."

"Should I start calling you Pollyanna?" he joked.

You're being too cheery for him. Listen more.

"Hey, I haven't initiated the Glad Game yet, but I could if that's needed," I quipped.

"And how does that go over with the homeless teens?"

"I don't know; I haven't tried it, but I'm pretty sure they'd tell me to go fuck myself."

My response must have caught him off guard because he started to cough and laugh at the same time. We slowed our pace down and eventually stopped as he tried to catch his breath.

"Are you okay?"

He was bent over still laughing and coughing. He took a deep breath and looked up at me.

"I was not expecting you to say 'fuck.' Maura, what would Father Sean say?" Thomas feigned disapproval.

I shook my head.

"Please," I dismissed. "You ready to keep going?"

I started to walk backwards as he stood up. I turned and resumed jogging and soon he caught up to me.

"You're telling me you use such language around a priest?"

"Not lately, but I know Sean's heard me cuss."

"Sean?" he caught me not using the title.

"Sorry, Father Sean," I corrected.

"So, what's the deal with that?"

He was quickly turning the tables on me.

"The deal with what?" I forced him to define exactly what he was asking.

"Must be weird, dating the guy and then having him become your priest," he reflected.

"He's assigned to the Newman Center at the University. It's not like he works at Blessed Sacrament that often. I don't really think about it much." I said exactly what I had been saying for the past six months whenever anyone asked.

"So you guys weren't that serious?"

I didn't say anything, because I couldn't bring myself to lie; knowing that looking at engagement rings counted as serious to most people.

"It was a long time ago. I was a junior in undergrad."

"How long did you go out?"

"Oh...like a year." I hoped the casual way I answered would downplay the idea that the relationship had been more serious than I was letting on. Simultaneously, I sped up our pace, almost as if it would help me speed through this part of our conversation. Thomas' longer legs handled the pace adjustment without any trouble.

"You consider a year nothing serious?" he asked with slight disbelief.

I let a moment of silence pass.

"Let's talk about something else," I stated cheerfully.

I was breathing heavier after stupidly changing up the pace. Luckily, there was less than a mile left.

"Sure," he said easily. "So, what's the deal with that Ethan guy? You sleeping with him?" His bold question startled me out of my train of thought.

"What?" I blurted out, shocked by his audacity.

I slowed down and looked over at him; he continued to stare ahead with a small smirk, letting me know he'd gotten the reaction he was looking for.

"What? I thought I was supposed to change the subject? Was it inappropriate for me to ask that?" he said innocently.

"I liked it more when we were talking about you."

"Of course you did; social workers are nosy," he teased, not realizing how unsettled his questions had made me.

My mind was racing because I realized he'd made a misconception about me. I knew it really shouldn't have shocked me because I was twenty-five and well aware that it was common for people my age to have had sex. However, usually once people found out how involved I was in church, they were able to conclude on their own that I was probably a virgin. For some reason, Thomas had assumed otherwise. I wasn't sure if should have corrected him, and part of me wondered why, for the first time in my life, I was embarrassed by the thought of admitting it to someone.

"So, doing anything else today?" I prayed I could get things back to a less personal topic.

"Family dinner at six."

"Oh, with everyone?"

"Yep, every Sunday since I've been back," Thomas didn't sound thrilled.

"Well maybe you can talk to Michael about your work schedule," I suggested with a cheesy smile, predicting that he would think it was a horrible idea.

"How about you come over and start that conversation? He seems to like you more, and then maybe you can lead us in a round of the Glad Game, followed by affirmations."

"You know, I would, but I can't; I have to go to mass. Raincheck?" We rounded the corner to the last stretch of the lake. I sped up and he mirrored my pace. Neither of us said anything for the remainder of the distance.

I gradually slowed down once we got to our starting point. He slowed down as well until we were walking side by side, both of us catching our breath. He stood still for a minute with his hands on his hips.

"You want to grab something to eat?"

He grabbed the bottom of his shirt and lifted it up to wipe sweat off his face. I caught myself staring at his abs and then quickly looked away. I wondered if I had always been a prude and was just now realizing it.

"I didn't bring any money," I started to decline.

"It's cool; I owe you for the beer on Wednesday anyway."

"Okay, there's a coffee shop over there," I motioned down the street.

He nodded, still catching his breath. I led us out of the park. As we walked by the basketball court, we heard someone shouting.

"Tommy! Tommy! O'Hollaren!"

Thomas and I turned to see who was calling to him. A dark-blond haired guy in a zip-up hoodie and basketball shorts was heading towards us.

"Shit man, I thought that was you," he said, smiling.

He reached out and shook Thomas' hand.

"Hey, man," Thomas greeted him. "What's up?"

"'What's up'? What do you mean 'what's up'? What's up with you? I didn't expect to see you around here. I thought your ass was still in New York."

"Nope, I'm back."

"So like back, back? For good?"

"Probably," Thomas said simply.

His friend looked over at me and introduced himself. "Hey, I'm Tyler."

I shook his hand and said my name quickly, which I don't think he heard because he went back to looking at Thomas.

"So, hey man, I heard about your dad. Sorry about that. Is that why you're back?"

"Yeah, working at the shop now."

"Well shit, man, we've got to get together now that you're back! I'm sure everyone would love to see you."

It was interesting how quickly Tyler shifted from communicating his condolences to sounding like he was ready to party with Thomas.

"Yeah, definitely," Thomas agreed without sounding committed to the idea.

"You still have the same number?"

Thomas confirmed with a nod.

"Alright then, I'll text you and we'll get something going. Excellent."

Tyler reached out and shook Thomas' hand and then pulled him into a manly half hug, saying, "I'll catch you later, man."

He then turned to me and smiled. "Nice meeting you."

With that, Tyler headed back to the basketball court. Thomas didn't offer further explanation as we resumed walking.

"Thomas," I said, "shit man, are you a bro?"

He smiled at my inflection mirroring Tyler's.

"I went to school with Tyler. We took our business classes together," he explained.

"That guy was a business major? Shocking," I said sarcastically.

Tyler looked like the stereotypical business school guy; preppy, always shaking hands, a little too enthusiastic to ever seem genuine. Thomas knew exactly what I was thinking.

"That must have been draining, splitting your time between the business majors and the art majors," I reflected, thinking of the polarity of people represented by each academic focus.

"You have no idea," he sighed. "Throw in working part time with a bunch of mechanics and it leads to feeling like you've got multiple personalities."

"At least you're well-rounded, right?"

"There's that Pollyanna-side coming out again."

"Sorry," I apologized.

"No," he quickly responded. "It's good. I think I like it."

THOMAS

IT WAS THE FIRST TIME I HAD GONE FOR A RUN SINCE returning to Seattle. I tried to think of the last time I had run at all while I headed to the coffee shop with Maura. It had been the same day I'd found out that my dad had died. I'd gone for a run that morning and had come back to find the message from Michael on my phone.

It was strange that I hadn't thought about that morning until now. Probably because everything that had happened that day and that week seemed like a blur. Every now and then a small piece of it would pop into my head.

I wondered if Maura was going to ask me why I hadn't gotten in contact with Tyler or any other friends since returning. However, I think she picked up from our brief interaction with Tyler that he was pretty much just a drinking buddy from the past. I hadn't really been up for partying with anyone since I had returned. Then again, now that I had run into him, I knew Tyler would follow up with me. That wouldn't be the worst thing. If I went out with him, I would probably get laid. He always was a good wingman.

It had been over four months since I had had sex and I was closing in on five. Obviously, the death of your father and moving back into your mom's house interrupts your ability and desire to score. But in all honesty, I had hit my drought well before moving back home.

About three months before my dad died I had broken up with a girl I'd been casually seeing. It was purely physical, and I guess it got old for her after a few months when I wasn't 'valuing her mind and spirit,' as she put it. According to her, she had no choice but to end it.

At the time, I hadn't been in a rush to go out and find anybody new because of all of the bullshit you have to go through just for something casual. I had not anticipated that I was going to have to move back into my mother's house and work all the time. But like any man, I had my limits, and five months was way too long to go without sex.

The urge to get laid hit me hard after hanging out with Maura at the bar on Wednesday night. She wasn't as put together as some of the other girls I had dated over the past four years, but I considered that a good thing. She didn't seem to care if I was listening to the right band, knew about the latest performance artist featured at the hippest gallery, or if the beer she was drinking was organic. She had a good sense of humor and it didn't hurt that she was nice to look at, even if she was religious. That week I had determined that I was so horny, I was willing to overlook it.

It was obvious she was the type of girl who would be more effort than I was used to putting forth. But for some reason, with her it didn't feel like bullshit. Okay, maybe getting up and running three miles on my one day off was a little bit of bullshit to go through, but with my new steady diet of my mom's cooking, it was only a matter of time before I would have to start exercising again anyway.

I was glad she agreed to go grab some food after we finished running so I had the opportunity to show her I was not a total freeloader, despite living at my mother's. She went to grab us a table after I got her order, and I waited to get to the front of the counter. I was trying to figure out a subtle way to find out if she was currently dating or interested in someone. My attempts during our run had failed, but they'd left me with the sense that she was not completely unattached. I seriously hoped she wasn't in love with that priest. I couldn't compete with that. Then again, I could be the perfect distraction for unrequited love.

I grabbed the bag with our bagels, my black coffee, and her latte, and found her in the corner of the crowded shop.

"I guess we weren't the only ones who wanted bagels this morning," I commented on the crowd as I sat down and handed her drink to her.

"Thanks. Nothing better post-run than some empty carbs and caffeine."

"Maybe we'll get smoothies next time."

"Only if they have whey powder and wheatgrass," she mocked the trend.

"I'll start doing my research."

"You know, if you want a good breakfast, you have to go to 14 Carrot," she said.

"Aw man, I haven't been there in forever," I let out a sigh. "You've got me thinking about the sourdough pancakes now."

"I know!" she exclaimed, widening her eyes. "So good."

"So screw the smoothies. Pancakes next time," I declared.

I took a sip of my coffee, wondering if I should ask another question or wait to see if she would ask me something. I soon regretted waiting.

"So, I asked how your mom is, but how are you doing?" she looked at me with concern and I realized what she was alluding to. I had managed to avoid anyone specifically asking me how I was handling my father's death since the funeral.

"I'm fine," I said, but I didn't know if I really was. I'd never had a parent die before, so I wasn't sure how I was supposed to feel. More depressed? Less guilt? Should I have cried by now?

"Have you talked to anyone about it?"

"I'm not really a big talker," I said honestly.

"I know it might be off base, but I just thought I would offer to listen if you ever decided you needed or wanted that. I don't know if you've had a bunch of people pestering you, so it's fine if you don't want to talk about it. I tried to think of what I would want if I were in your shoes, and honestly I wasn't really sure." Maura sounded so genuine that I couldn't be annoyed with her.

"There's not much to really talk about," I said casually.

She nodded but continued to look at me, her eyes probing, trying to figure out if I was telling the truth.

"I guess you could say it's complicated…just like you and Father Sean."

She gave me a stern look.

"You see what I did there?" I smiled. "I brought up something you didn't want to talk about after you brought up something I didn't want to talk about," I said proudly before taking a sip of coffee.

"I guess we're even," she remarked simply and looked out the window.

"Of course, I might be willing to share about my complicated situation if you were willing to share about yours," I prompted.

She was fidgeting, hesitant to agree to my terms.

"I mean, I think it's only fair." I looked her earnestly in the eyes.

It was obvious that she was the type that would do just about anything if it meant she helped someone. Of course, it was foolish of her to think getting me to talk would actually help me, but she didn't need to know that. I was willing to bet that altruism acted as aphrodisiac for someone like her.

"Alright," she declared. "You go first."

"The last time I talked to my dad was three and a half years ago, right before I moved to New York." I said the words coolly.

I wondered how horrible of a person she thought I was. Maybe it was a miscalculated move to share that fact if I was trying to sleep with her, but now seemed as good a time as any to finally say it out loud. Especially since no one else in my family was willing to acknowledge it – at least not to my face.

"Why?" Her tone was neutral. That caught me off guard.

"He didn't want me to go; said I was making a huge mistake and that I was going to fail miserably, so I decided I was done with him. I think I even told him that."

"And how do you feel about that?"

Surprisingly, I couldn't tell if there was any judgment behind her question. She appeared to be simply concerned with how I was handling the situation. I wasn't ready to admit to her, or even really myself, that I was beginning to regret just how negative my relationship with my father had been, so I shrugged and lied.

"I don't know. It doesn't make a difference how I feel about it. I can't change anything."

She nodded. I waited for her evaluation but she didn't give it to me. She just stared at me with those beautiful blue eyes, the same way she did at the funeral. If she kept looking at me like that, I was going to talk more about that asshole – I might even share how pathetic I was when it came to being alone in that stupid house. I wasn't about to let that happen. She had gotten enough from me.

"So, your turn. Why is it complicated with Father Sean? You in love with him?"

"No," she drew out the word and I could tell she was choosing her next words carefully. "When a guy becomes a priest, his commitment is to the Church, the same way as it would be if had he married another woman. So essentially, I get to see who and what he left me for every time I'm around him.

"Then you add the reality that there are expectations about how he should act around me, so the only solution is to pretend like one of the most important relationships of my life never happened... which is just kind of sad and lonely, living in a separate reality than everyone else."

"So why not switch churches? Blessed Sacrament isn't the only Catholic church in Seattle." I thought it was the obvious solution.

"I've thought about it, and I may end up doing that, but it just seems like it would cause more drama than it's worth. Church folks like to talk. Anyway, I've gone to Blessed Sacrament since the sixth grade; it seems silly to leave because of an ex-boyfriend."

"It's obviously not bothering him if he chose to come back here and was making jokes about it the other night."

"He doesn't get a say. He goes where the Dominicans tell him to go and they wanted someone younger at the Newman Center to work with the college students. When he first found out he was coming back, he sent me an email and said that he gave them full disclosure and tried to get placed somewhere else. They said they felt that it wouldn't be an issue and it would be a good exercise in obedience for him. And honestly if the other priests at Blessed Sacrament knew about what he shared on Wednesday, he probably would've gotten reprimanded for being inappropriate."

"It sounds to me like those Dominicans are causing a lot of their own drama," I declared. "But I mean, it is kind of their MO when you consider that whole Spanish Inquisition thing." I managed to make her smile. "But you know, nobody ever–"

"Expects the Spanish Inquisition," she finished the line before I got a chance to.

"Exactly. I don't think I technically count as part of your church, so if you ever want to tell me stories about the days of yore when Father Sean used to hold your hand and recite love poems to you in the meadow, I guess I'm willing to listen."

She shook her head at my ridiculousness.

"But you'll have to spare me when it comes to recounting what he's like in bed, because that's a little weird, even for me."

She stopped smiling and suddenly I realized I had miscalculated.

"Sean and I never…" her voice trailed off, uncomfortable finishing the sentence.

"Oh, I just assumed since you dated for a year," I tried to justify what I thought was a natural assumption.

She looked down at her cup. Suddenly I realized that she wasn't just talking about her past relationship with Father Sean.

I leaned in and said, "You don't do that at all do you?"

"No," she said simply, and I knew I hadn't successfully hidden the surprise on my face. I leaned back in my chair. I paused for a moment; she stayed silent but was still looking at me, waiting for me to say something.

"So, never?"

She shook her head in confirmation.

"Huh," was all I managed to get out.

I realized I was probably making her more uncomfortable, so I tried to recover. "So, you're like, waiting 'till you're married?"

She nodded. I hadn't asked a girl that question since high school. "Huh," I said stupidly again.

I had many questions going through my mind, most of which I knew were none of my business.

"So you're like…one of those really good kids," I stated my revelation out loud.

"Oh please," she said, rolling her eyes.

"I'm serious! I mean, I knew you were a good person with all the homeless and church stuff, but this, this officially makes you too good of a person to hang around me."

"Shut up," she stared at me, unaffected by my teasing. "Thomas, it's not that big of a–"

"Hold on," I interrupted her. "I'm going to need a minute here."

I sighed heavily and took a drink of my coffee. "I don't think I've ever hung out with anyone as…pure as you. As a matter of fact, I don't think there was a time when I was as pure as you – ever. And then you've got this whole noble thing going on with trying to protect the priest ex-boyfriend and getting the jerk whose dad just died to talk about his feelings…I'm a little worried you're going to catch the sin radiating off of my body right now as we speak."

"You done yet?" she said flatly, unaware that I was legitimately impressed by her.

I paused and smiled at her because of the new information I'd gathered.

"Really, it's not that big of a deal," she reiterated.

"It's just that you seemed so normal," I said honestly, thinking of how socially awkward people who were virgins had been in high school and college.

"And you seemed like a gentleman before," she shot back.

"Guess we fooled one another. So, you still want to hang out with a lowly sinner like me?"

"I guess," she sighed. "Someone's got to show you that God loves you…and I don't think it's going to be Tyler." Her tone had humor in it, but I wasn't sure if she was completely joking. I laughed anyway.

"No, probably not."

I came to terms with the fact that I would never have sex with her, and it did not disappoint me as much as I would have expected. For some reason, friendship with her seemed more interesting, anyway. I got the sense that she felt the same way about me, although I had no idea why.

MAURA

IT FINALLY HAPPENED. AFTER MONTHS OF SPECULATION, Ethan finally asked me out on a date...at least I thought he had. I got the usual text asking if I was going to Wednesday night mass. Originally, I said yes, but ended up having to provide suicide intervention for one of the kids I worked with. Eventually the kid was taken to the hospital and placed on a 5150 hold. I texted Ethan around five o'clock when I was at the hospital waiting for the kid to be admitted, since it was clear that I would not be making it that night. I got a response from him asking if I wanted to get drinks the next night. A non-church event with just the two of us. Clearly a date...right?

I chose to meet him at Teddy's, the bar around the corner from my apartment. The cleverly named Teddy's is located on Roosevelt Avenue, and is what comes to mind when I think of a manly bar. It is not at all flashy. The walls are covered with sports posters – mostly from the '90s – pennants, and even baseball cards on the ceiling, along with the standard alcohol advertisements. But it's far from a sports bar, because there are no TVs. There is one pretty scuffed up pool table and two dart boards, so maybe it could be classified as a pub, but they don't serve food, which I think is a standard for a pub. Perhaps I would classify it as a tavern.

However, when I think of a tavern, I think of old seafaring men as the main patronage, and over the past year, Teddy's had been taken over by newly legal hipsters who were "so over" the scene in the U-District and too poor for the Belltown bars and clubs. I guess it was appropriate that I picked a location that I couldn't classify correctly in my head since I couldn't even tell whether or not the thing I was meeting there for was a date.

It was a Thursday night, so I was hopeful it wouldn't be overflowing with skinny jeans, beanies, and beards. I picked Teddy's mostly because I could walk there and I wouldn't have to stress about what to wear. I left my apartment right at the time I was supposed to meet Ethan because I knew if I got there before him and was given too much time to myself, I would start over-thinking things and be nervous and awkward by the time he showed up.

Overthinking was a specialty of mine, especially in the last two years when it came to men. When you only date religious people, dating is never about having fun. Dating is about finding out if the person is supposed to be your spouse – from day one. No pressure. Yeah right. It was exhausting to try and figure out whether you wanted to marry someone before you'd even kissed him. Not to mention how self-conscious it made me feel to know that I was constantly being evaluated as marriage material. But it seemed to be the price I had to pay if I ever wanted to marry a Catholic man – at least one who actually went to church and who didn't consider 'no sex before marriage' to be a deal breaker.

Currently, I was on a very cold streak in the world of Catholic dating. There had been two boyfriends since Sean, but they'd both ended up leaving me to marry their ex-girlfriends, even though they had claimed to break up with me because they were discerning the priesthood.

There had been a few men – *Don't lie Maura, you know that there were exactly eight of them* – in the young adult group who had done what Ethan had been doing with me, texting and occasionally hanging out with me at group events. But I ultimately failed to meet whatever criteria they had for me to be deemed worthy of the coveted title of "dateable."

It's fine, I didn't like them much anyway.

71

At least that's what I told myself. When eight men could make you feel like you'd been dumped without ever even buying you dinner, it was a little discouraging. Hence my hesitancy to become excited about Ethan's apparent interest in me. He just seemed so orthodox and I was so obviously not – my prediction was that he would lose interest the minute I admitted I didn't see the point in Latin mass. Which was too bad because he looked like he would be nice to kiss and I hadn't kissed anyone in sooooo long.

There you go, objectifying again – strike two, Maura, strike two.

As I'd hoped, Ethan was sitting at a booth waiting for me when I walked into the bar. He was dressed in work clothes, black slacks and a light blue button-up shirt, but he had taken the step to look a little more casual by rolling up his sleeves. He had his glasses on, which of course I appreciated.

He stood up to greet me, in true gentlemanly fashion.

"Hey," he smiled and went in to hug me before I could decide if I was going to hug him or not.

This was more initiative than I had expected. I said my hello and took a seat across from him.

"I went ahead and ordered a beer, but I didn't know what you wanted," he said.

I turned to see the taps while the waitress made her way over to us.-

"I'll just have a Stella," I ordered, and then looked back at him. "So, what's new?"

"Not much," he said and looked down at the table before looking back to me. "I feel like I haven't seen you in a while."

In addition to not having seen me the previous night, he was referring to the fact that for the past two weeks, I had not gone to Sunday ten-thirty mass like I normally did. This was because I had chosen to go running with Thomas instead and had gone to the evening mass as a result. Also, I had not gone to midweek mass the week before because I'd had dinner with my parents.

"Yeah, I know," I agreed, unsure if I needed to go into an explanation.

"It's kind of been a downer."

"Are you sure it's not just because it's Lent?" I joked.

He let out a half laugh as my beer arrived, "Yeah, I'm pretty sure. So, what've you been up to?"

"Not much, just work. We've had some pretty busy days and yesterday was kind of intense. Tried to give up caffeine for Lent, failed miserably, thought about giving up alcohol instead, but quickly got over that and went back to failing to give up coffee. I switched up my mass time to five forty-five p.m. You know, trying to keep things interesting in my old age."

I felt like I needed to tell him I wasn't skipping mass altogether, because I thought he might have been worried about that and it would have ultimately ruled me out as a potential wife, err, I mean girlfriend. Best to get the focus off myself before I said something stupid.

"So hey, you have that big ski trip this weekend with the group. You excited?" I asked.

"Yeah, it should be pretty fun. I haven't been skiing in this area since I moved out here. I heard we're going to have a bigger group because Father Sean and some of the grad students from the Newman Center are coming too. That's actually what I wanted to talk to you about."

When he paused, I immediately assumed he was going to ask me questions about Sean in response to gossip he had gathered from the group.

"I just wanted to see if I could try to talk you into changing your mind at the last minute? I really want you to go. I think you'd have fun."

I was relieved that that was all he wanted to know. However, the thought of going on a group ski trip was even more unappealing now that I knew Sean would be the resident priest there. I envision him being the "cool" priest with all the grad students, showing off his athleticism on the slopes, following it up with a humorous, yet heartfelt homily before consecrating the Eucharist. He'd probably even move people to the point of wanting to receive the sacrament of reconciliation, which he'd offer impromptu style on a couch in some private corner of the cabin.

The thought shouldn't have annoyed me, but it did. I realized I hadn't responded to Ethan's invitation and he probably thought I was actually contemplating it.

"You know," I started with a smile, "that's really sweet of you, but I really, really don't like skiing...or being cold."

"But you're forgetting one thing: you've never been skiing with me."

He smiled and stared into my eyes and I was surprised by the amount of confidence he was showing.

"I'm pretty sure we can make a fire at the cabin to solve that cold problem."

"Maybe next time," I maintained my stance.

He sighed.

"I knew it was a long shot. That's why I wanted to make sure I got to see you before I left."

"Whelp, here I am," I said awkwardly and took a drink. I was nervous. I don't know if it was justified or not. Why did dating have to be such a big production for Blessed Sacrament guys?

"Maura, I know I don't know you really well, but I've been thinking and praying a lot about it and I would really like to get know you better one-on-one." He paused and waited for my response.

I didn't get why he had to be so serious about it. I mean, I didn't have a problem if he'd prayed about dating me, but why did he have to tell me about it? I guess I was just an old school Catholic and liked to keep the things I prayed about to myself.

Furthermore, if he wanted to date me, why not say that instead of the whole "one-on-one" thing? I realized it would be snobby and kind of stupid for me to turn him down just because I didn't like his phrasing. He was a nice, employed, Catholic, and not at all bad to look at. There was really no good reason for me not to date him... especially if I wanted to get married someday.

"That sounds good."

Really, Maura, that's most eloquent response you can come up with?

Thankfully, he smiled and didn't seem put off by my casual answer.

"So...how do you want to get to know me better?"

"I don't know," he laughed, presumably at my awkwardness. "I hadn't thought past what I just said because I was half expecting you to tell me no thanks."

"Really?" I said, feigning surprise.

Admittedly, I hadn't been the most encouraging with his attention. But can you blame me? I had gotten to the point where getting excited about the crumbs of courtship these devout Catholic guys offered was pointless because it never added up to anything meaningful.

"I don't know, sometimes you're hard to read and, well, I wasn't sure if you stopped coming to ten-thirty mass because you wanted to get away from me?"

"Me? Hard to read?" I laughed. "You just haven't been around me long enough to witness me rambling on about everything going on my head," I shared.

Lately, I had kept this nervous habit under wraps when hanging out with the Blessed Sacrament young adult crowd. Sean had found it endearing and used to joke that I was the only person in the world who could have an argument with myself. But after the fourth Catholic pseudo-suitor determined I was not even worthy to take on a date, I categorized neurotic rambling as an undesirable when it came to qualities for a potential wife. It was a risk to even bring it up to Ethan, but if he was really going to date me, it was better to warn him now.

"I imagine that's been helpful to guys you've dated in the past." His positive take on the subject caught me off guard.

"Maybe," I deflected. "Usually they found it annoying." I took a drink of my beer before I made the mistake of sharing every quality that past guys had found undesirable. There was a lull.

Great Maura, you actually called yourself annoying. It's like you are trying to give him reasons not to date you.

"So," Ethan broke the silence.

I thought he was going to ask me how else I irritated people.

"I think what I really need to know before we take the next step of going out to dinner is what your confirmation saint name is?" He smiled and I felt my muscles relax.

"Wow, I haven't heard that pickup line in a while," I said coolly, but really I was so relieved that he was being less serious than I had expected. "It's Saint Monica."

"Patron Saint of Lapsed Catholics?"

I nodded.

"Why did you pick that one?"

"I was a huge fan of the show Friends," I said sarcastically. "No, I just loved the idea that she never gave up on Augustine and never lost faith that he would turn his life around."

He nodded, appreciating my reasoning.

"What's yours?"

"Saint Isidore of Seville," he said sheepishly.

"The patron saint of computers," I laughed.

"Yeah, I know it's kind of lame. I am impressed you know that, though."

"I guess some of us knew what they wanted to be early on in life."

"You didn't always want to be a social worker?"

"I didn't even know what a social worker was until high school. But my mom likes to tell people about how I used to wrap myself up in a sheet and play Mother Teresa with my stuffed animals when I was little."

"Are you serious?" He was grinning, so he must still have been finding me amusing.

"Oh yeah, I even wrapped them in bandages – which were actually my socks – and I would lay them out in rows on the floor like they were on gurneys...and now that I'm sharing this, it sounds kind of weird."

"No, I think it sounds pretty adorable," he stated genuinely. "You don't think this was an early call to religious life?"

I shook my head.

"No, I think it was more a calling that I needed a sibling to play with," I joked off discussing anything having to do with vocation, afraid it would lead to talking about the break up with Sean.

We paused for a moment and stared at each other. He had dark brown eyes, that until that point, I had been careful not to appreciate. I was starting to feel more comfortable around him.

"You sure I can't talk you into coming with me this weekend?" he tried to persuade me with his smile.

Unexpectedly, I considered it briefly, but determined I'd rather wait and hang out with him next week without all the other people around – "other people" mostly being Jessica and Sean.

"Yeah, I'm sure. It'll give you something to look forward to next week."

"Sounds good," he agreed and then reached across the table and to gently place his hand on top of mine. This was not a big deal in the secular world, but I knew it was a big step for a guy like Ethan.

THOMAS

IT WAS SATURDAY NIGHT AND I WAS GETTING READY TO meet up with Tyler and Jeremy, another guy I went to college with. I knew them initially from high school when we played baseball together, them we'd reconnected in college when we all took the same business course.

Tyler and Jeremy had started off living in the dorms and eventually rented a house off campus. This had made them great to party with, since my parents demanded I live at home while attending college to save money. I spent most of my Thursday, Friday, and Saturday nights crashing on Tyler and Jeremy's couch after some of the heaviest drinking of my life.

After I moved to New York, I lost touch with them. No shock there, since our friendship was based purely on drinking and helping each other get laid. Nonetheless, I was certain it would be easy to pick up where I'd left off with them, bullshitting and trying to get laid.

Tyler texted for me to meet them at Kell's in Belltown. I wasn't thrilled about dealing with parking my dad's large Chevy truck on a cramped downtown street just to get a drink in a loud, crowded bar on a Saturday night. But it was better than the alternative: staying with my mom while she babysat my sister's kids.

I probably could've been guilted into helping her had it been my brother's four crazy kids, but Margaret's two girls were considerably more mellow than Michael's boys. My mom seemed excited to hear I was meeting up with Tyler and Jeremy. It was like I'd just told her I made a new friend on the first day of school.

In contrast to the past, I was considerate and told her I'd probably be out past midnight or I might stay at Tyler's until morning. Unexpectedly, she didn't protest like she had when I was younger. My mom understood that this would be part of me moving back and living with her, and probably would have agreed that it was a better alternative to stumbling in drunk with a girl at three a.m.

As I expected, it took me a good twenty minutes to find parking. I headed into the pub and spotted Tyler and Jeremy already half done with their pints.

Tyler saw me walk in, held up his arms and belted out, "Tommy!"

Jeremy joined in.

"Come here you snobby New York mother fucker!" Tyler called me over to their table. Even knowing my dad had just died, Tyler's demeanor hadn't changed, and I loved that.

"I was just telling Jeremy here that you finally fucking gave up your pastels and shit and are back at the shop."

"Yep," I confirmed. "But that's old news. What have you guys been up to?" I asked, not wanting to talk about New York or working at the shop.

"We're both working for Alexander Hutton, here downtown," said Tyler, the more talkative of the two.

He started to pull out his business card when I grabbed his hand.

"Don't fucking pull out your card. What the fuck I am going to do with an investment banker? Who's the fucking snob now?" I didn't even have a drink in my hand yet and I already sounded exactly like Tyler.

"I don't know, bro. You may have assets I don't know about."

Just then the waitress, a young, petite blonde, came up to the table and took my order. Tyler and Jeremy unabashedly checked her out.

"Speaking of assets," Jeremy commented with a grin. "Seriously, bro, that is happening tonight. We got the Prodigal Son back; we have to go all out!" Tyler grabbed my shoulders and started to wring them. "Thomas O'Hollaren, are...you..ready...to chase some tail?!"

Tyler may have sounded drunk, but this was just his personality. I didn't respond as enthusiastically as he had hoped. I had to ease back into being around Tyler and his obnoxious bro-ness.

"Dude, what's the deal? Are you pussing out on me tonight?"

"Nah, man, it's not that."

"Oh, wait, are you tied down? Is there some bitch back in New York?"

Tyler's very limited experience in New York left him with the impression that all the women there were bitches. I would argue in their defense that they simply could see through Tyler's shit more quickly than he was used to.

When I shook my head again, his eyes widened. "Wait, nah, man, is it that piece you were with at the park last Sunday? I can respect that. She was pretty fine, in a girl-next -door kind of way."

"No, she's nobody," I simplified who Maura was for the sake of not having to call her a friend and catch shit from Tyler. "It's just been awhile since I've gone out," I admitted, not intending to allude to my dry spell.

Unfortunately, Tyler and Jeremy saw through me.

"Dude, yeah, we get it. Your dad died," Jeremy said in the most heartfelt way he could.

"Shit, man, no big deal, just a month, right?" Tyler said, having just finished his pint.

I didn't respond.

"Longer than a month?"

"Jesus, man, at least let me get a drink before you start hassling me."

"Dude you gotta give me the number."

I sighed and rolled my eyes.

"I'll keep guessing and I'll be able to tell," Tyler threatened.

I didn't want to fess up, but Tyler and Jeremy were probably the best people I knew to lament the drought with. Everyone else in my life would probably hear the number and say, "That's a good start. Keep going until you find someone to marry."

"Five," I said, avoiding eye contact.

"Five weeks?" Jeremy tried to clarify.

I didn't answer.

"Oooohhhh, shit, bro!" Tyler exclaimed, grabbing my shoulder. "We're talking months!"

He and Jeremy burst out laughing, just as I'd expected. Tyler finally regained his composure. "Well, fuck, Tommy, I'd say you came out with the right guys tonight," he pulled out his phone and started texting.

"What're you doing?" I asked, looking over at him.

"Wing-manning, like the old days, my friend," he completed his text and lifted his hand up to Jeremy. "Up top."

I shook my head while they high fived.

"You'll see. I know some horny bitches in the U-District we can meet up with. You'll be thanking me by the end of the night," he stated confidently and winked at me.

After closing out, we arrived at Finn McCool's in the U-District a little after ten o'clock. The bar hadn't changed since I had been there in college. Complete with the same tacky Irish pub decor hung throughout and one-dollar High Lifes – the poor college student's version of Kell's.

I turned to Tyler and Jeremy after the bouncer stamped our hands.

"You really think this is a good idea?" I asked, feeling reservations about going to a college bar when we clearly were no longer in college.

"Yes!" Tyler answered, exasperated.

He pulled me to the side of the bar like a coach prepping a quarterback for a big game.

"You've been out of the game for a while. It would be stupid to stay in Belltown and try to pick up actual, grown-up women with jobs."

· We paused and took a break to order our beers. Luckily, it wasn't busy and we could start drinking sooner rather than later. This helped me tolerate Tyler and his pep talk.

"Your confidence in me is overwhelming," I responded flatly.

"No, no bro, you know it's not like that. All I'm saying is the last thing we need tonight is entitled, stuck-up, bitches. What you need is a girl looking to be shown a good time by a slightly older, experienced man who can afford to buy her drinks. Someone who just wants to have fun and isn't hung up on all that serious shit like commitment or whatever the fuck Oprah's telling them they want."

"You realize Oprah's no longer on TV?"

"You're killing me, Tommy!" Tyler said, shoving me. "Be sure to open with that line if you want to go home alone and jerk it in your mother's house for the millionth time."

"Maybe I'll just go jerk it at your mother's house," I said.

"Ohhh," Jeremy exclaimed into his rolled-up fist.

Instead of punching me, Tyler pulled me in and patted me hard on the back.

"See, there's my boy, there's my boy. Save some of that wit for the ladies. Speaking of which…" he said, looking over my shoulder to three young, attractive girls heading our way.

He walked up to them and gave the tall, blonde one a hug and pulled back to admire her.

"Hey, it's so great you ladies could meet up with us tonight," Tyler said as he walked them over to Jeremy and me. "I want to introduce you to my friends. This is Jeremy and Tommy. We go way back, like, all the way to high school. This is Michelle and her friends" he said, looking to Michelle to introduce the other two.

"This is Sabrina," Michelle said, pointing to the equally blonde, slightly shorter one, "And this is Natalie," she pointed to a shorter brunette on her right. "So, what're you guys up to tonight?" Michelle asked.

"We're actually celebrating tonight, so you ladies need some drinks. Go over and order whatever you want. It's on me; just give them my name. I already started a tab."

The girls looked impressed by this gesture. I didn't remember Tyler needing so much bravado in the past. Tyler picked up on what I was thinking and gave me a look to convey that I should trust him. Jeremy continued drinking his beer looking completely content to follow Tyler's lead. Michelle, Sabrina, and Natalie made their way back to us with various mixed drinks in hand.

"So, what are we celebrating?" Michelle asked, flipping her hair back to reveal her cleavage.

"My boy, Tommy, here"–Tyler put his hand on my shoulder holding his pint glass up in his other hand–"has finally come back from New York and we are so fucking glad to have him back in Seattle-fucking-Washington. The true big apple!"

Before anyone could see my look of confusion for Tyler's bizarre declaration, the four of them lifted their glasses with him and cheered. Finding no way out of it, I joined in. Because I had spent the last few years trying to fit in amongst the coveted New York art community, cheering for anything, particularly mundane things, had become unfamiliar. I mean, a true artist was above that shit. At least, that's what it seemed like when I was there.

"Oh my God! I love New York!" Natalie exclaimed.

I could tell she wasn't wearing a bra underneath her well-fitted T-shirt. I realized Tyler was trying to do me a favor, introducing me to this college girl, but it felt almost predatory given that we were specifically seeking out younger, more naive girls to hook up with. Then again, there I was, five months dry, craving sex, so wasn't it supposed to feel animalistic? Was five years difference really that big of a deal?

Ultimately, my penis overruled my scruples and I decided to play up the "I lived in New York" card. Tyler, reading my mind, led the rest of the group away to a corner booth.

"Oh? What do you love about New York?" I countered, hovering over her with my Mac and Jack's.

Her face was almost perfectly round, complimenting her large, doe-like brown eyes. She was considerably shorter than me with a very small frame, but her shirt and jeans accentuated what little curves she had. Conveniently, someone passed by us, forcing me to press a little closer to her.

She shot me a sly smile.

"Um, only, like, everything!" she exclaimed. "But I've only been there once for, like, New Year's, two years ago. I'm Natalie by the way."

She reached out her manicured hand to shake mine. I didn't know why she felt the need to reintroduce herself. But it was clear looking down into her eyes that she was attracted to me, so I just went with it.

"It's hard not to love New York once you've been there," I said. Not wanting to be a buzzkill, I held back the details about how uninspired and unsuccessful I had felt there for the past four years. It's not like this girl would've understood what I was talking about anyway. "But you know, it's always great to come back to the Northwest. It's not quite so pretentious."

She nodded, raising her drink to her lips without breaking eye contact, leaving it to me to continue the conversation.

"So, you loved everything about New York? You didn't have any specifics? Like a homeless man yelling at you? Or getting groped on the subway?" I asked, curious how she would respond to my humor.

"Ew! Ick! No!" Natalie playfully slapped my arm. She shook her head, keeping her smile. "I really liked the shopping. The stores and shops were phenomenal! Plus, it was just so great being in the same place as Carrie Bradshaw."

She took another drink, glancing back at my eyes again. She was fully aware of her physical assets. She made a point to keep her eyes as open as possible and hold her chest high, pushing it against me. It was impossible not to get turned on by the intensity of her stare.

"That was totally the same reason why I liked it," I said, hoping she would pick up on the sarcasm. She began to giggle.

"Yeah, I bet you are a huge Sex and the City fan" she laughed, taking another drink.

She paused and smiled with the straw still between her teeth. I knew she had used this move before. I couldn't fault her for it. Innocent meets sexy. A killer combination.

"For sure," I said. "I'm totally a Samantha."

I had no idea what the hell that meant. I was just grasping at straws in my memory of what girlfriends had said about Sex and the City over the years.

"That's good news, because I am totally a Samantha, too," she whispered.

Before I knew it, she leaned in and kissed me. I felt her tongue enter my mouth, not aggressive, but definitely assertive. This was way more than I anticipated for a first kiss from her.

She pulled back and giggled, "I bet you weren't expecting that."

"No, I can't say that I was," I smiled and tried to gather myself.

Most of the blood had flooded from my brain and I stared at her lips and wondered what she looked like naked. Since it looked like this was headed there, I decided it was time to figure out how crazy or slutty she was. I had hoped it wasn't too much of either.

"So," I sighed, "let me take a minute to gather myself," I said honestly and smiled, knowing that this gee-shucks approach would probably work on her.

While I wasn't being entirely insincere, over the years I had discovered that playing this up seemed to attract women, because the neurotic nerd was not the player at the bar who they had to be weary of.

"And what else should I know about you, Natalie? What do you do?"

She laughed and raised her eyebrows, hinting that the question could be taken in a naughty direction, but then she answered seriously, "I'm a senior here at UW. I'm finishing up my Bachelor's in Communication."

I nodded, realizing that it had been a long time since I had been in a conversation with someone about their major.

· "Don't ask me what I want to do with it after June, because I haven't figured that part out," she smiled and shrugged her shoulders in a carefree manor. "What about you? What's your major?"

The bar had become packed at this point and we were shouting at one another to be heard over the crowd. I saw Tyler sitting in the corner with Jeremy, holding court with Michelle and Sabrina who didn't know any better. He briefly gave me a thumbs-up, which I think was more of a symbol of him congratulating himself than celebrating my progress.

"Um, well," I smiled, reflecting on how four years seems to make quite a difference when you're in your twenties, "when I was in school, I majored in Art and minored in Business, here at UW."

"Oh? You graduated? When?" she shouted.

We had been moved up against the wall as more and more people had entered the bar. I wondered if she was concerned about what a twenty-six-year-old was doing at a bar in the U-District if he wasn't in grad school.

"A few years ago. I've been in New York working as an artist for the past three and a half years." Knowing that I was walking the line of being either a creepy loser or an intriguing older man in her eyes, I used the one piece of information I'd told myself I wouldn't use for something as superficial as getting laid.

"Yeah," I leaned in, making a point to make eye contact with her, "I moved back here about two months ago because my dad passed away and they needed me to help with the family business."

As the words left my mouth, I felt a little less respect for myself, but was pleased when the meaning of what I'd said registered in her eyes. She touched her hand to my chest and looked at me with the same stare I'd been seeing for weeks, every time I told someone about my dad.

"I'm so sorry to hear that. Gosh, I don't know what to say. Is that why you came out with Tyler tonight? He was trying to cheer you up and get your mind off things?"

She was now standing extremely close, despite having some extra room around her. I nodded, pointedly not bothering to let her in on the fact that Tyler's main agenda was to get me laid. Feeling a little guilty that I'd chosen to make things heavier than the average bar pick-up scene, I tried to get things back on track without showing that I was using my dead father as a play. I decided to go with being endearingly awkward and obvious.

"Wow, I'm sorry to be such a downer. What guy brings up shit like that when he meets a hot girl?" I rubbed the back of my neck and stared at the ground.

"No, don't feel bad. Here," she grabbed my empty glass, "I'm going to get you another drink. Because, you know, life is short, and we should celebrate the good times," she attempted to sound wise.

As Natalie backed away to make her way towards the bar, she kept her eyes locked on mine.

"I like your philosophy, Natalie." I gave her a small smile.

While Natalie was at the bar, Tyler appeared next to me.

"So, how's it going?" he pounded his fist softly on my chest.

His face was red; even now, he looked the same drunk as he had when we were freshmen together.

"It's going," I responded simply.

"Yeah, yeah, man," he nodded. "I think – I think we've done good work here tonight."

"We'll see." I didn't want to jinx anything.

"Well, Jeremy and I are heading out. We've convinced Michelle and Sabrina that it's better to drink for free at our apartment."

I looked over and saw the two girls that Natalie came with sharing the same plan with her at the bar. She was smiling and nodding and then they looked over at Tyler and me. They started laughing when they caught us staring at them.

"See, bro, I thought of everything. I am a great cock facilitator."

I raised an eyebrow at him.

"It's the opposite of cock blocking," he said matter-of-factly and slapped his hand to my shoulder, grabbing and shaking me, "Tommy's gonna get some pusssaaaaay tonight!"

I was thankful that the bar was so loud that only I could hear him. Jeremy walked up and said he was ready to go, giving me a knowing head nod as he left with Tyler to close his tab, and then the two of them headed out with Michelle and Sabrina.

I turned to see Natalie standing next to me holding two double shots.

She handed one to me.

"So, you've heard we've been ditched," she smiled and raised her shot to a cheers position.

"To being ditched," I smiled and clinked the glass to hers before shooting.

"Whiskey," I commented.

"Of course. I thought about getting you a Cosmo in honor of our shared love of Sex and the City, but I just couldn't see you drinking that."

"Well thank you for preserving my image as a man."

We placed our empty shot glasses on a nearby ledge.

Natalie stared into my eyes, suddenly looking more mature than before.

"So," she leaned in, making me bend my head down to hear her whisper, "how about we take off and see what being Samanthas together will lead to?"

Unable to offer a verbal response, I nodded. What followed was a blur of intensely making out with her; against a wall outside of the bar, then in my dad's truck to the point where I thought we were about to have sex in the truck. However, she pulled back from a long kiss and asked where I was going to take her. I freely shared that I lived with my widowed mother and could not take her back to my place, which surprisingly appeared to be more of a turn on than a turn off, judging by the way she kissed me more deeply and then directed me back to her apartment. I wasn't sure how well pity sex was going to turn out, but so far it was looking pretty good.

Natalie unlocked her front door and squinted at me with a look which I assume she intended to be seductive. I paused, trying not to laugh at her exaggerated attempt to create a sensual atmosphere, probably modeled after movies she had seen, but I decided I could go with it. I reached around her slender waist and pulled her in for a deep, long kiss. She let out a whimpering moan.

"I want you, Tom" she whispered into my ear.

It was a cliché thing to say, and I never really went by that nickname, but I wasn't turned off by it. Instead, I felt more assertive, wrapping my arms around her tighter, pushing myself against her while she let out another moan. Natalie unbuttoned my shirt and removed it, along with my undershirt. She let her hands trail down my chest and went for the button on my jeans.

Feeling confident, I stopped her, grabbing her hands and whispering into her ear, "Take me to your room."

She pulled back and kept her gaze on me, raising a mischievous eyebrow, while she led me to her bedroom. I grabbed her waist and enveloped her in another deep kiss. She fell back on the bed, pulling me on top of her, moaning despite the fact that I had hardly done anything that would constitute that level of pleasure.

At this point, I granted myself permission to explore her body, letting my hands wander up and down her torso, removing her shirt, confirming that she was not wearing a bra. I put my mouth to her small yet still intriguing breasts. I felt her writhe underneath me, which again I thought was overly dramatic, but I kept my mouth on her breast, demanding a continued response. She didn't disappoint. She took a brief break from her theatrics to direct me to the drawer where she kept her condoms.

Soon, she was saying my name again, pleading for me to enter her. I removed her jeans, followed by mine, and then pressed my hand between her legs, hearing an exaggerated moan once again and feeling a thrust of her pelvis. Not one to engage in any more foreplay than I had to, I gave her what she wanted.

The minute I entered her, I felt myself drawn into the dramatic scene she had been encouraging me to play into. Her moaning was now enticing me to press harder at a faster rate, yet experience reminded me to keep a steady, tried and true pace. This only seemed to excite her more. I started to think I was as good as she was leading me to believe I was as we finished together, and she caught her breath. I laid next to her and watched her breasts moving up and down at a rhythmic, hypnotic pace.

"Oh my God," she sighed. "That was so good."

I couldn't bring myself to respond with any words; every response sounded entirely too cocky in my head. Before I had to be bothered to think of something to say, she propped herself up on her elbow and turned to me.

"Do you want to spend the night? Maybe do it again in like an hour?"

I was surprised by how matter-of-fact she was. My experience had been that people were usually hesitant to spend the night after a first-time encounter like that, not wanting to come off as clingy.

It occurred to me that she might never have had a guy tell her no. I didn't know if it was a good idea to stay, since I didn't want her to think there was anything more between us than sex. However, I didn't have any compelling reasons to pass up more sex given my recent dry spell.

I smiled and ran my hand through her hair.

"Sure, sounds like fun."

"Well alright then," she laughed and curled up next to me.

It suddenly struck me that I missed sleeping next to a woman. It may not have been manly to like cuddling, but I was glad I could indulge in it for one night.

As I stared up at the ceiling, trying to go to sleep, out of nowhere the thought of Maura entered my mind. I wondered whether she wouldn't want to hang out with me anymore if she found out what I had done. The small amount of time I had spent with her led me to assume that using the story of your father dying to get sex from a stranger would be something she considered unacceptable behavior. I wondered why I cared what she thought.

I had never felt guilty after sex before, not even after I lost my virginity at seventeen in my parents' house while they were away tending to my dying grandfather. I reminded myself that Natalie was a grown-up, and what had occurred, while definitely not love, was consensual and enjoyable for both parties. No harm done. I drifted off to sleep only to be awoken, as foretold by Natalie, exactly an hour later. At that point, Maura was the last thing on my mind.

MAURA

I STOOD ON THE CORNER, WAITING FOR THOMAS. LAST Sunday he had said, "See you next week," before he headed home, as if running with me on Sundays was a set routine. I didn't think I'd needed to double check that we were running, but as I stood there five minutes after our meeting time, I began to wonder if maybe he had forgotten. I checked my phone to see if I had missed a message from him. Nothing. I contemplated texting him, but thought a five-minute delay was a little early to start pestering someone.

I felt silly waiting on the corner wearing running gear and just standing there while everybody else was running and moving around me. It was unusually sunny for early March, and in typical northwest fashion, everyone had flooded outside and the park was filled with people. Just when I thought I might take a walk around the block to keep myself busy, I looked up and saw Thomas running up to me.

"Hey," he greeted, out of breath. "Sorry I'm late."

He took another breath.

"I'm ready," he announced. "Let's do this."

"Do you want to head up and run around Ravenna to switch it up?" I motioned up

Sixty-fifth, referring to another park, thinking it would be less crowded.

"Sure," he nodded.

We began running up the street. Strangely, I felt the urge to tell him that Ethan had officially asked me out, but I decided to wait until it seemed more appropriate to bring it up.

"For a second, I thought you were going to flake on me," I said honestly.

"Nah, what else could I possibly do with my one morning off? Go to church?" he said sarcastically.

"But I did want to tell you, you were totally right about Colleen telling Michael our sixty-five hour a week schedule wasn't doable. He's going to open at six and go home at three, and I get to work the nine to six, which means," he paused for dramatic effect, "I get to sleep in until eight on weekdays!" he exclaimed.

Thomas was more animated than I had ever seen him before.

"We're also going to switch off every other Saturday."

"Exciting. See, I knew it wouldn't last forever. Wives can be incredibly convincing."

Before I could say anything else, Thomas asked me, "So, did you do anything fun this weekend? Bible study? Rosary club? Rave?"

"A rave? Do people even go to raves anymore?" I looked at him skeptically.

He smiled and shrugged as we ran.

"I don't know. It sounded clever."

I could not get past how different Thomas was acting. His happy demeanor was definitely out of character. Although I had really only started to get to know him. Perhaps Thomas was working through the grief process and was back to his normal self. But something still seemed odd about it.

"What is up with you?" I asked expectantly.

"What do you mean?" he feigned cluelessness and continued to smile.

"You're acting different."

"Different?"

"Yeah, you're acting...happy."

"Is that a bad thing?"

"No, it's just not what I was expecting."

"Well, maybe you're rubbing off on me, Pollyanna," he knocked his elbow against mine. "So, tell me about your weekend."

"Didn't do much. The young adult group went up to Snoqualmie so everybody was out of town. I hung out at my parents.'"

"Where do your parents live?" he motioned to the surrounding neighborhood, assuming that my parents lived nearby.

"Lake City."

"Why do they drive all the way out to Blessed Sacrament for church? There must be a closer church."

"They're kind of groupies. They like Dominicans." Blessed Sacrament was the only church in the Archdiocese, in addition to the Newman Center Chapel at the university, that was run by Dominicans.

"So you went to Nathan Hale?" Thomas asked about my high school alma mater.

I nodded, caught off guard by all of his get-to-know-you questions. It seemed so out of character.

"What do your parents do?"

"They're both teachers at Hale."

"Really? And here I thought I had overbearing parents."

"It wasn't that bad," I shared. "I've always gotten along with them."

"And we add yet another item to the list," he laughed.

"What list?"

"The list of qualities a ridiculously saintly person would have. Absence of teenage angst; check. Lack of conflict with parental figures; check." He made a checkmark motion with his hand and smiled at me.

I rolled my eyes. I had gotten past the point of trying to downplay things he insisted made me overly good.

"Why all the background questions this morning?"

"I don't know," he said honestly. "Maybe if I poke around long enough I'm going to discover something dark and sinister about you."

I raised an eyebrow at how hopeful he sounded.

"But I highly doubt it," he smiled as we ran at a faster pace, approaching the park.

I wondered where all his energy was coming from. The run was turning out to be much more rigorous than I had anticipated. I started the conversation back up in hopes that it would force him to slow down.

"So, I met up with Ethan on Thursday."

"Yeah?"

"Yeah, we went to Teddy's on Roosevelt. I think he asked me out finally."

"You think?"

"Well, he said he wanted to spend more one-on-one time together."

"Sounds thrilling," he said sarcastically. "Have you seen him since?"

"No, he's with the others at Snoqualmie."

"And why didn't you go?"

"I hate skiing and snowboarding." I left out my other reason for not wanting to go: Sean was going to be there.

"You could have just hung out in the Jacuzzi, getting drunk and making out...oh wait, no, that's what I did on my last ski trip."

"Something tells me Ethan wouldn't have been into that."

"False," he said quickly. "Every guy wants to make out with a girl in a Jacuzzi. It's what Jacuzzis were made for," he said matter-of-factly.

I shook my head.

Instead of veering left on the trail to run around the park, he took the trail that led back up to the street.

"Where are we going?"

"My house. I'm starving. I thought we could grab the truck and go get some pancakes," he explained.

I didn't disagree and followed his lead.

Once we made it back up to the street he began again, "Anyway, as I was saying, you may think that Mr. Ethan is an absolute gentleman, but deep down inside we're all just trying to bust that nut and would gladly make out with a girl in a hot tub."

Part of me liked that Thomas was being so candid with me. I felt like he accepted me as a friend. On the other hand, I found it a little disappointing how jaded he was about all men, on top of talking to me like I was naive.

"Didn't your parents ever tell you that boys are after only one thing, Maura?"

"Of course," I said emphatically, "a nice girl to take home to meet their mom and go to church with."

He knew I was being sarcastic, but it didn't stop him from condescendingly responding, "There is much I need to teach you about life."

He led us through the neighborhood streets; taking shortcuts to get to his house.

"I feel just like Friedrich in The Sound of Music when he sings to Liesel about being older and wiser."

"Um, excuse me, you mean Rolf," I corrected him.

"What? No, the blond kid who becomes a Nazi who dates the hot daughter."

"Yes, Rolf."

"No, Friedrich," he restated.

"Friedrich is the oldest brother. Rolf is the Nazi."

"No, Friedrich is the Nazi, trust me, I know this. I saw that movie several times growing up."

I couldn't believe how confident and clearly wrong he was.

"As did every other cradle Catholic in the country, but apparently some of us paid better attention, because Friedrich is the brother."

He paused and considered my words.

"No, I'm pretty sure he's the Nazi."

"You willing to buy my breakfast if you're wrong?"

I already knew I had won the bet. I was curious if my confidence would make him back down. It didn't.

"Why stop at breakfast? I'll throw in dinner too."

"Okay," I said simply, picking up my pace so I could get to proving him wrong more quickly.

"Yeah, I hope you know how to cook, because I like my dinner's homemade," he said cockily.

We ended up racing up the hill to his house. I fell a little behind because of his long legs but kept up for the most part. He started to slow when we approached an old white truck. He put his hands on the hood with his head down, catching his breath.

I immediately pulled out my phone from the arm strap to search the character list from The Sound of Music. He started to pace, still catching his breath. I found the page and held it up to his face.

"Boo-yah!" I exclaimed.

He examined it and sighed heavily, dropping his arms to the side and holding his head up to the sky.

"Ugh, it *is* fucking Rolf," he shook his head and then looked back at me.

I gave him a cheesy grin and did a celebration dance.

"The hills are alive, bitch!" I took my phone back from him.

"Clever," he commented flatly and then sighed again. He started to walk up the steps to his house and I almost thought he was being a poor sport and leaving me there.

"I've got to grab my wallet," he called back as he opened the door.

He left the front door open and within seconds was heading back out, but I could see Jackie right behind him.

"Good morning, Maura," she smiled and waved.

"Good morning, Mrs. O'Hollaren," I waved back. "How are you?'

"I'm good. I'm so glad you've been able to get Tommy out and exercising."

Thomas was unlocking the truck door for me, encouraging me to get in quickly.

"Oh, it's been good for me, too," I smiled and failed to take Thomas' cue. "Are you going on that women's retreat at the end of the month? My mom's going. She's pretty excited about it."

"Oh yes, it took some peer pressure from Judy Buckley, but I will be going."

I nodded, but before I could say anything else, Thomas started to wave.

· "I'll be back in a little bit." He moved over to his side of the truck, unlocked the door, and got into the driver's seat.

"I'll see you around, Mrs. O'Hollaren," I waved and got in the truck before Thomas drove away without me.

THOMAS

⌒⌒

I WOKE UP IN NATALIE'S BED AROUND NINE. EVEN though she kept me up until well past one, I awoke from the best sleep I'd had since returning home. The energy and tension released from having sex was just what I'd needed. We ended up going another round right after I woke up, which didn't require much convincing from her. When I glanced over to see that it was almost ten, I realized I was supposed to meet Maura that morning to run. I wondered how much longer Natalie could honestly want to keep me there and was surprised to see her smile at me just as she had done before initiating things when we woke up. Before she could offer to go yet again, I sat up and started putting my clothes back on.

"I gotta get going. I'm supposed to meet up with someone this morning." I stood up and then turned back to her.

"Oh, how mysterious," she teased and stretched her arms out over her head, exposing the top of her naked body.

I finished buttoning up my shirt and then leaned down, my face hovering over her.

"Thank you for last night. It was fun," I kissed her, but broke away before she could deepen the kiss.

"Yeah, it was," she smiled, her large eyes staring into mine. "So... do you think you would want to have fun again sometime?"

"With you? Of course," I stood up, knowing if I stayed that close to her, I would end up with my clothes off again.

I gathered my keys, wallet, and phone. Natalie quickly sat up and grabbed my phone out of my hand. She smiled playfully at me and entered something on the phone before she handed it back to me.

"There, now you have my number."

I looked down at the contact and pushed the call button. Her phone started to ring, and I hung up, staring back at her.

"And now you have mine," I gave her one last kiss before seeing myself out.

That was how I generally operated when it came to women. I let them decide if they wanted to spend time with me and went from there. I found that if I put too much energy into pursuing them, they would get the wrong idea and think I wanted a more serious relationship than I actually did. Things would be no different with Natalie. If she wanted to see me again, she now had a way to contact me. I hoped she would, because I wasn't the type who liked to rack up one-night stands. So far, my record was pretty good – I'd only had two.

I rushed back to my mother's house to change into my running clothes and then had to sprint to avoid being late.

The feelings of guilt that had crossed my mind the previous night had been alleviated by the overwhelming sense of relaxation and energy I now felt throughout my body. Maura even noticed my change in demeanor, but she didn't seem to put together that it was the result of getting laid. However, the amount of physical exertion from the night before quickly caught up with me and I was suddenly starving. It didn't take much convincing for her to join me for breakfast, but it probably helped that I had lost a bet and was now paying for the meal.

I looked over at Maura as I drove us to 14 Carrot Cafe, memories of Natalie sitting in the same spot the previous night coming back to me.

"So, was this your dad's truck?" she asked.

"Yep. Let me tell you, it is so much fun to park around the city," I said sarcastically. "But you'll get to witness it first hand in a second when we get to East Lake."

"We could go to Ballard; there are more restaurants over there with parking lots," she suggested helpfully.

"Nonsense. I've been dreaming about sourdough pancakes from 14 Carrot ever since you brought it up two weeks ago. And if I have to buy, I get to pick."

"Such a gentleman," she said flatly.

Amazingly, we found parking on the street immediately. It seemed like everything was going my way, with the exception of losing that stupid bet with Maura. However, there were worse ways to lose a bet than buying someone a couple of meals.

"So that's neat that your mom is going to go on that retreat," she said while we waited for our food.

I nodded, not really knowing what else to say.

"Has she gone to anybody for bereavement counseling?"

"Not that I know of. I can't really picture anybody in my family getting counseling. We're not a big touchy-feely group."

She nodded.

"So, will you be joining my mother and your mother and Judy Buckley on this retreat?"

I asked.

Maura smiled at my silly question.

"It's specifically geared toward women in their forties and older, so probably not."

"You'll probably have more fun spending time not making out with Ethan," I teased.

"I never said I didn't kiss," she defended.

"You minx," I retorted.

I wondered how far she was actually willing to go when it came to the physical side of a relationship. It seemed like even girls I dated in high school who held out on me were at least willing to get off with cliché teenage dry humping and hand stuff. Surely that wasn't off the table when it came to dating her. Not that I was interested; I just could not wrap my brain around how someone could simply choose not to have sex. Especially after the night I had with Natalie.

Our plates were placed down in front of us. I was relieved to finally get food in my stomach and stopped thinking about sex as I took my first bite. But only momentarily.

"So, do you know if Ethan shares your state of purity?"

I knew it was none of my business, but I thought that talking about sex made her uncomfortable, and that amused me.

"How is that any of your business? Are you interested in dating Ethan?" She called me on my shit. I liked that about her.

"No, but I'm curious if that's a deal breaker for you. I imagine the older you get, the harder it is to find someone who's held out."

"No, it's not a deal breaker. I've dated guys who've had sex before," she said casually as she took a drink of water.

"So how does that work?" I asked with genuine curiosity.

"What do you mean, how does that work?"

"I don't know," I shrugged. "It just seems like it would be challenging to go from having it to not having it."

She shrugged back.

"I guess I'm not the one who's ever had to deal with it, so I've never really thought about it," she said matter-of-factly. "That, and I'm just a really awesome girlfriend, so clearly it's worth the sacrifice," Maura joked in an over-confident tone, but she probably really did believe this about herself.

I let out a laugh but before I could set her straight on reality, my phone buzzed, alerting me to an incoming text. Maura went back to eating her pancakes, so I pulled out my phone and saw a message alert from Natalie.

I opened it to see she had sent a picture of herself. She was topless, but her arm was covering her breasts. The message underneath read:

Wanted to thank you again for having fun with me last night. Hope this can provide some fun until I see you again. XOXO-Nat.

Without realizing it, my mouth had dropped open. I had not been expecting that. But I liked it.

"Thomas? Is everything okay?" Maura called me back into reality. "Did something happen?"

At this point, it would have been more convenient had I been at breakfast with Tyler and he could high five me over this development. Instead, I quickly put my phone away, knowing Maura would not have the same reaction as Tyler.

"Yeah, yeah, everything's fine," I said quickly.

"What was it?"

"Nothing," I tried to maintain a sense of innocence while knowing I probably had the same expression on my face now as I'd had when my mom found a PlayBoy under my bed when I was thirteen.

"You don't look like it was nothing."

I decided the best course of action was to give her some information without giving her all the information.

"Oh, it was just some girl I met when I went out last night," I said.

She smiled and looked both interested and happy for me. My guilt returned as I knew she probably thought my actions with this girl were more G-rated than they had been.

"Oooooh," she teased. "What's her name?"

"Natalie."

"Where'd you meet her?"

"Nowhere," I started to say, but I could tell she wouldn't accept that as an answer. "At a bar."

She didn't ask which bar; thank God. I was still slightly ashamed that I had followed Tyler's predatory advice to pick up girls at a college bar.

"So, what does she do?"

I was starting to regret sharing any information.

"I don't know," I lied.

She looked at me with disbelief.

"You gave her your number and you don't even know what she does?" she said skeptically.

"Not everyone knows everyone's life story when they hook up."

And that's when it slipped out.

She stared at me as she realized what I had just shared. Then she went back to eating.

"See, I didn't want to tell you about it because I knew you would judge me."

"I'm not judging you. Did I say anything?"

Now I gave her the same skeptical look.

"Hey man, up top, way to get some ass," she simulated Tyler's bro voice and held up her hand for a high five.

I didn't reciprocate and rolled my eyes.

"So, what made you want to hook up with her?"

"Please," I laughed. "Like you'd understand."

"What? I don't get a turn to ask you questions about your sex life?"

She had a fair point. I was sure she wouldn't like the answers she would get from me, though.

"I hadn't had sex in five months; she was good-looking, not a total idiot, and willing." Maura nodded. "Was it good?" she asked pointedly.

I thought for a minute about how I would rate the overall experience in comparison to other partners I had been with.

"Eh, pretty good. She moaned a little too much for my liking and her rhythm was a bit jerky, but by the third time she was a little bit more fluid," I said honestly while I watched Maura, trying to detect her level of offense.

"Well, I hope you used a condom," she said seriously.

I had expected her to be more upset by my casual rating of the event.

"Of course. I'm not an idiot. But I thought Catholics didn't want people using birth control?"

"This Catholic realizes that not everyone can keep it in their pants, and would rather people avoid getting STDs if they're going to be treating sex like a handshake."

"Are you done with your public service announcement?"

"I'm serious. Do you know how many teens I've worked with who have AIDS? Too many. Not to mention herpes and gonorrhea."

She spoke at a normal volume, catching me off guard, since we were sitting in the crowded restaurant.

"Yes, I know, it's all fun and games until someone gets the Clap." I must have been the uncomfortable one because I started joking.

She didn't smile, so I tried to reassure her. "Maura, it's fine. No glove, no love, I got it. You know, I went to public school too. I'm starting to wonder if that's how you keep yourself from having sex; going on WebMD and looking up all the diseases that are out there."

"So, are you going to see her again?" she ignored my teasing.

"Probably. We'll see," I said, staying noncommittal.

"Well, maybe next time you can find out a little bit about her before getting naked. Just a thought," she suggested breezily.

"She's a senior at UW, she's a communications major, and she likes Sex in the City," I offered quickly to prove to Maura that I did learn a little something about Natalie before jumping into bed with her.

"As opposed to having it in the country?" she asked without guile.

I started to laugh. "The TV show, Sex in the City. Not the action of having sex in the city. Although probably, judging by last night, she likes that, too."

Maura rolled her eyes.

"I thought you'd be a little more judgmental about the age difference."

"I started dating Sean when I was twenty and he was twenty-five," she said simply, once again not using his title. I wondered if she just did that when she was with me. "I guess it's the maturity level that matters," she gave me a small smile and stared at me, proud of her good-natured insult.

"Yeah, that Father Sean does seem like he is kind of immature," I fired back.

"Touché," she responded quietly, taking a drink of water. "So you just let me know when you want to schedule a double date with Ethan and me." Her sarcasm was clear.

"You think we can get Father Sean to come too?" I threw back and made her laugh.

· "Yeah, that wouldn't be a disaster waiting to happen at all."

"No, not at all."

I changed the subject to the different classes we took in college. I no longer felt tense about being honest with her about my sexual decisions. Maura clearly didn't approve, but she didn't condemn me or try to convert me to her way of life. I had gotten the sense from when I first met her that she was a genuinely nice person, but I had still expected her reaction to be more combative. She continued to surprise me.

MAURA

ETHAN ENDED UP GOING TO SUNDAY NIGHT MASS WITH me after he got back from the Snoqualmie trip. I thought for sure they would've celebrated mass as a group at the cabin that morning but didn't protest when he suggested meeting me at Blessed Sacrament.

At some point during the Liturgy of the Word, he reached over and put his hand on top of mine. I found it a little distracting because instead of listening to the readings, I was trying to figure out how I felt about him holding my hand. As far as I could tell, I didn't feel any butterflies in my stomach, but then again, maybe I had gotten too old for butterflies.

I wondered how long it would take for Ethan to actually kiss me. It would be easier to decide how I felt about him if he would just kiss me. Did that count as objectifying him? Really there was no rush to figure things out and it was more important to just get to know Ethan better as a person. While I waited – impatiently – to be kissed.

After mass he walked me to my car, holding my hand. We paused as I stood by the door. This would've been a good time to kiss me and he must have been thinking the same thing, judging by the way he lingered.

"So, you had a good time this weekend?" I asked.

"Yeah, it was great. Except that, like I expected, I really missed you."

Should I say that I missed him too, even though it wasn't the truth? I decided to keep it honest.

"That's sweet of you."

He was still holding my hand. Part of me felt awkward about it, but I went with it.

"So, would you let me take you out to dinner this week?" he asked.

"Sure," I nodded.

"How about Wednesday? We can grab something before mass?"

I nodded again. *Will all our dates involve mass?*

"Great, I'll pick you up around five thirty," he said cheerfully, and then leaned in to give me a quick hug before saying goodbye and heading off to his car.

The next few days at work were pretty standard. Thankfully, there were no crises that resulted in even more paperwork than normal.

I made sure to update Sydney on all the developments with Ethan. She'd been wary of all the Catholic guys I'd dated since Sean had broken my heart. The other two Catholic boyfriends who'd left me to marry their ex-girlfriends didn't do much to cure her skepticism. But she knew there was no use telling me to date non-Catholic men. It was a priority for me, regardless of how many times it had bitten me in the ass.

Once I filled her in on the situation, she theorized that the reason I was not feeling super smitten with Ethan was most likely a response to how often I had been burned by guys in the past. She thought it was a defense mechanism. Her insight was, once again, spot on.

On Wednesday, our boss, Ann, called us into her office. We walked in to find Sean sitting across from her, of course wearing his Dominican habit. Sydney did a double take. She had not seen him in over four years, and it was her first time seeing him in the habit.

"Sydney!" he exclaimed, smiling. "How are you?"

Sean and Sydney had never been friends, but Sean knew she was probably the closest thing I had to a sister and was always cordial towards her.

"Doing well," she reached out and shook his hand. "I see you got some new clothes," she commented coolly.

"Yeah, I really think in a few years it's going to catch on with everybody," he joked and then turned to me with his hand out. "Maura," he smiled.

I shook his hand.

"Please have a seat," Ann invited us.

Sydney and I sat down, my face expressing more confusion than Sydney's ever-impressive poker face.

"Father Sean has been meeting with me and discussing some ideas that he has about the Newman Center becoming more involved with the youth center."

"Yeah, I've been talking with Archbishop Bennett about how the Newman Center is the closest Catholic church to the youth center," Sean explained, "and because the youth center was established and funded by Catholic Community Services, it only makes sense that we encourage our students at Newman to get involved with this ministry. I already have about ten students who are interested in coming over here and helping."

"Father Sean was hoping one of you could coordinate with the Newman Center's community service chair to organize a regular volunteer program," Ann informed us.

"In what capacity were you thinking they would volunteer?" I asked, my tone hinting at my concern. "I think we should consider that many of our youth are in the same age range as the students at the Newman Center, and that could pose some problems in terms of boundaries on both sides."

"And that will be considered when determining how much interaction they have throughout the center," Ann answered calmly. "But, Maura, it's not a reason to turn down potential help sorting and organizing our donations. We've been running low on volunteers for months. And you will provide training which will specify all the necessary policies we have for protecting our teens. Also, need I remind you, that when you started here, you were the first undergraduate intern we ever took and that turned out fine." Ann's tone communicated clearly that this meeting was more of a notification than discussion and consideration.

"Also, some of our older parishioners were interested in providing a donation to your program for the purposes of building a vocational program," Sean added. "I had mentioned that one of our very own former Newmanites," he motioned towards me, "was a case manager here, so they asked for me to coordinate a meeting to discuss how you guys would want to develop a program like that."

And now it became clear. If money was attached to a potential vocational program for the homeless youth we served, Ann was going to do pretty much anything Sean asked, whether it be taking on green volunteers or making me represent us to 'my people.' Since I was the only practicing Catholic on staff, she always had me act as spokesperson when we were soliciting donations at masses around the city. It didn't normally bother me, but sometimes I felt like I was being used – albeit for the greater good, but used nonetheless.

Ann went on, "So, I will need you guys to develop a report on a potential program – projected cost and ways to track and evaluate the intervention's success – for Maura to present to the potential donors."

"Sounds great," Sydney said convincingly. "We can probably get Ashland involved in this, too," she said, referring to the graduate student intern who came in three days a week.

"Is it possible to get these meetings scheduled today so we can get going sooner rather than later?" Sean said as he pulled out his smartphone. "I'd really like to get our students set up before they leave for spring break in a few weeks."

Apparently, the vow of poverty didn't keep the Dominicans from having modern technology.

Of course he wants everything completed in two to three weeks. He isn't the one doing any of the actual work.

"Of course," Ann acquiesced.

"How about next Tuesday at ten?" he looked at me and Sydney hopefully.

I remained silent, realizing I would be working over the weekend.

"That'll work," Sydney spoke for us. She stood up and I followed her lead. "Anything else, boss?" she turned to Ann.

"No, that'll be all, thanks."

"Good seeing you," Sydney shook Sean's hand.

I awkwardly mumbled goodbye and headed back to our office. I stood by my desk, and Sydney, knowing me all too well, closed the door behind her.

"So...that was interesting."

"Ugrhhh!" was the only sound I managed to get out. I slumped down in my chair and lowered my forehead to the desk.

"You think he's doing this to be closer to you?" she asked.

"Hardly," I sighed, sitting up, knowing Sean's intentions were completely, frustratingly, genuine. And then my rant began.

"That's exactly what's so aggravating. He is so utterly clueless and insensitive about why this would be a less-than-ideal situation for me. All he's thinking about is his damn students doing more to help the poor, never mind me having to deal with being around him and his stupid face."

This was the reality that I had done my best to accept over the past five years. At the end of the day, Sean cared more about the Church and what was best for Its people than he did about me. His sense of contentment and joy was so obvious ever since he came back to Seattle, further supporting the fact he had made the right choice and was clearly winning the break-up.

I continued, exasperated, with my arms up in the air. "And now I'm the asshole who's being selfish and doesn't want more volunteers or a vocational program! This is just so typical of him to think of some big idea and then just expect others to do all the coordinating and planning in a ridiculously short amount of time while he just keeps coming up with more big ideas to make more work for everybody else. And now it's worse because he has a stupid collar and he's totally going to play the priest card to keep people from telling him no."

Ironically, it was his leadership qualities and excitement about helping people that had attracted me to him initially. This thought was equally aggravating. I took a deep breath and held it while I pursed my lips.

"Okay, so let's figure out the positives," Sydney was calm. "When volunteers are properly trained and supervised, it can be a good thing. We already have a training that we can use, and we'll just have to set up one meeting to get them all trained. He didn't say anything about wanting to volunteer himself, so we probably won't see him that much after the initial meetings take place. And finally, Maura, you know we've been dreaming of being able to offer a vocational program. Think of how amazing that's going to be for our kids."

I sighed at the truth of this statement and looked over at her.

"Yes, but why did he have to be the one to find the money for it?" I realized I was being incredibly immature and petty.

"Because he's a charismatic mother fucker with a nice smile," she said matter-of-factly.

"Just be glad our kids are benefitting. You know, Mother Teresa took money from the mob all the time."

"Yes, this is exactly like that," I responded flatly, letting out another aggravated groan.

"Hey, I get you," she agreed. "But, once again, we're just going to have to suck it up and do it for the children," she said dramatically, making me smile. "And I will be readily available to listen to you vent while Sean continues to be clueless and insensitive with a stupid face, as you like to call it."

"Thank you," I sighed.

"No problem," she patted my back and moved over to her desk. "And, this may not be the best time, but I just want to throw it out there that this would not have been a problem had you listened to me and dated someone your own age five years ago."

"That's just because you thought I was too young to get married," I responded quickly.

"I'm just keeping it real," Sydney said dryly.

There was a knock at the door. I prepared myself for it to be Sean and took a deep breath.

"Come in," Sydney called out.

Ashland opened the door and walked in.

"Hey guys, thanks for letting me come in late. The amount of term papers I have for finals week is insane." She lifted her messenger bag off her shoulder.

Ashland Andersen was a first-year graduate intern earning her Master's in Social Work from the University of Washington. During the five months that she'd been with us, the thing she loved to share most about herself was that she grew up in a commune in Portland, Oregon. She had piercings in her nose, tongue, and belly-button. Sydney and I had both had the pleasure of asking her on more than one occasion to cover up the naval piercing when working with our youth. I had only seen her wear sandals, regardless of the weather. Her long dark brown hair was always extremely smooth and perfectly contrasted her bright blue eyes.

When I first met her, I thought maybe I was intimidated by her because she was so attractive. But then I realized she just made me uneasy because she was always so dismissive and clearly preferred Sydney over me. Don't get me wrong, Sydney is awesome and she's a great mentor, but it still drove me crazy that I'd always been nice to Ashland and couldn't for the life of me figure out what I had done to rub her the wrong way.

"So, did you guys check out the hot monk that Ann was walking around with?"

I couldn't bring myself to answer her.

"That's Father Sean from the Newman Center," Sydney said. "We were actually just talking about that."

"Don't tell me," Ashland cut in, "Maura thinks he's hot too? Is that like a fantasy that Catholic girls have?"

As always, Ashland's level of professionalism was inspiring.

Sydney moved on, knowing it was in Ashland's best interest to not speak anymore.

"We are going to be training about ten undergraduate students from the Newman Center and there is a possible donation to start up a vocational program here on site," she explained.

· "Cool," Ashland said simply, taking a seat and pulling out her laptop.

I turned to my monitor deciding to get back to work, wishing I could feel as nonchalant about the whole thing as Ashland.

MAURA

RATHER THAN MAKING ETHAN DEAL WITH FINDING A place to park on my street, I told him to call me when he got to my building so I could come down to meet him. He called just as I was second guessing the pencil skirt I had put on.

I didn't want to wear tights but wanted to look like I was taking the date seriously, especially since I knew he would without a doubt be wearing a dress shirt and slacks. It was good that he showed up when he did, because had I been given five minutes longer, I would have ended up back in my jeans – dressy jeans, but nevertheless denim – and of course would have felt underdressed next to him.

Ethan was standing outside of his car when I came down to meet him, waiting to open the door for me. I thanked him and got in. It seemed overly formal, but I could appreciate him being a gentleman.

Once he took his place in the driver's seat, he started the car and turned to me.

"So, I was thinking Italian tonight? Mamma Melina's?"

"Sounds good."

He nodded and began to drive. I put my hands in my lap, feeling awkward without really knowing why.

Can we just skip to the part where we feel comfortable around each other? Silences never felt this weird with Sean. I caught myself before my mind went any farther in that direction. *Shut up, don't think about Sean. Ask Ethan about his day.*

"So, how was your day?"

"Oh, pretty good. Working on some pretty exciting code," he said.

I had nothing to offer that conversation.

Maybe I should read up on computer programming over the weekend...ugh. Why couldn't he be like a zookeeper or something interesting? I wouldn't mind reading up on polar bears...except how global warming is melting their homes. That's depressing. Shit, I need to think of something to say about his work.

"It's okay," Ethan assured. "Most people don't really have a response when I tell them about my day. Tell me about yours."

"Uh, pretty typical; had one new kid show up, saw some of my regulars. We found out that there's a potential donation to start a vocation program."

He nodded, looking like he was interested in what I was saying.

"So, you're going to put the homeless teens to work?"

"Yeah, we call it the Oliver Twist plan. It's super economical," I joked.

Ethan didn't laugh, but briefly looked at me.

"You're being sarcastic, right?" He was smiling but didn't sound completely sure.

I was almost tempted to continue with my joke but decided against it.

"Yeah, uh, actually, they would use the center as a training site for different vocational skills to help them build up their resumes. But we have to get approval from the donors, so..." I sighed, "I get to work on the proposal this weekend...yay." My tone was flat.

Ethan pulled into the parking lot of the restaurant.

"Well, let me know if you need any help making an exhilarating PowerPoint," he offered, turning off the car.

"Thanks, I'll be sure to keep you in mind."

Once we were at dinner, I started to relax a little more, thanks to a glass of red wine. Because of all the time I had spent with Ethan at Young Adult events, I already knew most of his answers to traditional first date questions. His dad owned an investment company and his mom had stayed at home with the kids. He had four brothers and two sisters, and he was the fourth born. His parents and five of his siblings still lived in Spokane. He had one brother who lived in San Diego.

He knew all the same information about me. I had frequently referenced being an only child in the past, along with the fact that my parents were high school teachers. Normally, you'd think this would make things easier on a first date, but I was having a hard time thinking of things to talk about. He didn't seem to mind the repeated gaps in conversation, but kept smiling at me, at one point reaching across the table to touch my hand. Thankfully, I knew we only had an hour to eat dinner in order to get to mass on time.

We made it through the meal with only a few major lulls. The final one came while we were waiting for the check.

"So..." I said awkwardly, "what's your favorite color?"

He raised his brow at my juvenile question. "Uh, I guess blue."

I nodded. "I think I read a statistic somewhere that said seventy-five percent of the world's population's favorite color is blue."

He stared at me.

"So, you have something in common with a lot of people," I went on.

"And you?" he reluctantly joined in on the frivolous conversation.

"Me? Oh, I'm a weirdo; I like purple."

"Because of your school?" he asked, probably referencing my enthusiasm at the basketball game we had gone to the month before.

"No, I liked it before I went to Washington, but maybe I picked the school because of the colors...or the mascot. I do prefer dogs to cats. Aren't those really the things you're supposed to look at when considering a college?"

The waiter handed him the check. I went ahead and assumed that Ethan was paying. He got out his wallet and handed his card over to the waiter.

"For me, I think I was interested in a Catholic education, but I guess I like bulldogs, too."

"Now, bulldogs are a very high maintenance breed," I informed. "I had a friend in middle school and she had a bulldog named Charlie and they were always taking him to the vet and she had to, like, clean out his wrinkles and creases on a regular basis so they wouldn't get infected."

I had no idea why I felt the need to share that information with Ethan, especially after we had just eaten a meal. I looked up to see him smiling at me with an amused look on his face.

"What?" I asked, puzzled.

"Nothing," he laughed. "I just wasn't expecting to get random facts about bulldogs tonight." He signed the receipt the server had just handed him.

"Yeah," I sighed, "I can turn a little Rain Man when I get nervous."

He once again raised his brow, looking confused by the reference.

"You know, *Rain Man* with Dustin Hoffman and Tom Cruise?"

His expression didn't change.

"Come on," I exclaimed in disbelief. "You haven't seen *Rain Man?*"

He shook his head and I responded by shaking mine. "It's a good movie. Hoffman has autism and states all these random facts throughout –" I realized my synopsis wouldn't do the movie justice and stopped. "Anyway, it's a good movie."

"Well," he sighed, "I'll have to take your word for it. Ready to go to mass?"

I smiled and nodded but was still surprised that he didn't understand the reference. Then again, maybe I was the weird one for reserving space in my brain for random 80s movies when I could have been focusing on remembering more religious and important things like encyclicals or bible verses. Obviously, dating Ethan would be good for me because he would be interested in talking about more spiritually relevant things, and that's what I was supposed to be looking for, right? Not someone to quote movies with...because, although it was an impressive skill, being able to name all of Tom Hanks' films in chronological order wouldn't get me into heaven. I was thankful that silence was a built-in, natural part of mass; it would give me time to regroup and think of something Ethan would consider worthier of conversation.

Once we had parked at Blessed Sacrament, Ethan turned off the car, then paused for a moment. I unbuckled my seatbelt but waited to open the door.

"Hey, I was thinking, instead of going out with everybody tonight at the bar, how about we spend some time alone?" he suggested.

"Sure," I nodded.

His tone was sincere, so I resisted the urge to make a joke. Humor was my default response when I felt awkward. I got the sense that he would've been confused and it would only lead to more awkwardness. Lord knows, no one wanted more of that.

Once again, we sat next to each other during mass and I found myself having trouble concentrating. I kept wondering what Ethan would want to do once we were alone. At the same time, I felt pressure to pay attention because of my newfound determination to be ready for on-the-spot discussions about all things holy – and if he asked me what I thought about the readings or the homily, I figured answering "Gee, I wasn't listening because I couldn't stop thinking about whether we were going to make out or not," would surely rule me out as marriage material before the date even ended. However, my inability to focus was only made worse because he was holding my hand again in clear view of Felicity, whom he used to date, and Jessica and Marie, both of whom I was sure wanted to date him. I began to feel uneasy, thinking that all three of them would be better matches for Ethan, given how traditional I knew them all to be. And all of them would've been classy enough not to talk about a dog's gross skin infection during dinner.

Good one, Maura.

I started to miss attending mass alone, realizing it was much easier to pay attention when I sat by myself.

Ethan and I quickly made our exit from the church before anyone could even ask if we were meeting up with them at Latona. I had to admit, I felt a little excited about sneaking off with him. It crossed my mind that we might kiss, but the realist in me knew it was unlikely. We got in his car and drove the short five-minutes to my apartment. He parked and turned off the car, then turned to me.

"I forgot to tell you that you look very nice tonight."

"Oh thanks, so do you," I smiled.

I ordered myself to suppress the urge to ramble and try to be comfortable with the silence. He reached over and held my hand without saying anything and rubbed his thumb over the top of it. It took all of my willpower, but I managed to sit in the silence and wait for him to say something.

"I've been thinking, and I know this may be a little fast, but–" immediately my mind went to filling in the blank with various possibilities, most of them inappropriate, "I think we should talk about our pasts."

I stared at him, waiting for him to elaborate before I jumped the gun.

"I mean, I'm twenty-nine, and you're twenty-five, so clearly there have been other people that we've dated. I just think that if we're going to do this, we need to be totally honest about what those relationships meant to us and whether we made any mistakes while we were in them."

His words sank in. I knew the type of guy Ethan was, and I knew that when he said "mistake," he really meant "premarital sex." He was trying to find out if I had had sex with anyone before. Well, if he wanted to have a conversation that intimate, he was either going to have to flat-out ask for the information or be the first to talk about his past.

I nodded to let him know that I understood what he was talking about but remained silent and waited for him to share.

"I've only had three serious girlfriends," he said. "The last one lasted for about a year before I moved out here."

Again, I didn't say anything, waiting for him to share more.

"Thankfully, all the women I've dated have been strong Catholics, and with every one of them, we always made a commit to remain chaste throughout the relationship."

I knew that I should have appreciated this information, and maybe even congratulated Ethan, because I knew it was a difficult standard to maintain.

However, I also wondered whether he was telling me because he thought I wouldn't date him if he wasn't chaste; or rather, he wouldn't date me if my status didn't match up with his. The troublemaker in me wanted to lie and say I was not a virgin, just to see if he would reject me, but I knew that was not fair to him or to myself. He was looking expectantly at me, waiting for me to talk.

"Uh, well, I've dated five guys since high school. Three of them serious, two of them casual. I didn't sleep with any of them." My terminology was a lot more matter-of-fact than his.

"So, three out of the five became priests?" he clarified, referencing the night at the bar with Sean almost a month ago.

"Well, yeah, but not really. Father Sean is the only one who's made his vows. The other two are still in formation for like, two more years, and I dated them in high school and my freshman year of college. Plus, they joined seminary long after we broke up. Sean was the only one who told me he had to break up with me because he was called to be a priest."

I paused and then remembered the other two who married their ex-girlfriends. "Well, technically there were two more who said they had to break up with me because they needed to discern their vocation to the priesthood, but they ended up getting married to other girls."

Ethan looked sympathetically at me. I was surprised. Usually it was only the non-Catholics who validated that track record as upsetting.

"So, I guess it's good that we're having this conversation now, because I gotta say, if you are in the process or think you will be in the process of discerning the priesthood, I don't think I can handle another one," I stated honestly.

"No, no, I think we're good there. I mean, I did think about it for a bit right after college, like all Catholic young men are supposed to do, but I ruled it out. Unless the Holy Spirit has some crazy surprise waiting for me." He laughed, but I knew better than to tempt fate.

His face turned serious. "So, we're on the same page with staying committed to purity?"

I really wanted to ask what exactly that meant to him. I didn't think I could date a man without kissing him, but I felt like I would come off a little trampy if I asked him to clarify the parameters. Instead I just nodded, because it seemed like the more appropriate thing to do.

This was the first time I had ever had a discussion like this with a guy I had dated. In the past, it had always been assumed that we wouldn't be having sex and would figure out the exact limits as we went. It was becoming very clear that Ethan was not going to be the type of guy who pushed for "everything but."

Not that I was a really a big supporter of that concept, but over the years, I had dated more than one guy who subscribed to and enthusiastically encouraged pushing the boundaries. I had come to expect that that was how most guys in Ethan's position functioned. However, maybe this was a healthier way to go about things – set all the limits from the beginning and avoid temptation. I really couldn't argue with that logic.

"I feel really good about this," he announced, squeezing my hand.

I was beginning to understand why he had been holding my hand so much.

"I did want to ask you something before you go," he said, looking into my eyes.

All I could think was that he was finally going to ask to kiss me. Despite the last moments of our conversation providing evidence otherwise, I was still hopeful.

"I wanted to know if you would pray the rosary with me?"

What?

No, I had not been expecting that question at the end of the date. This was definitely a first. However, I felt like I really couldn't say no without it being weird, and I didn't have a legitimate excuse for not praying the rosary.

"Sure," I said in my best nonchalant voice. I told myself there were worse ways to end a date.

I considered the possibility that maybe I had gotten lax when it came to the spiritual effort I had been putting forth. Was Ethan meant to be a positive influence in my life? Being with him could make me a better person – definitely a holier one. As we said the Hail Mary together, I found myself thinking that I was never going to find anyone to spend my life with unless I was totally open to whoever that was supposed to be. I recognized that I had been hesitant for some time about falling in love, and in that moment, I asked Mary to tell God that I was ready to try again.

THOMAS

I LET OUT YET ANOTHER YAWN WHILE I SAT DRINKING coffee on my break, wishing it were Friday instead of Thursday. I had spent Wednesday night at Natalie's after she sent another text even more revealing than the first. I hadn't realized how late she intended to keep me up until after I got there. She didn't empathize with the fact that I had to work the next day; she still lived in the fantastic world of college and didn't have class until one in the afternoon.

I knew it wasn't a good idea to continue the weekday sleepovers, but I also knew it wouldn't take much for Natalie to convince me to do it again. She was just too easy and convenient to pass up. I regretted sitting down because it had given my body and mind time to recognize just how tired I was. I took a deep breath before heading back to the floor.

When I walked out, I saw a beautiful, black Chevy Camaro pull into the shop. I wasn't the only one who noticed the car. Two other guys on the floor, Will and Jason, stopped what they were doing to watch it pull in. What caught our attention more was seeing Father Sean in his white Dominican robe and large rosary beads around his waist step out of the car.

Will mouthed, "What the hell?" to Jason and myself.

I walked up to him, since he had requested to be put on my schedule. The car, or more likely the Dominican priest, had caught

Michael's eye too, and he was now walking towards Father Sean as well.

"Hey, Thomas," Father Sean greeted me and shook my hand.

I could see Michael's confusion that a priest knew my name.

"Hey," I greeted back. "Uh, this is my brother, Michael. Michael, this is Father Sean, the director of the Newman Center at the University."

He turned and shook Michael's hand.

"Michael and his family go to Blessed Sacrament," I explained.

"Oh, okay, good to meet you," Father Sean smiled. "Newman keeps me pretty busy, so I don't really do the Sunday masses at Blessed Sacrament, but sometimes I help out on weekdays or with young adult stuff."

Michael nodded.

"Glad to meet you, Father. So, you talked to Thomas about bringing your car in?"

"Yeah," he turned to the Camaro, "Here she is."

He looked at me with pride.

"My nephew's getting ready to head off to college next year and I told him he could have her. I just wanted to make sure everything was good before he flew out to drive her back to Iowa. She's a 2010."

"It's a good-looking car." Michael had his arms crossed and was looking over the Camaro.

"Yeah, when you said you were giving your old car to your nephew, I figured it was a junker," I commented frankly. "Or something…"

"More befitting of a priest?" he finished my sentence, smiling.

"Exactly," I laughed. I caught Michael giving me a stern look, displeased that I could have potentially insulted a man of the cloth.

"Seriously," Father Sean agreed, "I foolishly bought it about three months before I went into the seminary with the inheritance I got from my grandfather," he explained. "The other option was to let the Dominicans have it, and I just don't see Father Jack or Father Bernard driving it. I mean, I already know I look ridiculous in it now," he motioned to his outfit.

"Well, we'll get you set up, Father," Michael said responsibly. "Give us about an hour to run through everything."

"Great," he handed me the keys and started to turn towards the waiting room but stopped. "Oh, and Thomas, I have a few questions for you when you're done, if you have time."

"Yeah, I'm sure we can fit that in," Michael answered for me.

I knew he did that because he anticipated I would come up with an excuse not to. I couldn't blame him for thinking that, based on my history when it came to all things Catholic.

Once Father Sean was in the waiting room, Michael turned to me expectantly. "You didn't feel the need to tell me we had a priest coming in?"

I was entertained by how worked up he was about it.

"It's on the schedule," I said calmly.

"He's not listed as Father," Michael seemed to be offended by this.

"I didn't schedule the appointment," I shrugged. I moved over and opened the car door.

Michael stopped me by touching my arm. "But how do you know him?"

"Maura McCormick introduced me. We went out and got beers last month," I answered nonchalantly. I loved that he was both envious and confused that I was seemingly more buddy-buddy with a priest than he was. I drove the Camaro over to the pit so that we could get a look under the car in addition to everything else. Michael met me as I got out of the immaculate car.

"What does he want to talk to you about?" he pressed.

I shrugged. "I don't know, maybe he wants to talk to me about becoming a priest," I said dryly, but suddenly worried that could be a possibility.

"Whatever, just don't be a smart-ass with him," Michael warned more than advised with his expression. He turned to walk back to the office.

"You're welcome for bringing in new business, by the way," I called out after him.

I turned and saw Will and Jason standing by me, waiting for me to open the hood.

"This should be fun," I said.

Throughout the tune up, Jason kept trying to get me to come up with an excuse to take the car out onto the freeway. I was tempted, but knew we had a busy afternoon and taking two mechanics off the floor would throw us off schedule for no good reason.

It was the first time one of the mechanics was actually looking to me for permission and the first time I had actually made a decision about what was best for the business. I knew it wasn't really a high stakes situation, but I still acknowledged it to myself and was proud of my sense of responsibility. Honestly, it was an easy decision to make; I knew if we got behind, it would be my ass staying after-hours because I would have to pay everyone else overtime.

Not surprisingly, everything checked out on the Camaro. Whoever Father Sean's nephew was, he was incredibly lucky to be getting a car like that for free. I headed out to the waiting room with the keys. I found Father Sean sitting there, thumbing through his smartphone, another odd sight. I caught two other customers glancing at him, unsure what to make of him. He seemed completely oblivious to their stares.

"You're all set, Father," I called out. He looked up and came over to the counter.

"How's she look?"

"Fine. Everything looks good. We went ahead and changed the oil, just to be safe. And we rotated the tires because you said you never had, but it doesn't look like anyone has ever driven it."

"Probably 'cause no one really has. I didn't even drive it down to Oakland for seminary. It's been sitting in a garage for almost five years."

"You know how pissed my guys would be if they knew that?"

Father Sean laughed and held up his hands in surrender.

"I know, I know; believe me, I'm just as upset at myself. Hopefully Anthony has better luck using it than me."

"When's he coming out to get it?"

"He's flying out with my sister for spring break around Easter, and they'll drive it back together."

I nodded, handing him the service report. He handed me his card.

"So, do you have a spot where we could meet?" he asked after signing the form.

I looked out the window across the floor into the office where Michael was sitting.

"Uh, there's the office, but it looks like Michael's finishing up some work in there."

"That shouldn't be a problem; you guys are co-owners anyway, right?"

"Yeah." It still felt odd to confirm that aloud, especially since I wasn't sure if Michael thought of me that way.

I led him through the floor over to the office, wondering what he could possibly want from me and Michael. I was afraid he was going to offer to pray with us about our dead dad. It seemed unlikely, but I was really didn't know anything else priests did besides pray.

Michael looked up from his desk when I opened the door, quickly sitting up straight when he saw that Father Sean was with me.

"Hey, you got a minute? He wanted to talk to both of us."

"Sure, sure; of course," Michael scanned the room, embarrassed by the clutter on the desk across from him.

Before my father passed away, he and Michael had shared the office. Michael had remained at his own desk, which was incredibly organized and clean. My father, never a fan of organizing anything besides tools, had historically kept a desk with papers and books stacked everywhere. Logically, I should have been using the desk by now, but I had been waiting for Michael's instruction to clear it off. It hadn't come yet. Neither of us had talked about it, and except for the occasional search for something we needed, we tried to avoid the subject of the desk all together. It was just another reminder that my dad was gone and Michael was stuck with me.

"Sorry, about the mess," Michael apologized. "We're still trying to get organized with Dad being gone and all," he explained openly.

I wondered why it was so easy for him to say this to a complete stranger, but couldn't even make a plan with me about what he wanted to do about the damn desk.

"Go ahead and have a seat," Michael motioned to the chair in front of his desk.

I sat on a chair propped against the wall.

"Of course," Father Sean took the offered seat. "Everyone at the priory continues to send their condolences and prayers for him and your mother and your whole family."

"We were very pleased with the service Father Jack put together for him," Michael said in his even tone.

This was the only time I had heard him reference the funeral since it had happened.

"I'll let him know," Father Sean nodded. He then turned to me, "So, thanks for being willing to meet with me without any notice. I have a few questions for you guys about being a mechanic."

"You thinking about switching professions?" I joked.

Michael didn't smile, but Father Sean did.

"Nah, man. I don't know if you've noticed, but I'm pretty committed to what I do. Actually, I was wondering what type of schooling and training someone would need to get a job as a basic starting mechanic?"

Michael and I looked at each other and shrugged.

"Well, Father, it depends," Michael answered formally. "Every shop's different. We started our training at fifteen because our dad was the owner. But if you don't have any connections or anyone willing to take you on as an apprentice, you probably have to pay for a certificate. For the most part, when you're starting, it comes down to who you know, and then the more advanced training comes later."

"But it doesn't require any degree or official certificate to start with, like, tire rotations and changing oil and spark plugs and stuff like that?"

"Well, you could be like Tommy and go get an art degree with a business minor, but we don't recommend or require it," Michael said flatly.

Father Sean nodded and was quiet for a moment. Michael and I were waiting for him to ask us to hire someone, which we did not have the funds for, but I was still interested in seeing how Michael would tell a priest no.

"We have these older parishioners at the Newman Center that have approached us with a potential donation, but they want it to go towards young adults who are less fortunate than our usual crowd at Newman. I've suggested partnering with the University Youth Center to set up a vocational program. I've been trying to think of vocational skills they could use to build a resume without having to pay to go to school. I just wanted to confirm that an older teenager or young adult could potentially work in an auto mechanic setting without having to pay for a specific certificate."

"Theoretically," Michael answered. "It depends on what the owner is looking for, but yeah, a kid could potentially get started at a Jiffy Lube or Les Schwab with just experience and a recommendation."

Father Sean was nodding again. "Are either of you available this Tuesday at ten a.m.?"

He quickly realized Michael and I were not following his train of thought.

"We have a meeting with the potential donors and one of the Youth Center staff, Maura McCormick," he looked over at me. "It would be really helpful to have someone there to speak to what kind of training a starting mechanic would need, and what kind of materials would be needed for the program."

I looked over to Michael, leaving the scheduling decision to him.

"Uh," he paused, showing his hesitation.

"It should only take an hour, tops,' Father Sean assured.

"Tommy?" Surprisingly, Michael deferred to me.

Father Sean looked at me expectantly.

"Sure, that should work out, I'm the late starter anyway."

"Great," Father Sean stood up, followed by myself and Michael. "Thanks so much. I really appreciate getting your expertise on this. I'm sure everyone else will appreciate having someone there with first-hand knowledge, too." He shook Michael's hand.

"Nice meeting you, Father," Michael said.

"Pleasure." Father Sean turned to me and shook my hand. "Thomas, thanks for working on the Camaro, and I'll see you Tuesday at ten at the Newman Center."

He let himself out. I closed the door and turned to Michael.

"Under no circumstances are we in a position to hire anyone," was the first thing out of Michael's mouth. "I don't care how homeless they are."

"Are you quoting Jesus right now?" I joked.

Michael moved his hands to his hips. A vein in his brow appeared.

"I'm serious, we need to stay cautious right now."

"Michael, I looked at the books last week; we're doing fine," I assured, but knew the chances of him trusting me were small.

"We're doing okay, but I just want to make sure Mom is taken care of. She's getting dad's retirement, and now on top of your paycheck..." he trailed off.

"Which I have gladly reduced to a starting salary until things level out."

I had offered to cut my salary from the beginning. It made sense because I was getting room and board from my mother. There were times when I sensed that Michael was waiting for me to demand more money since he had maintained his manager's salary. Clearly, Michael thought his brother was an asshole who wasn't able to factor in the fact that he had a mortgage, a wife, and four kids to take care of.

"Listen, I know we can't take on any new people. It makes total sense to send the heathen to the meeting to tell them no," I said matter-of-factly.

"That's not why I'm sending you," he answered, then paused. "You're better with people," he admitted. "Especially a university crowd."

He didn't look at me when he said it, but I believe it was the first compliment he had ever given me.

"Just don't cuss when you're there."

I knew our moment couldn't have lasted long.

I opened the door and then turned back to Michael, "Got it. Maybe I can make a trade: we'll hire one guy if he gives us the Camaro?"

He shook his head, but his face didn't have the same gruff expression I was used to. I took it as a win. It wasn't a huge business decision that we made, but it was significant to me because it was the first time we had ever talked as partners.

MAURA

I SLUNG MY LAPTOP BAG OVER MY SHOULDER ONCE I got out of my car. Of course it was raining on a day when I actually wore a dress to work and made the effort to straighten my hair. It seemed like the moment I stepped out of the car it began to rain harder. My rain boots would've been a better choice instead of what I'd thought were sensible flats at the time I'd gotten dressed. Hopefully my hair could hold off the frizz at least through my presentation. I hurried through the parking lot and the brick entryway up to the large wooden double doors of the Newman Center.

Walking into the lobby felt like I had stepped back in time. I hadn't been there for at least three years, but it still smelled the same. Instead of pews, they still had wooden chairs lined up in rows facing the altar. To my right were the same old leather couches in front of the fireplace where I had attended dozens of planning meetings. I pulled down my hood and continued to stand there, knowing I was a good fifteen minutes early so I could allow myself a moment to let memories come back.

"Good morning," Sean called me out of my daze.

I turned and saw him standing in the hallway.

"I was in my office. I saw you run in."

"Morning," I said politely.

"It's kind of a trip, isn't it?" He knew full well where I had just gone in my mind.

I wished I didn't know the exact chairs we had both been sitting in the first time I turned around and shook hands with him during the sign of peace. Or where the table I stood at was when he came up to me and introduced himself for the first time while signing up to volunteer at the soup kitchen downtown.

"I would've expected you'd have put in stained glass windows by now and at least five more statues of Mary," I joked coolly.

"No, so far just one new statue of Mary in the front," he pointed. "And maybe I'll get the windows with next year's donations...the kids don't need a fall retreat anyway. But hey, look," he smiled, "we've still got Jesus here," he motioned behind himself to a floor-to-ceiling statue of Jesus on the cross.

I simply nodded and stayed rooted where I stood, not wanting to give up the twenty feet between us.

"We're going to meet in the back room," he pointed down the hallway.

I nodded again and walked towards him to head down the corridor. "Did I get here first?" I asked.

"Yeah, but I expect the Warrens and the Paulsons will be here any minute," he said.

"Those are your donors?"

We walked into the meeting room where Sean had already set up a table with chairs, and another table with coffee and pastries on the side. I knew the Warrens and Paulsons from my time at Newman; they often provided generous donations to our community service projects and fundraisers.

"Uh-huh. Why do you think I asked for you to come?" Sean responded confidently.

I moved over to the table and set down my laptop bag. "Do you guys still have a projector? So I can set up for my PowerPoint?"

"You know, I don't think that will be necessary. I was thinking we should keep it kind of informal."

My jaw clenched. This would have been helpful to know before I spent all weekend putting together a PowerPoint which I had practiced presenting three times, once to Ann and twice to Sydney.

He read my frustration.

"Maurie," he coaxed, trying to soften me with a name he hadn't used in years, "you know the Warrens and the Paulsons. They're going to want a conversation, not a presentation."

"You could have mentioned this last Wednesday," I said calmly.

"You think your boss would've taken me seriously?" he said knowingly. "Listen, pull up your info on the laptop and we can refer to it if we need to."

"We? Hmm, so what part did you have in putting this proposal together? Or did you come up with your own that I'm just going to nod along to?"

"You know I would've wanted to meet and put this together... together," his lack of articulation was a small victory. "Just trust me; this is going to be awesome for the Youth Center."

"Any other surprises?" I sighed and pulled out my laptop.

There was a brief silence. I shot him a look warning him not to mess with me anymore.

"Well, I did invite a local business owner to give us his perspective and potential buy-in."

I raised my eyebrow. His words didn't entirely make sense to me. He saw someone walk past the large window overlooking the courtyard, then went to the exit door and opened it.

"Hey man, we're in here," he called over to the person walking toward the front door. I looked over in time to see Thomas walk in.

"Thomas," Sean grinned, "Good to see you." He shook his hand.

Thomas took his hood off and unzipped his dark green North Face jacket. I was surprised to see him wearing an Oxford shirt along with khakis.

"I was just telling Maura I invited you to this meeting. Help yourself to some coffee and doughnuts."

"I thought they only let you have that after mass," he joked.

Sean laughed his salesman laugh. Thomas was unaware, but I knew Sean was plotting something. Sean excused himself to wait for the Warrens and the Paulsons in the lobby.

Thomas met my gaze. "Morning. You look nice," he commented on my navy dress.

"Had to look professional today," I informed.

"I tried to wear my coveralls, but my mother insisted it wasn't appropriate." He poured his coffee. I found it endearing that he didn't hide the fact that he lived with his mom.

"So, I assume Natalie was the reason you cancelled our run on Sunday?" I said to get my mind off of trying to figure out Sean's scheme. Thomas took a sip of his coffee.

"Well, one, it was raining on Sunday, and two," he paused, staring at me, "yes, she also factored into the decision. Someday you, too, will understand how staying in bed with someone is more appealing than running four miles in the rain. Anyway, you said you had to work on a presentation all weekend."

I motioned to my laptop, which was warming up.

"Ah, I see," he said. "Well, this better be good. I gave up my weekend run for it." He took a seat at the table with his coffee.

I heard Sean's voice approaching down the hallway and turned to the door, quickly smoothing my dress. He walked in, followed by the two older couples; Irene and Harold Warren, and Patty and Mark Paulson. I smiled to greet them.

"You guys remember Maura McCormick," Sean gestured to me while I reached out and shook their hands.

"So good to see you, Maura," Irene exclaimed. "You look so grown up. We were so excited to hear from Father Sean that you've continued your commitment to social justice by working at the shelter."

"It's good to see you all again," I returned the pleasantry with a smile.

"How about you all help yourselves to some coffee and doughnuts and then we can get started." Sean moved over to the table and took a seat next to my laptop.

I had pulled up the PowerPoint earlier and now I saw that he was quickly scanning through it to familiarize himself. Good to know he didn't feel the need for boundaries in this particular situation.

Apparently, we were a team again. I moved over and sat down in front of the laptop.

"So, I assume I'm following your lead?" I said quietly.

"Trust me," he whispered.

I figured I had no other choice and waited patiently for the meeting to begin. Once the two couples had taken a seat they noticed Thomas sitting at the table, quietly drinking his coffee.

"Oh, this is Thomas O'Hollaren. His family attends Blessed Sacrament. He and his brother, Michael, are owners of O'Hollaren Auto."

"Oh, I know where that is," remarked Patty. "I had no idea there was a community connection."

"We've only advertised in the Blessed Sacrament bulletin," Thomas explained.

"Thomas is here to give us some feedback about the feasibility of a vocational program at the University District Youth Center," Sean informed.

And there it was.

I saw in Thomas' eyes that this was news to him. Luckily for Sean, no one else noticed. The Warrens and the Paulsons nodded, accepting his explanation without question. Thomas sat up straighter and appeared more alert, almost as if he was getting ready to be called on in class.

"Maura created this wonderful proposal for us to review, but I was thinking maybe she could start with sharing a little bit about the work that she does."

Everyone's eyes turned to me.

"Well, as you know; we serve the homeless, at-risk, and street-involved youth population, which includes teenagers as young as thirteen through young adults aged twenty-two. While some identify us as a shelter, we are considered more of a drop-in center as we do not provide overnight housing. What we do provide is a place for youth to go to and access clothing, laundry, showers, and bus tickets, and also participate in activities. For example, our graduate intern is currently running an art program for those youth who are interested.

· Should youth who come to the shelter decide they want to participate in case management, educational, or drug treatment programs, we provide those in-house for them through myself, a few other social workers on site, licensed drug and alcohol counselors, and teachers and tutors provided through an educational nonprofit." I paused to see if anyone's eyes had glazed over. The Warrens and the Paulsons still looked interested, but I knew Sean wanted me to get to the meat.

"What we've found in providing case management services is that for our older teenagers and young adults, one of the greatest needs they identify for themselves is obtaining employment. We all know that the cycle of poverty is greatly linked to accessing education in order to access a well-paying job. However, many of our youth feel that they are so behind in school that they don't believe they can be successful and don't know where to start. The idea would be to provide a program that is skill-based, related to specific jobs that youth can get training for at the center. They would then be able to apply for jobs using their experience at the center in their resume and as a reference."

Both the Warrens and the Paulsons looked captivated. I paused, giving Sean the opportunity to jump in, which he took.

"Ultimately a program like that is going to help these kids transition into independence in the long run. The whole thing about teaching them to fish versus giving them the fish," Sean appealed to the more conservative Paulsons.

"So, when considering something like this," Mark Paulson spoke up, "what kind of program expense would we be looking at?"

"That's exactly what I was going to talk about next," Sean smiled. "I've been thinking about this, and that's why I wanted to bring Thomas in today. Obviously, when you're starting something new, you don't want to overextend yourself, but you still want to have a vision of where you want to go, right?"

There were murmurs of agreement from the group.

"That's what Maura's presentation is about. It's about the vision, the hope of what the program will eventually develop into: offering multiple vocational training opportunities, bringing in instructors from certificated programs, and partnering with local businesses; which is great, and I know one day we'll get there.

But what I was thinking was for us to start with one specific program, like auto-mechanics, and partnering with one local business," he looked over at Thomas, "to come on site at the center and work with six to ten youth for the next few months. Then we can evaluate and see where we're at.

So, Thomas, I was hoping you could tell us what kind of materials would be needed to execute something like that, so we can get an idea of cost," Sean wrapped up his speech and turned the attention of the group over to Thomas.

Thomas leaned forward and paused, looking like he was choosing his words carefully. "Well, that depends," he stalled, unaccustomed to being put on the spot by Sean.

"Just ballpark. Think about the things you needed and used when you first started."

"Uh," he sighed, "well, to start you need a couple of cars to work on for a consistent amount of time; something you could take apart and put back together. You'd need a standard set of tools – probably more than one set if you've got a group working together – a couple tire jacks – really, tire stands if you have them – at least two creepers, manuals to the cars…" he paused but it seemed like he could have continued.

"Do you have any idea of cost?" Harold Warren asked.

Thomas looked towards the ceiling, calculating in his head.

"Well, depends on how usable you want the cars to be to start with. You can get some really run-down cars for five hundred to eight hundred dollars, but if you want the kids to actually fix the car, you have to consider auto parts, and the cost of that can be anywhere from twenty-five to a thousand dollars, depending on the part."

I worried that Sean's plan of bringing in Thomas to represent the auto mechanics industry was backfiring. If he had talked to me earlier, I would have suggested bringing in a baker or pastry chef. However, I know Sean would've argued that, due to our larger male population, mechanics made more sense, to which I would have replied, 'that's sexist.'

"I know," Thomas laughed at people's expressions as he continued to break down the cost of various parts. "Now you know why we have to charge you so much when you bring your car in. Really, it's the car taking all your money," he said, making the Warrens and Paulsons laugh. "Um, I'd say you're probably looking at the thousands."

"Do you think it could be done with ten thousand?" Harold Warren clarified.

"Oh yeah, easily," Thomas remarked confidently.

I stared at him. This was the first time he really looked like a grown-up to me. The Warrens and the Paulsons looked at one another, seeming pleased with the amount. I couldn't help but think how nice it must be to be able to donate that amount of money like it was a regular rainy Tuesday.

"Will you be the one at the center to provide training for these kids?" Irene asked, smiling hopefully at Thomas. He seemed to have won her over.

"Easy Irene, I told Thomas he was just our consult for today," Sean laughed, but he might as well have paid Irene to ask that question in front of everyone. "I mean, I would love for Thomas to take part in this project, but I haven't had a chance to talk with him yet."

"It depends on the time commitment," Thomas responded, unknowingly opening himself up to more than he'd bargained for.

"Well, what do you think, Maura?" Sean pretended to care about my opinion. "I was thinking someone coming out once a week for one to two hours would be a good start."

"Sounds good to me," I knew it was best to agree with Sean in front of the donors, especially if we were taking this minimalist approach in the beginning. Thomas looked at me, almost smiling as he began to recognize what had happened to him.

"Of course, we would provide that person with extensive support so they wouldn't feel overwhelmed when they started, especially if they've never worked with at-risk teens before." I figured at this point I could join in on Sean's grand plan to get Thomas involved, knowing it would be good for him.

Thomas started to nod. "I will have to talk to my brother to make sure the time commitment is okay with him."

"Oh, good," Irene and Patty both exclaimed happily. It was funny to see how the older women seemed to be quite taken with him.

"So, who should we make our checks out to? Newman or the UDYC?" Mark focused back on logistics.

"UDYC," Sean and I both answered.

"And I will be checking in with Maura and Thomas on a regular basis to monitor the progress of the program, and we can put together a report for you guys in about four months?" Sean verified.

Mark and Harold agreed, pulling out their checkbooks.

"Sounds good," Mark confirmed.

"Tell me, Thomas," Harold said, "does your shop work on BMWs?"

"We do. I actually have a mechanic who's pretty experienced with Beemers."

"For the past month, ours has been making this weird sound when I accelerate and I've been putting off getting it checked."

Thomas reached into his wallet, pulled out a business card and handed it over to Harold.

"Give us a call and we'll get you set up."

"Can I get one of those, too?" Patty asked quickly. Thomas smiled and reached back into his wallet.

"Sure thing," he handed her the card.

"Thomas just finished tuning up my old Camaro that I'm giving to my nephew. He and his guys did a fantastic job," Sean vouched for him, almost in repayment for using this meeting to strong-arm him into volunteering.

"It was a great car to work on, seeing as how it looked like you never drove it," Thomas said with a laugh.

I was reminded of how that stupid car was my first real hint to knowing it was over with Sean. He bought it only two days after looking at engagement rings with me and discussing putting a down payment on a house with the money he'd inherited from his grandfather. Of course, he told me I was being ridiculous when I told him that his rash decision was clearly communicating that something was wrong. Three months later he was gone.

The group stood up and Harold and Mark handed me their checks for five thousand dollars each before the couples said their goodbyes. Sean walked them out to their cars. I shut down my laptop along with twenty hours of work I didn't get to show anyone, so glad I had put all that energy into researching studies and statistics. I looked over at Thomas.

"So, were you in on this?" he asked.

"In on what?" I asked innocently, although I knew what he was referring to.

"You trying to turn me into a better person by getting me to volunteer?"

"I had no idea you were coming to the meeting. That was all Sean," I said fervently.

"Looks like you got Finley-ed. It's okay, it happens to the best of us." I packed up my laptop and put on my coat.

"What does that mean?" he asked.

"Sean is all about seeing people in terms of resources. He thinks it's his God-given duty to make sure people are given every opportunity possible to share their resources with others, particularly when it benefits the Church or the poor...and even if they're not quite sure if they are ready or willing to share their time, talent, or treasure – more commonly known as money – he finds a way to make them do it anyway. How else do you think I ended up running one of the most active community service social justice committees in the history of Newman my junior year?"

I imitated Sean's voice, "Maura, have you thought about getting the group to do this? Hey, Maura, I think if we get everyone to do a bake sale we can double our donation to El Hogar. Maura, I really think if we set up a table on campus, we can get the word out about the Fair Trade movement."

Thomas looked amused at my impression.

"So, he warned me about you, but you didn't feel the need to warn me about him?" he asked, pointing out my oversight.

"Who I am to question the judgment of a priest?" I said sarcastically.

"Well maybe I'll have to use that line on Michael when I ask for two hours off a week."

"We're an afternoon program," I reminded. "Just switch the morning shift with him one day a week and you can be at the center by three thirty."

"It seems like I've been McCormicked now."

"If that means not taking weak-ass excuses for not helping the greater good, then I'd say I agree," I remarked cleverly.

He feigned shock. "McCormick and Finley, the gruesome twosome."

"Come on, Thomas, it's for the children," I said with exaggerated piety.

He zipped up his coat and was about to say his goodbye.

"Actually, before you go, we need to set up a time for your training."

"Of course," he sighed and pulled out his phone.

"I just talked to Sydney this morning and she's going to be training some undergraduate volunteers this Friday at the center at four."

"I'll have to run it–"

"By Michael," I finished for him. "You send Michael my way if he has questions."

Thomas raised an eyebrow at me, doubtful of how persuasive I could be.

"Oh, and do you want to go and buy the tools and stuff Saturday or Sunday?"

He seemed caught off by my question about an additional appointment.

"We want to get started sooner rather than later," I explained.

"Jesus, I come to one meeting and you're taking up my whole calendar."

"He has a way of doing that," I said with a straight face.

Thomas rolled his eyes. "Okay, well, it's my Saturday to work, so I can't do it until after one."

"That's fine. I'll meet you at the shop and we can go from there."

He finished typing everything into his phone.

"Oh, and you'll have to get a background check done too, but I can give you the paperwork for that on Friday."

"So you're telling me that if I go and commit a crime I can get out of this?" he joked.

"Well, probably not if it's only a misdemeanor," I said seriously.

"Hmm, I'll have to consider whether a felony is worth it."

"I think you'll like it," I said knowingly, slinging my bag over my shoulder and heading back to Sean's office to debrief him and let him know the training date for the undergrads.

"Have a good day," I smiled.

I probably should've felt at least a little guilty about the position Thomas had ended up in, but I just couldn't seem to.

THOMAS

I PREPARED MYSELF FOR A LECTURE FROM MICHAEL once I got to the shop. He didn't like new ideas or change. Even though I gave Maura a hard time, I believed helping out with this voc-ed program was a good business decision. I went over my reasons on the drive back to the shop.

One: the shop did not have to provide any donations of materials as long as we kept it within the ten-thousand-dollar budget. Two: if Michael switched shifts with me one day a week, it wouldn't take away any manpower during regular business hours. Three: it gave the shop good publicity and could potentially increase clientele. As far as I could recall, the only positive community support the shop had ever offered was sponsoring little league teams. Four: it was the right thing to do.

I had begun to realize over the past couple of months how lucky Michael and I had been to be trained with a marketable skill at such a young age. It occurred to me now how much I had taken it for granted. Maybe my desire to pass on what my dad had taught me to those less fortunate was my way of trying to make amends. I hoped I would catch Michael on a good day and that he was willing to accept my opinion as valid. I decided to change into my coveralls before approaching him, thinking that if he viewed me as a fellow mechanic, it could possibly help my argument. Silly, but worth a shot.

I walked into the office and closed the door behind me.

"You got a minute?" I asked when he looked up from the desk.

"Sure. Don't tell me they asked you to hire a bunch of kids?"

Of course, he went to the worst possible scenario. I sat down.

"Yes, and I shouted, 'O'Hollarens don't do handouts!' at them before shoving the table over and storming out," I stated flatly to gage his attitude.

He stared at me with a stern look. Michael never seemed to appreciate my sense of humor.

"No, they didn't ask us to hire anybody. They asked if we could provide training."

I could tell that Michael immediately started envisioning a bunch of street youths running around the garage, tagging gang signs on the cars and walls.

"On site at the youth center," I calmed his fears. "It would be once a week for two hours in the afternoon."

"How much did they say it would cost us?"

"Nothing. They had two donors contributing ten thousand dollars for the whole program – to pay for the cars, the tools, the parts, everything. They just need a mechanic."

He sighed.

"They asked me if I would do it," I admitted.

"And you told them…?"

"I told them I had to talk it over with you."

I thought Michael would appreciate that I considered this a partnership. I hoped he would offer me the same respect as I attempted to sell the idea. He sat there, silently mulling over the information. After giving him a few minutes to process, I gave my opinion.

"I think it's a good decision. It gives us good publicity. It gives a few kids the opportunity to become employable. They didn't ask us to donate any of our tools or our space. I just need you to switch one morning shift with me a week."

Colleen had pushed so hard for Michael to get off at three every day. He would need time to consider this point.

"Or we could send Frank," I joked, looking out the window at Frank working on a truck.

Right on cue Frank yelled at the truck, "You goddamn slut fucker!"

"That's a new one," I remarked, turning back to Michael. "They'll not only learn about cars, they'll learn how to express themselves."

Michael let out a sigh and rubbed his forehead.

"I don't know, Tommy."

I knew Michael well enough to know that his hesitation was purely due to the unpredictability of the situation, paired with the still-recent changes of running the shop without our dad, in addition to my return. I decided to appeal to his desire to honor our dad.

"Don't you think Dad would've liked the idea of it? It's an opportunity to give kids who are less fortunate an opportunity to develop an employable skill, so they're not sucking off the damn government teat," I quoted something we had both heard our dad say many times before.

"Well, that is true," Michael acknowledged, smiling briefly.

We sat in silence for a moment.

"You swear we're not going to be on the hook to pay for anything or hire anyone?"

"Yes, I saw them write the checks and there was no mention of hiring."

"Okay," he sighed. "Let me talk to Colleen about what day I can switch to afternoons and I'll let you know."

"'Kay," I said, standing up. I reached for the door and turned back to him, "There was one more small thing."

He stared at me expectantly.

"They asked me to go to a volunteer training this Friday at four, so I'm going to need to either switch with you Friday or get off two hours early."

He was reaching his small limit of flexibility.

"Maura knew this was going to be a hassle so she offered to babysit to make it up to you and Colleen," I lied.

"Really?" He sounded skeptical, but then again, it was something Maura would be likely to do.

"Uh-huh. She said to let me know the time and date and I could pass it on to her."

"Huh," he reflected, considering the information. "All right, deal. I'll talk to Colleen and let you know."

I nodded and started to leave the office, but he stopped me. "Hey, did they give you a list of the stuff they wanted to use?"

"Actually, no, they left it wide open. I just have to make it fit into a budget intended for six to ten kids for four months. I was thinking at least two cars to work on."

Michael was nodding.

"Yeah, I'd say that's right. We could probably talk to Randy down at the yard to see if he would give us a deal."

"He could probably get a tax write-off for it," I pointed out. "I was trying to think of all the tools Dad had us using when we started."

"Tell you what, how about you come over for dinner tonight and we can write up the list."

Even as I said, "All right," Michael had already gone back to looking at the papers on his desk. That was about as warm and fuzzy as he was going to get, but it was a nice change, considering our interactions in the past. I went out to the floor, pleased with myself for not only convincing Michael that our involvement in this program was good business, but also for setting Maura up to babysit unknowingly. Granted, payback against her wasn't really warranted, but messing with her was just too damn entertaining.

———

I showed up on Friday for my volunteer training at the University District Youth Center. I had never been there but had passed by it dozens of times without knowing that it was an outreach operation. It was a large house with a couple of small portables surrounding it. There were several teenagers hanging around outside, some of them sitting on the porch, some of them playing basketball. I walked through the front door to see a sign with an arrow directing me to a backroom for training.

When I found the room, there were already about ten college kids, mostly female, standing around talking to one another in various circles. I signed in and then took a seat at the table by myself.

"Hi, I'm Gina," I looked up to see a brunette smiling widely at me and holding out her hand.

"Thomas," I said and shook her hand, not offering any other social invitation.

"So, are you here for the volunteer training?" She sat down next to me. Great. Apparently, Gina wanted to chat.

I nodded, keeping my interactions as brief as possible.

"Me too. I'm so excited. I think I really want to work with kids after I graduate. Do you go to Newman? I've never seen you there."

"No, I don't go to Newman. Just here for the training." I realized Gina was just trying to be friendly, but I had switched the early shift with Michael in ordered to be there. Paired with another Natalie sleepover, I was exhausted and just wanted to sit in silence.

"Cool. So what made you want to volunteer?" Gina was staring at me, genuinely interested in my reason.

"I'm just helping out a friend," I said simply. Hopefully I succeeded in killing the conversation by not returning the question.

Rather than offended, Gina looked confused by my pithiness.

Maybe I wasn't the right person to be working in this setting if I got annoyed by Gina and her level of pep. Maybe that was how you were expected to act when you hung around teenagers who were having a rough go at life. I thought of how much I had teased Maura about acting like Pollyanna and now I feared I would be playing the Glad Game while teaching kids how to work on junk cars.

In walked a woman with short dark hair, wearing jeans and a white button-up shirt with a tie. Her rolled up sleeves revealed some intricate tattoos. She was carrying binders.

"All right, go ahead and grab a seat so we can get started," she said assertively.

Everyone in the room did as she asked. She put the binders down on the table.

"Here, take one and pass them down," she instructed the woman closest to where she stood.

"These are your training binders; inside you will find this sheet," she held up a form. "This is the most important piece of the packet. This is the paper that you will take in when you get your fingerprints and background check done. After you do that, bring this form back to us. You will not be allowed to volunteer here until you have cleared your background check. Your group has stated that they want to start the first week of spring quarter, so I suggest you get this done before you go and get drunk in Cancun for spring break." She put the form down and put her hands on her hips.

"So. I'm Sydney Gregg. I'm a case manager here. I will be providing your training today. Let's go around the room real quick and just say your name. Just your name. I don't need to hear about why you're here and what you want to get out of it. Just names," she reiterated.

Quickly and efficiently, everyone went around the room and said their first names. Then Sydney started again.

"You should be here to serve in the appropriate capacity we ask you to, which may be cooking, sorting donations, or participating in activities with our youth. Very likely it will mostly be sorting donations and running our free clothing store. You will not solve homelessness while you are here. You will not keep our youth from making bad decisions by offering your limited insight or judgment. If you plan on saving anyone, this is not an appropriate place for you and I request that you find another place to volunteer. That being said, it is okay if you occasionally get warm fuzzies by treating our youth with dignity and positive regard; just please, for the love of God, do not hug anyone, but we will go over that more when we get to policies and guidelines. Please save your questions 'till the end."

Sydney then went right into explaining the operations of the center. I looked around the room and saw the expressions of intimidation on all the undergraduates faces. I, for one, appreciated her no bull-shit approach and started to feel more comfortable about agreeing to help with their program.

I went up to Sydney after the training was over. Even though I enjoyed her gruffness, I was still a bit nervous to approach her as a stranger. However, I wanted to confirm my meeting with Maura for tomorrow and share some good news with her before I left. I figured Sydney could tell me where she was at.

"Excuse me, hi. I'm Thomas O'Hollaren," I held out my hand. "I'm the mechanic who's going to be providing some training," I explained, hoping someone had told her about the plan.

She smiled for the first time in two hours.

"Oh right, right, good to meet you," she shook my hand.

"Is Maura here today? I need to touch base with her about something."

"Yeah, she should still be here. Come on, I'll take you back," she motioned for me to follow her down a hallway. "Sorry if I came off like a total bitch back there," she commented once we had cleared the conference room. "It's just that sometimes we get these volunteers who are little misguided on what they think they're going to be doing. We had a group a few months ago who were kind of forcing baptism on some of our kids, and what can I say? I get protective."

Unsure what to say, I nodded. We reached a door that was cracked open. Sydney knocked and then quickly peeked inside before stepping in.

"Look who made it to the training," she announced. Maura looked up at her desk.

"Hey," Maura grinned at me.

I was starting to feel like she greeted everyone this way.

"So, how was it?"

Sydney answered before I had to figure it out if she was asking me specifically.

"It was good. I think I sufficiently scared everybody into wanting to comply with our guidelines." She sat down at her desk and started gathering things up into a messenger bag.

"Did she do her whole no-nonsense spiel about how no one's going to be hero and cure homelessness?" Maura turned to me.

"I believe I was told several times that I'm not going to save anyone."

"Sounds about right," Maura sighed. "Well, you think we lost anyone?" she asked, turning back to Sydney.

"We'll see, but you were the one who was all worried about getting crappy volunteers with bad boundaries. I thought you wanted me to weed them out."

"That doesn't mean you can't throw an icebreaker in there somewhere," Maura said pointedly.

"We went around and said our names," Sydney countered.

"That doesn't count as an icebreaker." Maura turned back to me. "I should have sent you to the training next month; then you would've had me as your trainer."

"And it would've taken an hour longer and she would have made you color a name tag and then journal about your hopes and dreams," Sydney warned.

I was thankful I went through Sydney's version of the training.

"Some people happen to like my training style," Maura defended. "Oh here, Syd, one of the therapists stopped by and wanted me to give you this message." She handed a note across the desk.

Sydney stared down at it for a second, then looked back up.

"Shit. Really?" she asked Maura.

Maura nodded.

"Fan-fucking-tastic,. Whelp, I guess we'll see what happens after Monday," she sighed.

Clearly, they couldn't talk about whatever it was openly in front of me. I waited through their silent exchange of eye contact, not knowing if I should step out of the room.

Suddenly, someone walked in behind me. I moved to get out of the way and saw a slender young woman. She had dark brown hair in a long braid. Her loose knitted sweater hung right above her midriff, revealing a naval piercing. She bent down next to Sydney's desk, revealing a tribal tattoo on the small of her back. She was wearing flip flops, which I thought was odd, given the rain. She started talking, not really paying attention to the fact that I was in the room.

"Okay, so I am all wrapped up for today. I have finals next week, so I won't be coming back out until spring quarter starts up in two weeks. I think I might have to file an incident report before I go because I'm pretty sure Kendall and Pepper were smoking weed in–"

"Ashland," Maura quickly interrupted. Ashland paused and looked confused.

"We have a volunteer in here," she pointed to me.

Ashland turned around and looked me up and down before smiling at me with her piercing blue eyes.

"Hi, I'm Ashland, I'm the graduate intern," she reached out her hand, which I shook.

"This is Thomas. He's the mechanic who's going to be coming out once a week for the vocational program."

"Oh, exciting," she gave me a half smile. "Well, maybe I'll see you around when I get back."

Maura and Sydney exchanged another look before Maura stood up.

"We're going to go to the conference room so you guys can file that incident report," she announced to the other two before leading me out.

"Nice meeting you," Sydney waved. Ashland's eyes remained on me as I left the room.

"Sorry about that," Maura apologized.

"No need to apologize; it's your office." I followed her into the conference room. Personally, I thought it was pretty interesting to see Maura engage with people outside of a church setting.

We reached the conference room and she turned to me. "So, what did you need?"

"Just wanted to let you know that Michael and I talked to a contact we have at the junkyard and he is donating a Corolla and an Accord to the program. You just have to pay towing costs. He's going to drop them off here Monday around nine. I told him to make the invoice out to the Youth Center."

· Her eyes lit up and she started clapping her hands.

"Yay! That's awesome." She immediately hugged me. "Thank you so much."

"You know, I just went through a training that told me to refrain from full frontal hugs and to stick to high fives or side hugs," I remarked as she backed away.

"Whatever," she pushed my arm. "That's so great," she said, still excited about the news. "Was there anything else?"

"No. Just wanted to make sure we were still on for tomorrow at one."

She nodded.

"Oh, and there was just one more small thing; you're babysitting for Michael and Colleen next Friday at six."

She looked at me with confusion.

"Yeah, I told Michael that you felt so badly about any scheduling upset my involvement with this program had caused him and his family that you offered to babysit to make up for it."

My words registered and she stared me down.

"What?" I asked innocently. "That's not what you meant when you said to send Michael your way? It's kind of a bitch when people just schedule you to do stuff without clearing it with you first, am I right?"

She crossed her arms, realizing she had gotten played.

"You know what? That's fine. I'm so happy about the cars that I don't even care, and I love kids and helping people out, so there."

"There's that Pollyanna again," I laughed. "I'll see you tomorrow."

———

Our Saturday at the shop flew by, mostly due to the massive amount of people picking their cars up after being worked on over the course of the week. Twelve thirty arrived quickly and we began to shut-down for the day. Maura showed up right before one o'clock, just as Frank, the only employee left, was getting ready to clock out.

She walked in wearing jeans and a University of Washington hoodie, with her hair up in a high ponytail, looking like she could still pass for a sophomore in college. As expected, she was smiling.

"You ever feel like you're Billy Joel in the video for Uptown Girl?" she asked randomly. "'Cause I would."

"All the time. In fact, you just missed the big musical number we sing every day right before closing," I said with a straight face. "Usually we have Frank play the role of Christie Brinkley," I raised my voice in Frank's direction.

"I don't know what that means, but fuck you, Tommy," Frank called back, heading out the door with a wave.

"See you Monday."

I turned back to Maura.

"You ready to go get some car tool thingies?" she grinned.

She was going to be utterly out of place in the auto parts store. "Tell me again why we have to go together?" I asked.

"Because I have the company credit card so you either take me with you or get reimbursed a good month or two down the road."

She had a fair point.

"If you wear that, do we get a discount?" she asked, referring to the coveralls I had yet to change out of.

I couldn't tell if she was kidding, but I hoped she was, or it was going to be a long day. Her smile cracked and gave her away.

"Wait here. I'll be right back," I left to go change in the office.

Once I was back in my jeans and T-shirt, I remembered Michael had mentioned it would be wise to store the materials and tools at the shop until we started the program. He'd suggested using a storage garage we had on site and told me that the key was somewhere in my dad's desk, most likely in the top drawer.

I did a quick look-over on the surface and under some of the piles of papers. I felt like I was disrupting a sacred space by actually opening the drawer, which I had never done. When I did, I found it equally as cluttered as the top of the desk. I rifled around in search of the key, but froze when a piece of paper caught my eye.

It was a scene from Green Lake Park, done in watercolor and colored pencil. I knew because I had painted it in sixth grade. My initials were at the bottom of it. I didn't remember ever giving it to my father and I was shocked that he would have kept any of my artwork, especially at his beloved shop. I lifted the paper up, staring at it, trying to remember or understand why my dad had kept it over the years. I looked down and noticed a couple of other small paintings I had done, along with a newspaper clipping about the one moderately successful exhibit my work had been in two years before in New York.

Maura called my name from the floor, bringing me back into the world. I quickly resumed my search for the key and found it under my amateur paintings. I grabbed it and put everything back in order, feeling agitated. I suddenly had a stream of questions filling my mind and knew there wasn't anyone around who could even attempt to answer them. Really, there was only one person I wanted to talk to in that moment and I couldn't. Finally, it registered: my dad was dead and I would never have another conversation with him again.

MAURA

SHOPPING FOR TOOLS WITH THOMAS TOOK FOREVER. He seemed to be in his own little world once we got to the store, muttering about different sized wrenches and the brands of different things. He kept referring to his list and even called Michael a couple of times for his opinion. To me, it sounded like they were speaking in a foreign language. I tried to engage him in conversation a few times but my efforts fell flat.

He didn't even seem amused when I suggested buying the bubble gum pink tool kit and storage cart. He just looked up and simply said, "No," before going back down another aisle. Eventually, I resorted to pulling out my phone to look at Facebook and Pinterest. Thomas didn't seem to mind or notice. When we finished, I was shocked that it had only taken us three hours. It felt like we had been there for at least five.

It was weird seeing him in work mode. All my other interactions with him had been social, except when I saw him briefly to get my oil changed. I wondered if he was going to be this standoffish with the teenagers. Then again, it wouldn't be the worst thing to be serious when instructing young people how to use expensive materials. I told myself I should be glad he was taking the whole thing seriously.

But I still couldn't help but feel that something was off with him, given his usual tendency to joke around with me. He had joked around when I first showed up, but then as soon as he came out of the office he was super quiet and could barely hold a conversation on the drive to the store. I resolved to at least check and see if he was okay when we got back in the truck.

"So, did we get everything on the list?"

He nodded at my question.

"And you want to store it at the shop before we start?"

He nodded again. I let a period of silence pass.

Finally, he said, "You should probably invest in a pretty good lock or even security system for your garage if that's where we're going to be keeping everything with the cars."

"Yeah, I told Ann about that. We have our security company coming out this week to add a system to the garage."

No big surprise, he just nodded again. I paused and then finally asked the question I had wanted to all afternoon.

"Are you okay?"

"Yeah, fine, why?" he answered.

"You're just more quiet than usual."

"Sometimes I like to be quiet. You should give it a try."

Based on his tone, I first thought he was being serious, but then he winked at me. I didn't say anything and decided to let him have his silence. Unfortunately, I only lasted about three minutes.

"So, you got any plans tonight?"

He grinned, acknowledging that I couldn't keep my mouth shut even when I tried.

"I'm meeting up with some people tonight."

"Natalie?"

"She'll be among them." He didn't offer any more information.

"So, no running tomorrow?" I thought it best to confirm so I wasn't standing on the corner like an idiot waiting for him.

"Probably not."

I was disappointed but didn't think I should be. I wanted him to ask me what I was doing that night so I could tell him I had a date with Ethan, but he never did. When we pulled back up to the shop, he parked the truck and went into the front office to unlock the garage door. I stepped out of the truck as he walked back out.

"So where are we unloading everything?" I looked around.

"It's fine. I got it." He opened the driver's side door.

"You sure?"

As I anticipated, he simply nodded.

"Okay, well, I guess I'll see you next week. Have a good night."

"You too." He climbed in and drove inside the shop.

I walked over to my car, feeling awkward about the whole exchange, but unsure what to do. I tried not to analyze anything while I drove back to my apartment to get ready for Ethan to pick me up. Instead, I thought about how I really didn't want to change out of my jeans and sweatshirt. Amazingly, it was like Ethan had read my mind when I listened to a voicemail from him instructing me not to dress up for the night.

I ran down to meet him on the street when he called. Once again, he got out of the car and opened the door for me. He was wearing jeans, and what appeared to be an actual T-shirt underneath his red Columbia softshell jacket. His tennis shoes, although immaculate, were the most casual shoes I had ever seen him in.

"When are you going to let me come up and knock on the door like a gentleman?" he greeted me.

"I like to be hassle-free," I shrugged before sitting down and letting him close the door.

When he was back in the car, he turned to me.

"I never consider treating someone like a lady a hassle," he said earnestly. "Especially a pretty one."

"So where are we going?" I redirected, not knowing how to receive the compliment.

He pulled into the street.

"It's a surprise," he informed me.

He had been wise to not tell me until that moment because I would probably have pestered him multiple times before he picked me up.

"Does it involve food?" I asked because I was starving.

"No, I thought we could throw in an extra fast for Lent," he said seriously. He looked at me and realized I wasn't sure whether he was joking. "Yes, Maura, it involves food, but no more clues."

I refrained from revealing one of my more annoying qualities: wrecking surprises through repeated guessing.

"Well, I am a fan of food, so you're off to a good start," I said. "So, what did you do today?"

"I went to mass; I worked a little bit. You?"

"I had to work too, kind of." I felt the need to clarify. "I had to go out and buy all these tools for the voc-ed program at work. They decided to focus on just having an auto-mechanic training program to start."

"So, you went to the auto parts store and picked out a bunch of tools to work on cars with?" His tone was doubtful, clearly not believing that buying auto-mechanical tools was a skill in my repertoire.

"Well, not by myself. I went with the mechanic who's going to be doing the training, Thomas. You know him. You met him last month at Latona."

He nodded.

"I played on my phone while I followed him around the store, and then I used the agency card to pay for everything. So, yeah, it was exactly the same as you working on matrices and algorithms all day."

He looked over at me and grinned.

"Is that what you think I do at my job?"

"Well, sometimes I picture the movie Hackers and then sometimes I picture the movie Jobs, but with more current haircuts and clothes, and a different logo because I know you work for Microsoft." As silly as I sounded, I was being truthful.

Ethan laughed. "Someday I'm going to have to sit you down and show you what exactly I do for work."

"As long as I get to play on my phone. Speaking of, are you guys not allowed to have iPhones? Like, is that a no-no?" I asked out of genuine curiosity, but once again he looked amused.

"We're encouraged to use our products, but no, they're not doing body searches for Mac products."

I nodded.

I then noticed the parking lot that we had pulled into.

A large neon sign reading, "Lake City Bowl" lit up the parking lot. I had spent many a birthday party there growing up. I was surprised I hadn't realized sooner where we were driving. I turned to Ethan to see him smiling and smiled back, not knowing what else to do.

"I ran into Father Sean this morning and asked for advice on where I should take you tonight. He said you love bowling."

I tried to maintain my smile. Apparently, I didn't have a very good poker face because his smile disappeared.

"Wait, you don't like bowling?"

I paused and decided it was best to just be honest.

"I don't *not* like it," I said weakly. "It's just...meh," I shrugged.

His face fell in disappointment. "I can't believe this," he tilted his head back. "But why would Father Sean say you love bowling?"

"Because he loves bowling and probably has very fond memories of kicking my ass and me being a good sport about it," I said nonchalantly.

"But why would he keep taking you if you didn't like it?"

"He always had such a good time, I never told him specifically that I didn't like it," I explained.

Ethan shook his head.

"I'm sorry. I feel so stupid. I thought you were going to be so excited," he sighed.

"No, this is a great date idea," I tried to reassure him. "I'm just stoked that I'm in jeans and a sweatshirt," I said truthfully. "And I know there's beer and pizza inside, so, double-score."

He stared at me, his expression softening a bit.

"Anyway, I think it was very sweet of you to want to surprise me."

My words were sincere. He reached over and touched my hand, and I waited a moment to see if he was going to kiss me.

161

When he didn't, I joked, "But maybe next time, don't go to a priest for dating advice...especially my ex-boyfriend."

"Yeah, yeah, fair point," he said and rubbed his forehead. "So, you want to go in there and endure ten frames with me?"

"I thought you'd never ask," I grinned and turned to get out of the car. He met me in front of the car and grabbed my hand again as we went inside.

Once we got our shoes and were assigned a lane, Ethan ordered us food. I went in search of a ball. Logically, I knew the best bet was to pick a ball heavy enough to knock the pins over, but one I could still hold onto with one hand. However, I chose to ignore that logic and ended up picking a ten-pound ball because it had sparkles on it. Ethan didn't seem to notice, or if he did, he withheld from teasing me about my choice.

"Are we keeping score?" he sounded uncertain. Since I had been honest earlier, he was probably going to be walking on eggshells for the rest of the night.

"Well how else are we going to get to see the cartoons between each frame?" I answered as if it were obvious, trying to lighten the mood and put him at ease.

As he programmed our names into the machine, I wondered if he was going to let me win, which would be extremely hard to do while still making it look natural.

"Okay, ladies first," he motioned to the lane.

I grabbed my ball, accepting that there was no way I could leave tonight without embarrassing myself at least a little. It crossed my mind that Sean had suggested this as a small form of torture, but more than likely he was just clueless about the types of things I'd actually liked doing when we were dating. But that wasn't entirely his fault. I was so young when we started dating and he'd seemed so wise to me at the time. I'd wanted nothing more than to make him happy, and I thought the best way to do that was to make everything all about him whenever we went on a date. I thought it was unconditional love, but what it ended up being was blind devotion.

I let go of the ball, and sure enough, it rolled into the gutter.

"That's how I like to warm up." I turned around to Ethan.

I could tell he didn't know if I was really trying or not.

I had to give Ethan credit; he sat through seven whole frames without giving me any advice. It probably took a lot of self-control, seeing as how I had a score of forty-nine and he had already passed one hundred. The screen signaled that it was my turn. I grinned at him, knowing he had to be biting his tongue.

"What?" he laughed.

"You totally want to give me pointers," I called him out.

"What? No," he denied unconvincingly.

"Come on, you know you want to. I can tell. Many bowlers have tried to save me from my bad form."

He kept smiling and shook his head, refusing to take the bait. I threw him a bone, knowing he had probably thought the night was going to be more competitive.

"Ethan, would you like to help me with this next turn?"

"Do you want me to help you?" he was being cautious.

"I think I could tolerate it...at least I know my score could," I joked, picking up my ball.

"Maybe you want to pick a heavier ball," he hinted what he had undoubtedly been thinking the entire time.

"But this one has sparkles," I said.

He stared at me, trying to gage how committed I was to the sparkle ball, then bent down and picked up a twelve-pound ball.

"And this one is blue, like seventy-five percent of the world's favorite color," he quoted my statistic back at me.

He won me over by the reference and, well, just pure reason. I put the sparkle ball down, grabbed the ball from his hand, and moved into position.

"Okay, so here's what you want to do," Ethan moved up behind me and I was surprised to feel him put his arms around me, his hand resting over mine. "Stare at the arrows closest to you to get your bearings, and don't worry about the pins for the first roll. Then, when you swing your arm forward, you want your hand to move sideways like you're shaking someone's hand."

While I had heard everything he said, I was more focused on how nice it felt to be enveloped in his arms. I noticed for the first time that he smelled nice. I liked having his mouth so close to my ear, liked how strong his hands felt. And then it clicked: I had butterflies in my stomach.

"So, you ready to give it a try?" he asked confidently, clueless as to where my mind was. I only managed to nod.

He backed away, waiting for me to bowl the ball. I tried to focus on his instructions, which were all tips I had heard before but could never seem to get right anyway. I took my turn. Miraculously, the ball stayed in the middle of lane. It rolled slowly down the center, eventually making contact with the pins. To my amazement, all the pins collapsed. My mouth dropped open and I turned to Ethan with a large smile. He enthusiastically held up his hands, matching my excitement. I jumped up and down and couldn't for the life of me remember the last time I'd gotten a strike.

"See, I told you I was just warming up," I exclaimed proudly.

In my opinion, this would have been the perfect time to kiss me. Then again, there had been at least three occasions when I'd been with Ethan that I thought would have been the perfect time to kiss me. He simply gave me a high five.

"It's a wise strategy to wait until the seventh frame – like a sneak attack," he joked.

Then he took his turn, eventually picking up a spare. It didn't inspire the same level of enthusiasm that I'd gotten for my strike.

I made it through the whole game but was thankful when it was over. Most people don't recognize that rolling gutter balls gets pretty tedious and boring after a while. I managed to break sixty, making it not-my-worst bowling score ever. I must admit, I thought about asking Ethan for instruction again, merely to have him put his arms around me, but decided it would look needy and ditzy.

"So, are there any other activities you absolutely hate, so I can avoid future embarrassment?" he asked when we were driving back to my apartment.

I considered telling him how boring I thought the Liturgy of the Hours was, but refrained, knowing it was probably too soon to be that honest.

"Hmmm," I thought for a minute, "I don't like Chinese food."

He nodded.

"I like movies, but I have trouble not talking during them, so I wouldn't recommend taking me to a theatre," I admitted.

"Sporting events?"

"Yeah, you're good there, especially if it's Washington."

"I remember. You get a little intense," he commented, but didn't sound critical. Then again, I don't know, maybe he thought it was in poor taste for me to be that enthusiastic and loud during a sporting event. I figured time would tell.

"And unfortunately, you don't like skiing or snowboarding," he sighed. "I'm convinced I could change your mind, though."

"Maybe," I shrugged, not wanting to sound too inflexible, but knowing I never would care for either.

"I just can't believe Father Sean never figured out that you didn't like bowling...I mean, you're really..."

"Bad," I finished what he was too polite to say.

He laughed. "I was going to say 'not good,' but no use candy coating it now, I guess."

"Sean was kind of a clueless boyfriend when it came to stuff like that." For the first time, I didn't use Sean's title when referencing him to Ethan.

"And here I was worried that I had stiff competition to live up to," he confessed.

He found a place to park outside my building and turned the car off.

"No need to worry about that," I assured.

He stayed in the car and turned towards me. I started to anticipate another rosary invitation.

"Can I ask you something about Father Sean?"

I nodded.

"Did you want to break up with him?"

I let out a small nervous laugh. "I didn't really have a choice in the matter."

He continued to look at me. He was asking me if I was still in love with Sean.

"At the time no, but now looking back, I know it would have never worked. When we started dating it was great, but then gradually I kind of lost myself. It was like I became his sidekick."

Ethan looked at me with understanding.

"I think I needed to grow up a lot and Sean just wasn't the right person to grow with. Don't get me wrong, it's not like he's a jerk or anything," I wanted to make sure I didn't sound bitter. "You shouldn't worry about me comparing you guys...but, if I did, you're totally already winning because he never helped me get a strike."

His expression looked like he was relieved by my answer.

"Can I please walk you to your door like a gentleman?"

"Sure, I'll allow it," I sighed but then smiled.

I led Ethan into the building. While we were waiting for the elevator he took my hand, and he continued to hold it without saying anything as we rode up to the fifth floor. It seemed so silly to me that he wanted to make a point to walk me all the way to my door, especially since I knew he was not the type to come in after only going on a few dates with me. We made it to my apartment and I turned to him.

"So, this is it," I said obviously.

Ethan continued to hold my hand, looking down at it, fiddling gently with my fingers.

"You are not like any other girl I've dated before," he said, looking into my eyes. I wasn't sure what to say, so I stayed quiet, but when he didn't say anything else, I couldn't take the silence anymore.

"Is that a good thing or not?"

"It took me so long to ask you out because I was pretty sure you were going to turn me down. You're so confident and outgoing with your faith, not to mention beautiful...you're not really the type a computer geek like me is used to."

"Well, I guess a social worker nerd like me is all about equal opportunity," I said. While this statement was true, I don't know why I couldn't have said it more eloquently and let the moment be serious.

"I'm serious. I really don't want to mess this up. I don't want to let you down."

In my gut, I knew the reality was that I was probably not nearly as holy as he thought me to be. It was only a matter of time before I would be the one to let him down when he found out how much I actually cussed, or how many reality shows on E! or Bravo I indulged in on the weekends; that some months I chose paying extra on my student loans over tithing, in addition to the fact that I had voted for political candidates who happened to be pro-choice. Of course, I had voted for them because of reasons beyond the pro-choice factor, but I knew that it was still looked down on by many Catholics.

Before I could explain that there was no need for him to worry, Ethan moved in closer and placed his hand on the side of face with his thumb resting on my cheek. I willed myself to stay silent, hoping if I could keep from saying anything or ruining the moment, he would finally kiss me. He stared into my eyes for what seemed to be forever and I wondered if he was expecting me to lean in. Finally, I closed my eyes, hoping he wouldn't awkwardly back away to signal that I had read the situation wrong. Within moments I felt his lips on mine, pressing gently. I responded by pressing back. And then it was over, before I could even contemplate whether I should open my mouth or not.

"Good night, Maura," he smiled.

"Good night, Ethan," I managed to respond, confused by the quickest first kiss I'd had since middle school.

"Can I meet you for mass tomorrow?"

I nodded.

"You still going to five thirty?"

I nodded again. Was I that bad of a kisser?

"Okay, I'll see you then."

Almost as if to calm my doubt, Ethan leaned in and kissed me goodnight, repeating the same simple style of kiss.

"Good night," he said again, and took a few steps back, still looking at me.

"Good night." I unlocked my door and gave him a small wave goodbye before I walked into my apartment.

I turned on the light and went into my living room, dumbfounded that for the first time in my life, I was the party that was disappointed with the lack of physical contact on a date. It wasn't like I wanted to bring him in and make out on the couch, but I would be lying if I said I hadn't been craving at least a long kiss or two at my door.

Although there was really no reason to be surprised. After all, Ethan had taken a good four months to ask me out on a date. I sighed, feeling guilty for wanting more passion.

Eventually, I settled into watching trashy reality TV. The drama on screen was the best distraction from the guilt I felt for thinking that I had somehow misled Ethan into thinking I was holier than I actually was, and for not appreciating his commitment to respecting me and taking things slow.

THOMAS

IT WAS WEDNESDAY NIGHT. I SAT ON NATALIE'S BED watching her pack for her spring break trip to Puerto Vallarta. She was making a point to showcase the many brightly colored undergarments she was bringing with her. I had been sleeping with her for a little less than a month and knew that the relationship had basically run its course. But I couldn't tell if she had come to the same conclusion.

"I'm so glad you were able to come over before I have to leave tomorrow," she said without looking at me.

I was staring off into space, transfixed by how many outfits she was packing for five days – or was it six? I hadn't been listening that closely. She didn't notice that I was zoning out since she kept folding and packing.

"My brain is like, totally fried from finals. I'm so looking forward to just going and sitting on the beach with a margarita in my hand," she sighed dramatically. "I don't even want to think about next quarter's finals with graduation and everything. You're so lucky that you're out of school, Tommy."

She had started using my nickname one night after we went out with Tyler and she had heard him call me that when he was drunk. She finally noticed that I hadn't said anything.

"Hey," she smiled and walked over and began running her fingers through my hair. "I'm going to miss you."

· I didn't repeat the sentiment but nodded, putting my hands on her hips. She was dressed down in pajama shorts and a tank top.

"You know, there's still a chance to come with us," she said naively.

"Sorry, grown-ups don't get spring break," I informed her.

During my brief history with her, Natalie had suggested several times that I take vacation or call in sick. Her lack of understanding about my responsibilities was starting to annoy me. I also thought it was kind of weird that she was inviting me to go on an extended vacation with her after we'd only known each other for a short amount of time.

"I know," she whined. "I just wish I could have you there...I get really horny when I'm on vacation," she said, hoping to entice me.

When I didn't encourage her to elaborate, she paused and looked over at her suitcase. She broke away and went back to packing. "Speaking of...so you know I haven't been sleeping with anyone else since we started hooking up."

"Me neither," I stated.

Great, she was about to lead me into the 'defining the relationship' talk, and I was ready for the relationship to end soon.

"So, I'm just curious...if I'm going away for a while...for spring break...do you have any expectations?" I wasn't sure what she wanted from me so I took the easy way out.

"I want you to go and have fun."

It was a nice way to say I really didn't care what she did.

"Do you want me to have good girl fun or bad girl fun?"

The mere fact that she was referring to her actions as 'good girl' and 'bad girl' magnified the difference in our maturity. I know some guys, like Tyler, would eat that shit up. I had soaked up a month of Natalie's hyper-sexualized naughty school girl persona and was pretty much over it.

"I want you to have whatever type of fun you want to have," I maintained my laissez-faire attitude.

She put her bikini down in the suitcase and looked at me, wide-eyed.

170

"So you wouldn't care if I ended up having fun with another person?" She didn't seem upset by having to ask me to clarify this. From what I knew of her, it appeared she was starting to get excited. I thought that was weird, given my previous encounters with women. I'd found that they usually wanted you to care about what they did.

"Yeah, you do whatever makes you happy. I'm not your boy-friend." I wondered if I was hurting her feelings by being so blunt.

She moved over to me, maintaining eye contact. She strad-dled me. I thought maybe she was going to try to convince me to care more.

"I can't believe what a nice guy you are, wanting me to have a good time without you."

She was back to playing with my hair and I was now com-pletely confused. I hadn't expected her sound so happy about the whole thing.

"I'm going to do my best to stay good for you...but I feel like I have to tell you what happens when I try to be good when I'm on vacation..."

She stared at me with her wide eyes and then bit her lip. From the outside I would have considered this totally contrived, but in the moment, I was turned on by it.

"...I tend to make out with girls."

She locked her eyes with mine, waiting for my reaction.

"Funny, I tend to do the same thing on vacation," I joked, now pathetically transfixed by her.

"And sometimes," she was now whispering, "it can lead to more."

She began to grind her pelvis against me. My hands had found their way underneath her shirt and up her back, instinctively unfas-tening her bra.

"So, would it bother you if I did that?" She asked with a slight moan escaping her mouth.

I shook my head. She moved me down on my back, her face still close to mine.

"I mean, it's too bad you're not coming with me because you could watch me try to be good...with another girl," she said suggestively, trailing teasing kisses along my jaw.

She pulled away to gage my reaction again.

At this point, I could tell she wanted me to play along. I couldn't bring myself to reciprocate the dirty talk, although I couldn't deny I was entertained by it. I thought about how little I knew about her, and yet didn't really care enough to know more. For a brief moment, I thought maybe I should stop her from having sex with me, wondering if she deserved better. Natalie began to nibble on my neck and suddenly, I didn't really care about what she deserved, just what I wanted.

"So how about you tell me what I'm going to be missing out on for the next week?" I suggested.

A mischievous smile spread across her face and she eagerly obliged, offering an extremely descriptive account of past vacations with her friend Sabrina.

For the first time, I didn't spend the night with her after we had sex, insisting that it was best for her to get a good night's sleep before her trip and that I had to work early the next day. Neither were true. I kissed her goodbye and said I would talk to her when she got back.

By this point, I think she sensed that I was not going to see her when she got back. I convinced myself this was hardly heartbreaking news to her. After all, she was the one who had called me a nice guy after blatantly stating that I was not her boyfriend and I wanted her to be free to have fun. Clearly, she didn't want to be tied down either. While I drove home, it was strange; I'd never had to work so hard to convince myself that I had done nothing wrong.

———

"Hey, Tommy, you doing anything tonight?" Michael walked up to me at work a few days later. I was finishing installing brakes on a Dodge Caravan.

"Nope," I said, quickly glancing to the side at him.

He joined me under the car, casually inspecting my work. I hadn't made any official plans yet, but it was Friday. I had considered going out with Tyler and some other guys but wasn't fully committed to the idea.

I was torn, mostly because I knew any interaction with Tyler and whoever I would meet with him would be a highly superficial. I had little tolerance for that lately. However, the other option was to sit alone at my parents' house, because my mother was leaving for the weekend.

I still dreaded being alone in that house. Even more so since I had found my drawings and paintings in my father's desk. The desire to avoid the empty house had gotten so strong that I'd even volunteered to work on Saturday. Of course, Michael had no idea about the reason behind the offer.

"So, tonight's the night Maura is supposed to babysit," he began.

I kept working, waiting for him to spit out his request.

"Would you mind stopping in and checking on the kids while Colleen and I are out?"

I put my wrench down and turned to face him.

"Are you saying you trust me more than her?" There was disbelief in my voice.

"No, I trust her just fine. I don't trust my kids. I mean, you've met them. There are four of them," he stated the obvious.

Michael's kids were ages six, four, three, and one. All of them were boys and all of them were hyperactive.

"I don't want to traumatize her. I don't even remember the last time we had a babysitter that wasn't one of the grandmas. I have a feeling Gabriel's going to lose his shit," he said, referring to the three-year-old, easily the most sensitive of the four.

"Then once Gabriel loses it, he'll suck Andrew into it, and then Hunter's probably going to have a field day with her."

Hunter was the oldest and clearly the most rambunctious and mischievous of the four. Although, there were times when I looked at James, the one-year-old, and saw a spark in his eyes that made me think he was plotting something, but that could have just been the red hair.

I nodded in agreement.

"We're leaving at six, maybe pop in around seven and make sure they haven't burned the house down?"

"You know you're really selling the idea of fatherhood right now," I commented sarcastically.

He stared at me, waiting for my confirmation.

"Yeah, I'll stop in around seven and make sure Hunter hasn't declared mutiny and tied her up."

"Thank you." Michael walked away.

I went back to work. I knew Michael and I were still far from being close, but I had noticed a difference in the past three weeks. He was acting more like I was his brother rather than an acquaintance. It was a welcomed change.

I pulled up to Michael's house around seven, as he had suggested. I found it still standing, without crying or screaming being projected out into the front yard; a good sign. I brought pizza, figuring it would be good leverage if my nephews were misbehaving when I arrived.

I knocked at the door and immediately heard an explosion of sound, multiple little voices talking over each other and growing louder with every exclamation.

"Someone's at the door! Who is it? I bet it's a pirate! If it's a ninja I'm gonna beat him! Let's go get him!"

After a few moments, Maura answered the door, holding James in one arm and surrounded by the other three.

"Uncle Tommy!" The three older boys exclaimed in unison, pushing through to hug me.

Maura stepped back to let me enter the house with three mini-Michaels attached to me.

"Hi," Maura greeted, looking puzzled.

"Hey," I smiled, knowing I would have to explain Michael's request.

Before I could get a chance; Hunter, Andrew, and Gabriel began jumping up and down, grabbing at the pizza box I held in my hands.

"Pizza! Pizza!" they shouted in unison.

"Oh my gosh! Uncle Tommy brought us pizza!!!!!" Hunter bellowed, throwing his body down on the ground.

He was wearing what looked to be a Captain America costume. I knew Michael would be mortified, but I was more amused by his over-enthusiastic response and fashion choice.

"We just finished dinner," Maura informed me.

"But there's always room for pizza!" Hunter shot back up and ran to the kitchen table, quickly followed by Andrew and Gabriel.

"Funny, they didn't have the same reaction to the salad and fish sticks I made." Maura led me into the kitchen, still holding James.

The boys were still jumping around and grabbed at the box when I walked in.

"All right," I took command. "You guys need to take a seat if you want me to share any of my pizza."

Much to my relief, they moved to their respective chairs at the table while Maura placed James in his high chair. I put the pizza down on the counter and Maura grabbed some plates. When I opened the box, I caught Maura giving me a look.

"What?"

Without saying anything she started picking the pepperoni off the pizza, trying not to let the boys notice.

"Why are you taking all the good stuff off?" Hunter shouted, once again letting everyone know you couldn't get anything past him.

Suddenly it clicked: it was Lent and it was Friday...and of course that's why Colleen had told Maura to give the boys fish.

"I want the pepperoni!" Hunter erupted.

"Me too! Me too!" Andrew agreed with equal volume, followed by Gabriel. James, with that mischievous look, sat there laughing while his brothers began to pound the table in a chant. I realized that Michael's plan to have me help Maura was turning disastrous. Although Maura looked surprisingly cool under pressure, continuing to pick off the meat.

"You guys don't want that pepperoni!" I exclaimed, trying to regain control.

"Why?" Hunter demanded a reason.

"Because…" I paused, trying to think fast. "Because…it's Princess Pepperoni and it will turn you into a girl!" I exclaimed, hoping I was convincing enough.

"Noooo! Ewww!" Hunter threw his head back in dismay.

Yes!" I insisted, seeing that I had held their attention. "Princess Pepperoni that turns you into a girl with a pink dress and flowers for hair! I can't believe they put this on the pizza! Thank God Maura caught it before you all turned into girls!"

"Let's make James eat it and see what happens!" Hunter, ever the idea man, suggested. Maura served them each a meatless slice.

"No, I think your dad would be very upset with me if he came home and found out that we turned James into a girl," I said. "Anyway, do you guys really want a sister?"

"Nooooo!" they answered loudly in unison. They stuffed their faces with pizza. I guess they accepted my absurd reasoning.

"Girls are gross," Hunter declared.

"Yeah, girls are gross," Andrew readily confirmed.

"Yeah, they are," I agreed, smiling at Maura.

They settled down as they filled up their stomachs. Maura managed to get them to their rooms and start the process of getting ready for bed without protest, but still a fair amount of chaos. This was mostly due to Andrew's decision to start a game of tag while everyone was in the middle of changing into their pajamas. Luckily, I had witnessed bedtime at Michael's house before, so I could share with Maura that this was actually par for the course. The only difference was that Michael was not shouting at them to calm down, which was probably the reason why the bedtime process took an hour instead of thirty minutes like normal.

My four nephews were finally in bed and at least pretending to sleep shortly after nine. Maura, appearing to have just as much energy as the kids, immediately went to work cleaning up various toys left around the living room and then moved on to the kitchen.

"So, did you worry that I wouldn't be able to handle them?" she asked, wiping down the counter.

"Michael wanted to make sure they didn't traumatize you," I clarified. "And personally, I wanted to make sure you didn't throw a wild kegger...but if you did, I would at least get to participate."

She still gave me a doubtful look.

"Sorry about the pizza. I totally forgot."

"It's okay, heathen," she teased.

"Well, I never really understood that whole thing and why it matters."

"Me neither," she admitted. "But, it seems like a small, easy sacrifice when you look at the big picture. I'm sure God wouldn't have cared too much about a couple of little boys eating some pepperoni tonight."

Her comment surprised me.

"But, I didn't know how conservative Michael and Colleen are," she said.

"Well, I know Michael definitely wouldn't want anyone eating Princess Pepperoni, regardless of whether it's Lent," I said.

"Quick thinking. A little sexist for my taste, but I guess it's better than telling them they would go to hell if they ate it."

"That was my backup plan," I joked, trying to make her smile.

She leaned against the counter and stared at me.

"So now what?" she crossed her arms, looking at me, clearly wondering why I was still there.

The truth was I wasn't ready to go home.

"I don't know," I shrugged. "I've never babysat before."

She pushed off the counter and walked past me toward the living room. "Crappy Friday night TV it is."

I followed her and sat down on the opposite side of the couch. She turned on the TV. "Any preferences?"

I shook my head. A brief silence passed.

"Maybe we'll get lucky and The Sound of Music will be on and you can learn all the characters' names correctly," she joked.

"You're trying to lure me into another bet," I commented, not taking the bait.

"As I seem to recall, I still haven't collected on the last bet I won."

"Yeah, I paid for your breakfast that day," I defended.

"The wager was for breakfast and dinner," she reminded me.

"You're right. I do owe you dinner," I sighed.

I paused while she flipped through the channels. A solution to avoid being alone on Saturday popped into my head.

"How about tomorrow?" I asked.

She turned to me.

"If you're not doing anything, I could wipe my debt clean, clear my good name. Unless you have other plans," I said, hoping she didn't.

"No, Ethan's working all weekend, so I'm free," she said, finally settling on watching Dateline.

"Okay then, it's a date...you know, the kind you like; one that doesn't involve any sex or making out of any kind."

Maura didn't seem amused by my joke. "Hilarious," she commented flatly.

She didn't look at me but instead stared at the TV. Her silence might have been due to how quiet, or rather cold, I had been the last time I'd seen her when we went to the auto parts store together. I tried to make up for it without actually having to talk about it or apologize...like a true O'Hollaren man.

"So, Sydney told me I'm going to start working with kids next week," I said.

Maura nodded.

"You know any of them well?"

"Yeah, Sydney will go over who they are before you meet them."

She still wouldn't look at me, letting me know that the man who possibly murdered his wife for insurance money was more interesting than me.

"So...what time do you want to meet for dinner?"

"Whenever you want to," she said, unconcerned.

"Does six work?"

She nodded.

"Okay, so you want to meet at my house at six?"

She nodded again, refusing to make it easy on me.

"You're totally making me pay for last week, aren't you?" I decided to call her on it.

"Just trying to give being quiet a try," she said coolly.

"Cool," I sighed.

From what I knew of her, she wouldn't be able to stay silent for long. Out of pure stubbornness, I decided to wait her out and sat without speaking...watching Dateline. I was surprised when Maura lasted fifteen minutes without saying anything. I looked over and discovered the reason: she had fallen asleep.

For a moment I thought to wake her up and tease her for falling asleep on the job, but instead caught myself staring at her, thinking how peaceful she looked with her head resting against the back of the couch and her legs tucked underneath her. This was the perfect excuse to hang around until Michael and Colleen got home.

However, I definitely would be watching something else while I waited. I slid over to find the remote was tucked between her arms, a pretty defensive move for an only child, in my opinion. When I took the remote out, Maura leaned down further and nestled herself on my shoulder, still asleep. I didn't try to move away or reposition her. I just sat there, enjoying the fact that she was there and I wasn't alone... and that I didn't have to watch Dateline anymore.

MAURA

I CONSIDERED CANCELLING ON THOMAS MULTIPLE times throughout the day on Saturday. I could not shake the feeling that I had done something wrong when I'd woken up with my head on his shoulder the night before. Sure, he had provided me an easy enough explanation; I fell asleep and when he went to get the remote from me, I leaned my head onto him. But why let me stay there? How would Ethan feel about it if he knew? Should I even tell Ethan about it? Was there anything to tell?

The only thing that kept me from cancelling was the thought that if I did cancel, I would be admitting that I'd done something wrong or was doing something wrong.

To clear my conscious, I had texted Ethan earlier to check-in and let him know my plans to have dinner with a friend that night. He texted a thoughtful response wishing he could be there and encouraging me to eat some dessert for him, which he had given up for Lent.

I'd worn jeans and a fitted blue sweater and done my hair, trying to look casual, but not completely unkempt. I'd determined that if Thomas were to ask me where I wanted to go, I would pick some place where you ordered from a counter, like teriyaki. I also planned to bring up Natalie, knowing that hearing him talk about her and his contradictory relationship values would calm any of the neuroses

180

that had erupted in my head since waking up last night and inhaling the smell of his aftershave.

I walked up the steps to the O'Hollaren's house twelve minutes after six. It was a pathetically calculated decision to communicate that I didn't care that much about our date. Wait, no, not a date. A dinner thing. I knocked on the door.

Okay, Maura, take a deep breath. I told myself, waiting for him to answer. *God, that's ridiculous. Honestly, who does breathing exercises before hanging out with someone?*

"Hey," Thomas opened the door, dressed even more casually than I was, wearing a light blue Weezer T-shirt and jeans with Converses.

He took a step back to let me in. "What took you so long? Were you doing your hair?"

He playfully reached over and flicked my hair. I had straightened it and was wearing it down, but now I realized he had never seen my hair done to that degree.

Great, now he probably thinks I'm misreading things and trying too hard. Should I say something clever about how he looks like a slob?

I wasn't quick enough. Thomas had already closed the door and led me into the house. *Probably for the best; that would have been mean. What's that smell?*

The delightful aroma of roasted garlic and onions filled the air. Thankfully, my stomach successfully distracted me from the cluster of nerves that were exploding in my head.

We walked through the living room. It was immaculate but still cozy. My mother had always raved about how Jackie O'Hollaren had the best taste and always knew how to make things look nice. Her living room was a testament to that; a consistent color theme of grey, navy, and brown, with accents of white throughout. I felt like I was looking at a picture from Martha Stewart Living. What caught my eye most was a large oil painting that hung on the wall above the couch.

It was a scene from Pike Place Market. The sky had been captured perfectly. It was exactly what the Sound looked like on an overcast spring morning when natives knew that the sun would eventually peak through by the afternoon. The colors of the flowers being sold in the scene were vivid yet not overly loud, staying true to the lighting. I wanted to keep staring at the painting to take in all the detail. I looked over to see Thomas looking at me, but then he quickly walked into the other room. I had never envisioned the O'Hollarens as art collectors, but imagined that that piece, depending on who it was done by, probably cost a good amount of money.

I was about to comment on the painting, when I walked into the kitchen and saw multiple pans on the stove and other signs that Thomas had been cooking. I looked up at him in surprise.

"So, I hope you like Italian."

He checked one of the pans on the stove.

"We're having chicken cacciatore with gnocchi," he announced nonchalantly.

I couldn't hide my dumbfounded expression.

"What? You don't like Italian? Who doesn't like Italian?" he exclaimed in disbelief.

"No, no, I just wasn't expecting you to cook. I didn't expect that you even knew how to cook," I said.

"Hey, oh, easy now," he said in his best East Coast Italian-American accent. "How do you think I got to be my mother's favorite? Anyway, she always has so much food here, it made more sense to cook than go out and buy dinner, because, well, this was free," he stated proudly, before checking the pasta. "So, you still planning on giving me the silent treatment tonight?"

"Maybe," I said simply. "I haven't decided yet."

He pulled down two wine glasses from the cupboard and poured from an open bottle of Cabernet I assumed he had used for cooking. Not asking if I wanted any, he handed a generous pour to me.

"To loosening your lips," he clinked glasses with me and took a drink before going back to cooking.

I could tell he wanted to get back to our usual friendly banter. I took a sip, hoping I could let my neurosis go, but it just felt strange being in his parents' house, having him cook for me, on a Saturday night.

It's probably nothing, Maura. Just make some small talk.

"I like that painting of Pike Place in the other room," I said, remembering that he was an art major so maybe he would have something to share about it.

He strained the pasta; his back was turned to me.

"Where'd your mom get it? I've always wanted to have something like that in my living room but everything is too expensive or I just don't like the style."

He turned back around.

"Uh, well, I painted it," he said without looking at me.

I think my mouth dropped open.

"What?" I peered back into the living room to catch a glimpse of it again, trying to confirm that it was as good as I thought.

I turned back to him. He still wasn't looking at me.

"You painted that? Thomas, that's really good," I said clumsily, sounding almost like I was talking to a child.

He didn't say anything and pulled out two plates from the cupboard. I still wanted to know more.

"When did you paint that?"

"About six years ago. It was a birthday present."

"It's beautiful. I mean, your mom must love it." I was being genuine, no longer caring so much about trying to figure out if I was betraying Ethan by being there. I just wanted to know more about his talent that, until that moment, I had no idea was so impressive.

"Dinner's ready," he announced, finally making eye contact with me. Clearly, he didn't want to accept my compliment or talk about his painting anymore.

He scooped the pasta and the chicken on a plate and then handed it to me.

"Forks and knives are on the table." He motioned behind me.

I went to the table, trying to calculate whether I should press more about his skill. I tested the waters of altruism.

"You know, we have our graduate intern leading an art group at the center," I began, taking my seat with my wine glass and plate.

Thomas took a seat across from me.

"She's okay at it, but I'm sure the youth would really like it if you came in and–"

"So it's not enough you have me teaching about cars, you want me teaching them how to paint?" he laughed.

"Well, I didn't know you were so multi-talented." I wanted to go on with my sell but he stopped me.

"You're not going to pull a Father Finley on me now, are you?" he joked.

"How can I not? Clearly you're very good. I just–"

"Maura," he interrupted, "I don't paint anymore."

He made a point to make eye contact with me, indicating his seriousness.

"Why?" I couldn't wrap my brain around why someone with a gift like that would just stop using it.

He sighed.

"I just don't anymore. Look, can we talk about something else?"

I knew there was no point in pressing it further or I might have ended up with the same sullen Thomas I'd hung out with the previous Saturday.

"Well, not that it's of the same quality, but I did give my mother a paint-by-number picture for her birthday once, so you know, I totally get what it's like to be creative," I said.

"Yeah?" Thankfully, he looked amused. "Was it the one with the horses?"

"I think it was actually one with a cat," I recollected. "I've also made many a latch-n-hook in my day."

"What's a latch-n-hook?" he laughed, sounding unimpressed just by the name.

"Are you serious? You have a sister and you don't know what a latch-n-hook is?"

He shrugged, taking a drink of his wine.

"It's like this mat thing you get with holes, and different colors of yarn, and you latch and hook the yarn to the mat to make a picture."

He was looking at me like I was crazy. I had to admit, it did sound kind of weird.

"Never mind, I'll show you one someday. I think my parents probably still have some I made when I was younger."

"They must be very impressive if your mom and dad held on to them this long," he observed.

"No, that's just because I'm their only kid. I have this theory that having one child turns you into a bit of a hoarder. Seriously, they have everything from my childhood. It's kind of ridiculous. It's like the museum of Maura when you go into the garage or attic."

I liked that I was making him smile.

"What about you? Does your mom still have your old stuff?"

"How's your dinner?" Thomas ignored my question, but I figured he actually wanted to know how I liked the food. Okay, so it was delicious, but I wasn't going to fawn over it. His ego was healthy enough.

"It's good," I said simply. "You cook like this for Natalie?" I decided to bring her up before his obvious strengths fooled me into thinking he was more dateable.

"I never lost a bet with Natalie," Thomas responded, taking a bite. The conversation lulled while we sat there eating.

"So how is Natalie?"

"I don't know," he sighed, sounding uninterested. "Probably making out with some guy or girl somewhere in Mexico."

He looked up at me to gage my reaction. "You know how spring break goes." He paused. "Actually, you probably don't."

I chose to ignore his teasing.

"I think things are pretty much done with her," he stated reflectively.

"You broke up with her?"

"Can you break up with someone you were never dating?" he raised an eyebrow at me.

"Can you exchange bodily fluids with someone repeatedly and not call it dating?" I mimicked his tone.

"Well, see, the condom is supposed to prevent most of that, so I guess we're both right. Unless, you count saliva, and I checked – they don't make a condom for kissing, although I'm sure you would prefer it if they did." He looked pleased with his response. "Maura," he continued, using his condescending tone, "sometimes people just sleep with each other until one of them doesn't want to sleep with the other one anymore. It's just how it goes."

"How romantic," I exclaimed sarcastically. "Is that the line you use when you pick up girls?"

I looked down to see my wine was almost gone.

Let's focus more on eating and less on drinking, Maura. Before you make an ass out of yourself.

"Well, lately I've been using your gloom and doom approach about STDs, but for some reason it hasn't been working as well," he responded to my crack about pick-up lines.

I looked down at my food. It frustrated me how nonchalant he was being about the whole thing, even though I knew his approach to casual dating wasn't unusual and wasn't anything I hadn't heard from other friends. I didn't know why it was irking me more now than before.

"Listen, I know we're not going to agree on this, so why don't we just talk about something else?" he suggested.

"Like what?" I challenged.

"Like how I'm a better cook than Ethan," he responded cockily.

I rolled my eyes.

"And how is Mister Ethan?"

"He's fine." I wanted to offer more but didn't know what else to say.

"You guys make it to second base yet?"

"I thought we weren't talking about that stuff," I countered.

"With me. It's totally fair game with you," he clarified.

"Too bad it's none of your business," I tried to sound unaffected.

"So, does this mean you're not going to humor me with a rousing game of I Never?" he joked.

I rolled my eyes at him, eating my last bite of food. He stood up, grabbing my plate along with his, and moved over to the sink where he started to do the dishes.

"Are you starting or am I?" he asked.

I couldn't tell if he was being serious.

"I'm quite possibly the least interesting person to play I Never with," I said, walking over to the counter with my wine glass, watching him rinse and load the plates into the dishwasher.

He turned and refilled both of our glasses.

"I don't know. I think it might be interesting to me. I think I can win," he challenged. I gave him a doubtful look and then held up five fingers on one hand while I took a drink of wine with my other.

"I have never lost a game of I Never," I started us off.

He was scrubbing one of the pans now and looked up reflectively.

"Does one really lose at I Never?"

"Yes, when you have to put all your fingers down, you've lost," I explained.

"I thought that meant you've won?" he smiled, knowing that I was right.

"I guess if being a slut makes you a winner," I said bluntly, feeling the effects of the wine.

"Are you this judgmental with your kids?"

"I don't play I Never with the kids. What kind of poor boundaries do you think I have?" I said. "And you need to put a finger down and stop trying to cheat by distracting me."

"You're assuming I've lost this game before," he challenged playfully, finishing up the dishes.

"Yes, I am willing to bet that you have lost this game before; probably many times. Now put your finger down," I ordered.

He turned to me and leaned over, propping his elbow up on the counter, holding four fingers up on his hand. He held my stare while he thought of his "I Never" statement. I knew there was no possible way he could win the stupid game.

"I've never been Confirmed," he said.

"What?" I exclaimed, not expecting that. "That doesn't count."

"Maura, the game is just about saying things you've never done. It doesn't always have to be about sex," he said obviously, trying to feign innocence, like I was the one with a dirty mind.

"Fine," I sighed, putting down one of my fingers. I still knew I was going to win.

187

"I've never lived in New York." I tried to prove that I wasn't the one with a dirty mind. He put his second finger down.

"I've never made out with a guy," he smiled at me.

I rolled my eyes and put my second finger down.

"Oooh, scandalous, Maura," he teased.

"And I've never made out with a girl," I threw back.

"Really? Not even in your undergrad days when you were trying to find yourself?" he said wistfully, now only holding two fingers up.

He was quiet for a moment and was staring at the counter.

"It's fine if you want to give up now," I said coolly.

He stood up from the counter and took a sip of wine, still staring at me.

"I'm waiting," I said impatiently.

"I've never...been an only child."

"You know, I think you're really reaching here and not playing fair," I commented, putting my third finger down. "Because I could go for the easy one and say I've never had a sibling or I've never had a penis, but you don't see me doing that."

"No, but I see you being a poor sport," he said dryly.

"Fine, I've never been in a three-way," I said flippantly.

He laughed.

"And neither have I. You went right to a three-way? No, wasting your time on that obvious one-on-one intercourse," he exclaimed. "Wow, I gotta say, I'm kind of touched that you think I have that level of game. You do have a dirty mind."

"Whatever, I'm still going to win," I maintained, sipping my wine again.

"We'll see," he sighed, carefully calculating his next statement. "I have never had a close friend who was gay."

"You're just assuming that Sydney's gay?" I tried to distract him by challenging his stereotypical thinking.

"No, you're assuming I'm assuming," he corrected. "I know Sydney's gay because she introduced me to her girlfriend when I was there last Wednesday."

"Isn't Julie the best?" I exclaimed.

"Yes, she's fantastic, now stop trying to distract me and put your finger down." Thomas reached over and forced my finger down, so I was only holding my index finger up.

I was officially behind.

"I've never smoked pot." I took a calculated risk with my statement.

"That's probably for the best," he said smartly while he put a finger down. "I imagine you would be an extremely paranoid person when you're high."

I didn't respond, mostly because I had never considered what I would be like high.

"All right, here it is, the moment of truth, it all comes down to this," he stated dramatically.

"I have never..." he started.

"You better not pull some shit like worn a bra or worn a dress, because that's lame," I warned.

He waited for me to be quiet.

"I have never been in love," he stated. It felt like a confession.

I put my whole hand down.

"I don't believe that," I said firmly.

He put his hand down and shook his head.

"Not even with all the girlfriends you've had?"

"First of all, I haven't had that many girlfriends."

"Fine, girls you've dated," I changed the label for him. "You didn't love *any* of them. Not even the first girl you slept with?"

"Nope," he said simply.

I paused and looked at him; for a brief moment I saw the same sad look that had been in his eyes the day of the funeral.

"Well that's really sad. I feel sorry for you." Most likely the wine kept me from saying it more tactfully.

"You shouldn't. It's a good thing." He stood up straight.

"How can that be a good thing?" I asked in disbelief.

"How else would I have won this epic game of I Never?" he smiled. "Let it be written in the record books that I beat Maura

McCormick on this historic day, which according to you, officially makes you a slut," he proudly turned my words against me.

I let out a sigh.

"Now," he said, walking out of the kitchen, holding a fresh bottle of wine along with his glass, "if you'll follow me to the next part of our evening..."

I picked up my glass and followed him into the family room, confused that there were multiple parts of the evening planned. He put his glass and the bottle of wine down on the coffee table and then held up a DVD of The Sound of Music.

"Ta-duh! Look what I found in my mother's movie collection," he presented it to me proudly.

"Please, I have that shit on Blu-ray, fiftieth anniversary edition."

"I believe that's the first time anyone has ever trash-talked a copy of The Sound of Music," he said dryly. "Would you still be willing to watch this lowly DVD version of the movie with me?"

He must have been anticipating that my answer would be yes because he opened the case. I wanted to say yes, but knew how long the movie was, and knew if we kept drinking wine I was going to end up falling asleep on the couch next to him...again.

"I don't know," I sighed. "It's not that late, but it's a pretty long movie. I'm probably going to fall asleep," I said.

"That's fine," he shrugged, putting the movie in the player.

The confusion showed on my face while I pieced the night together; a homemade dinner, announcing Natalie was no longer in the picture, wine glasses that kept being refilled, the flirtatious game, and now a movie I knew he probably had no interest in seeing. I felt like I had enough evidence to call him out on what he was doing, but I was afraid of what would happen if I did. He turned around and saw the awkward look on my face.

"What?"

"I just – I just don't think it's a good idea if I end up falling asleep." I looked away from him, trying to decide if I should drive home now or if I had to wait a little bit.

"Why? It's not that big of a deal." He seemed so casual. "I'll probably fall asleep too."

"I don't think that's really considerate to Ethan."

"Ah, I see," he nodded.

"Well, I'll just wake you up when it's over," he said without concern. He sat down on the couch.

I remained standing.

"You going to watch the movie standing up?" he asked with a smile.

I sat down slowly.

"Thomas, what's going on?"

"What do you mean? We're about to watch a delightful family feature about Nazis," he said innocently.

"It seems like you're trying to get me to spend the night," I finally said what I was thinking.

"Yes, my strategy to get women to stay the night usually does involve Julie Andrews movies," he joked.

He was trying to deflect me but it wouldn't work. I stared at him and he sighed, rubbing his forehead.

"You're right, I am," he admitted.

I didn't know what to say.

"Don't worry, Maura, I'm not trying to have sex with you," he said as if stating the obvious. "I just–" he sighed. "I hate being in this house alone."

"Because of..." I didn't want to keep assuming things, but I thought this had to do with his dad.

"Because...I don't know, because–" he shrugged, "just everything."

"Do you want to go back to New York?"

"No," he said definitively. "No, it's fine for the most part when my mom's here. But when she's not, it's like all I can think about is him," he said, meaning his dad.

I waited a moment, not wanting to fire questions at him, knowing it was probably hard enough for Thomas to share with me what he just had.

"What kind of things do you think about?"

He looked forward and shook his head.

"Mostly how much we didn't get along, how much of an asshole I thought he was...but recently, I keep thinking how much of an asshole I was...or am." He let out a nervous laugh.

"What makes you say that?"

He kept looking forward, quiet for a moment.

"All I ever wanted was to leave here. I just wanted to go and paint, but that wasn't good enough for him. He had decided exactly what Michael and I were going to do the day we were born...and it just didn't fit...and I wasn't going to pretend that it fit. It drove him crazy, and over the years we started speaking to each other as little as possible...and then I left four years ago and didn't speak to him at all."

He stopped. I let the silence linger.

"And now – now that I'm back...and I'm at the shop, and I'm actually interested in it...fuck, it's like he was right the whole time and I was a spoiled brat who didn't care."

He sighed. "Sorry, I'm sure you weren't expecting to deal with father-son melodrama tonight."

"Are you still angry with your dad?"

"No...yes...some days," he said. "I don't understand why he had to be so stubborn about everything. And then," he laughed bitterly, "of course I was going through his desk last week and found all these pictures I had done when I was younger and a newspaper article about an exhibit I did two years ago. If he hated that I wanted to paint so much, why did he keep all that? I don't get it. And then part of me thinks it's stupid to even care; it doesn't make a difference with him gone now."

"Have you talked to anyone in your family about this?"

"About the stuff I found in his desk?"

I nodded.

"No," he sighed. "I don't think anyone really wants to revisit and analyze my relationship with my father. It wasn't particularly enjoyable for anyone around – especially my mother."

"Well, those are the only people who would have any insight," I said softly, not trying to force the idea on him. "It sounds like you're angry at yourself."

"I don't know," he reflected. "I've gone through my whole life thinking, you know, I'm an okay person – not a great person, but at least an okay one – but lately, I see all this stuff I've done or tend to do, and I'm starting to realize that I'm kind of a selfish asshole."

I didn't try to argue with him, even though I saw so much potential for good in him. It seemed counterproductive to refute his statement.

"It's the worst when I'm here by myself in his house. That's actually why I met up with you that first Wednesday night. I was here by myself, and all the arguments just kept replaying over and over again...and now it's shifting into constantly thinking about how I'm never going to get a chance to undo any of that. I didn't sleep at all last night. I can't turn my mind off when I'm here alone."

Thomas paused.

"I guess it's hard to run from good old Catholic guilt when you're born into it." He turned and gave me a small smile, trying to minimize what he'd just shared.

"I think sometimes guilt can be a good thing," I said truthfully.

"Of course you would; you're a glutton for punishment," he joked, still trying to lighten the mood.

I remained serious. "No, it makes us accountable. When you feel guilt, it means you know you're capable of more and you want to do better. It means you care about the effect you have on things."

"Well, I'm not sure what I care about."

"Maybe it's time to figure it out," I responded simply. "Once you figure that part out, then–"

"What? Things will get easier? The sun will shine again?" he said, playfully mocking me with clichés.

"No. It won't get easier," I broke the news to him, "but it gives a purpose to the guilt, rather than feeling hopelessly shitty all the time."

He didn't argue with me. I let another silence pass.

193

"I'm sorry you and your dad didn't get along better," I sympathized.

He shrugged it off. He was done with serious discussion but seemed glad that the door was open for future conversations, should he want them.

"Also, I can think of at least five or six people who are bigger assholes than you, so I wouldn't worry too much," I said confidently.

"Wow, five or six?" he remarked. "Well, I guess there's hope for me yet."

"Of course, none of them have flat-out refused to help homeless teens learn how to paint," I commented dryly.

He was smiling again. "You are ruthless."

"I'm just throwing it out there...but really, I think the best way for you to feel better is to paint me something for free...I will accept depictions of Mount Rainier, the Seattle skyline...oooh, the cherry blossoms in the spring," I teased him, knowing there was very little chance he would actually ever paint anything for me.

"Can't you just respect my choice to abstain? I thought that you were a fan of abstinence," he teased me back.

"Not as much as you're a fan of virgin jokes."

"Really I'm a fan of giving you a hard time," he admitted.

We paused for a second.

"Thank you..."

I got the sense that he wanted to say more but didn't have the words.

"Anytime," I responded easily.

"So, how about that slumber party?" he raised his eyebrows.

I hesitated.

"Come on, we've got some wine, Fraulein Maria, my unresolved relationship problems with my dad...I thought social workers lived for that shit. Who knows? I may even start talking about my commitment issues after I'm done with this next glass," he tried to sell the idea.

I took a deep breath, holding his stare, knowing I was starting to waiver.

"If you stay, I will go with you to mass tomorrow," he offered from out of nowhere.

I suddenly realized how badly he didn't want to be alone. He probably also knew that I would feel obligated to take advantage of the opportunity to get him to church. I gave him a look, doubting his sincerity.

"I promise."

I thought about how he could have just as easily gone out to a club or a bar and picked up a woman to avoid being alone that night, but instead he had chosen to have dinner with me and watch a G-rated movie. I'm not sure what, but that said something.

"Okay," I finally agreed, "but we are not sleeping on the couch together."

"No problem –"

"Or in a bed together," I interrupted, anticipating his solution.

"Um, may I remind you that you are at Grandma O's house and we have the perfect accommodations," he said, standing up and holding out his hand. "Come on."

I took his hand and he led me up the stairs to a room with a set of bunk beds, a solitary twin and a crib. Thomas turned back to me.

"Obviously, my mom encourages sleepovers," he said matter-of-factly. "You could say they are a few of her favorite things." He kept a straight face but winked at me.

"Come on, let's get this over with," I mirrored his straight face and went back down the stairs to the family room, hoping I was making the right decision.

THOMAS

I WOKE UP TO MAURA FORCEFULLY BOUNCING UP AND down on the twin bed I had squeezed myself into the night before. Groaning, I slowly opened my eyes, greeted by her obnoxiously peppy smile. The bottom bunk – the bed she had slept in – had already been made, with the T-shirt and basketball shorts I gave her to sleep in neatly folded on the bed.

"Good morning, friend," she greeted loudly.

"Morning," I mumbled, which turned into a yawn.

I closed my eyes, gradually remembering that I had made the deal that I would go to church in exchange for her spending the night.

"Time to get ready," she instructed happily.

I let out a pathetic whimper.

"Come on, I recall you making a promise last night," she reminded.

"That was before we watched the movie that would never end and you kept me up all night talking about your favorite Disney movies."

"I know, I get real chatty after that much wine," she reflected.

I had unfortunately discovered this fact the previous night around midnight. In addition to giving me a detailed argument on why Lady and the Tramp was the absolute best Disney movie, Maura had also insisted that I provide her with a list of all the women I've slept with and then rate them according to who I liked the best. She then proceeded to play a game of MASH using the inventory of

196

names to determine who I would marry in the future. It ended up being Penelope, my psychotic girlfriend from sophomore year. This, of course, happened after her rant about how I needed to get tested for HIV and chlamydia when she realized I had given her a list with eighteen names.

When I stayed in bed with my eyes shut, she started to nudge me.

"Thomas," she sing-songed, "get a move on. Daylight's a-burning, pilgrim."

Surprised, I turned onto my back to look at her.

"Did you just quote John Wayne? Are you like a seventy-year-old woman on the inside?" Then it registered that she was wearing different clothes than the night before.

"Hey, you changed your outfit."

"I went home and showered," she explained. "You didn't think I would do the walk of shame to mass, did you?"

"No, apparently just to your apartment, which somehow makes it better?"

She went back to nudging.

"Come on, I don't want to be late."

"Okay, okay," I said, finally sitting up.

"You have twenty minutes," she informed me, standing up and then heading downstairs. I sighed again and found my way to the shower.

Like a drill sergeant, Maura was standing by the door with her hand on the knob when I made my way downstairs, wearing khakis and a grey polo shirt. I then noticed that she was in jeans.

"I didn't know jeans were allowed at church," I said.

She was dressed more casually than I had ever been allowed to dress for mass. Maura opened the door, not giving me the opportunity to change clothes. I followed her out and locked the door.

"We're going to the Newman Center. It's more casual there. Anyway, my boots make my jeans look kind of fancy," she remarked, getting into her car. I got in on the passenger's side.

"Oh, the Newman Center, eh? Did you decide that I wasn't up to snuff for the fancy mass at Blessed Sacrament?"

"Exactly," she answered, starting to drive.

I knew there had to be another reason we were going to the Newman Center, a chapel meant for college kids, instead of Blessed Sacrament, but before I could ask her, I was distracted by the song playing on Maura's iPod.

"Maura, is this Apple Bottom Jeans by Flo Rida? Well, this is exactly what my mom likes to listen to when she goes to mass," I teased.

I picked up her iPod and scrolled through the playlist.

"Hmm, Dr Dre, Whitney Houston, Rush, Aerosmith, Adele, Journey, The Spice Girls," I announced, laughing as I read. "Could you be more all over the map? It's like all of the Top 40 exploded into one horrible playlist."

I kept scrolling. "Maura, some of these songs are diiirty. I am certainly surprised. If I would have had to guess, I would have expected a bunch of classical music and Simon and Garfunkel...nope, there we are, just found it, Homeward Bound. Well, I was right about one of 'em," I mused. "The girl who listens to The Chronic and goes to mass...interesting," I commented, putting the iPod down.

"Says the mechanic who oil paints and knows most of the lyrics to Edelweiss," she shot back.

"Touché."

"So," she said as we drove down the winding road towards the U-District, "I realized this morning that it's Palm Sunday," she announced and then stopped talking.

"And..."

"Well, it's probably been a while since you went to Palm Sunday..." she started to explain.

"Maura," I laughed, "I know what Palm Sunday is. They're going to give us palm branches."

"Yeah, but they also go through the entire crucifixion of Jesus. The readings are pretty long."

"You mean there's a time when mass isn't long?" I asked.

"I just thought I'd warn you. I mean, it's kind of a depressing one to go to after not having been in a while."

"Well, the last one was my father's funeral, so it's got some competition," I said dryly. "Then again, is there a time when mass isn't depressing?"

"You're the one who came up with this arrangement," she reminded, now searching for a parking spot on the crowded street.

"I know. What could I have possibly been thinking?" I reflected wistfully.

The truth was that I had been thinking that the quickest way to get her to agree to stay the night before was to make the offer to go to church with her. Also, I had to admit, I was curious to see what going to mass was like through her eyes. She was unlike any other Catholic I had ever met and that confused me. I wanted to see for myself if her eyes glazed over like the rest of us humans when we sat through a ridiculously dry service.

There were numerous people standing outside the church, gathered in a circle. I was surprised to see that while the majority of the people looked to be college-aged, there were also a good number of older adults. I saw Mr. Warren and his wife standing a distance away from us, recognizing him from the proposal meeting and also from when he brought his Beemer into the shop.

We were each handed a palm. I was about to ask Maura why we weren't going inside, but then I heard a familiar voice shout out over the crowd. Father Sean was standing at the center of the circle and suddenly it clicked that he would be the presider. This was going to be weird, finally seeing him act in the way I expected a priest to act.

Once he was done with the reading about Jesus entering Jerusalem and he had blessed the palms, we joined the crowd, herding ourselves into the chapel during the choir's opening song. I followed Maura's lead and hoped she wasn't going to make me sit in the front. Thankfully, she picked a spot in the middle, although I would have preferred the back. I was impressed that she knew the song without having to look at a songbook. When we took our seats, I was grateful that it was Palm Sunday, because the palm gave me something to fiddle with while I ignored the readings.

When it was time for the gospel reading, I reflexively stood up. Maura had not exaggerated when she said that the reading was long. Ever helpful and naive, Maura held her missal open in front of both of us, thinking I would want to read along.

I thought it was harsh and dark that the church attendants read the part where the mob said to crucify him. I didn't remember this from when I was a child, but I had probably been hiding in the bathroom at the time.

I was caught off guard when we all had to kneel at the moment when Jesus died. Good thing the book had instructions for us to do so, so I didn't look like a total idiot standing up when everyone else dropped down. It was completely silent in that moment. I looked over and saw tears rolling down Maura's face.

Was it appropriate the reach over and grab her hand or put my hand on her back? The moment passed and we were standing again, and then, of course, sitting again when the gospel reading was over.

Maura had stopped crying and I wondered whether her emotion was really connected to the reading. It baffled me that she could have that strong of a reaction about something that happened thousands of years ago, to someone she didn't know, whose story she had heard repeatedly throughout her life. I was just glad she was done crying and hoped she wouldn't start again. I wasn't ready to deal with that.

Father Sean stood up and started his homily. I anticipated that he wouldn't say anything very interesting—and wasn't looking forward to having to sit through it. More than likely, I wasn't going to agree with anything he said, and for the most part I thought he was an okay guy. I didn't want my perspective of him to change now.

Of course, Father Sean now presented an image of himself that was more serious than I had seen before. That was to be expected. After all, he was at mass and they just had read about the crucifixion of Jesus. What I had not expected was that he would start talking about Mother Teresa or a poem that was written on the wall of an orphanage in Calcutta.

I heard most of it, but couldn't recall anything beyond the first line, "People are illogical, unreasonable, and self-centered. Love them anyway."

He kept coming back to that line in his homily and I started to think of me and my dad and how we both fit the description in the first part of the line and failed at the second part. I appreciated that Father Sean didn't try to make the idea of loving people sound easy, regardless of their nature, but I felt uncomfortable when he used Jesus' death on a cross as an example of loving people in spite of the horrible shit they did, probably because I found it hard to believe that was possible.

I snuck a glance at Maura. Her eyes weren't glazed over. She looked more serious than I had ever seen her look before. I wondered how she was tolerating seeing Father Sean up front. She had mentioned before how complicated the situation was for her. If she had any negative feelings, she was holding her poker face pretty well, her gaze fixed on him.

Father Sean then recounted a story from his past in which he had stopped speaking to his brother because his brother had renounced Catholicism and gotten divorced. Father Sean told how he had been reminded by a friend that he was too caught up in judging his brother and needed to focus more on loving him.

Right in that moment, I caught it.

I'm not sure if anyone else besides Maura noticed it, but he locked eyes with her. Until then, I wasn't aware that he even knew that we, or rather she, was there.

It was over almost before I'd registered what had happened, and he then tied the sermon back to how people misinterpret Jesus' death as a basis for judgment of sins, when it was meant to be understood as an action of love. Jesus' ability to love the people who sentenced him to death, even as he was nailed to a cross and dying a painful death, was more profound and astounding than any righteous judgment that had occurred.

I would be lying if I said that the homily offered any great revelation for me. I found the whole talk of love a little cheesy, naturally, not being a big believer of the concept. However, it was more refreshing than a ten-minute lecture telling me I should feel guilty for killing Jesus when I hadn't even been around when it happened.

The rest of mass went by quickly, probably because there wasn't a five-page reading. I didn't recite the Creed, since I had never learned it. I did surprise myself though, when I discovered that I still knew the Our Father.

Maura of course hugged me without hesitation during the sign of peace. She lit up during this portion of the service, smiling and shaking everyone's hand, not caring that they were strangers.

I chose not to go up for communion. I thought that Maura would shoot me a look when I stayed seated, but she didn't seem to care. Oddly, I found myself feeling left out while I watched every-body else going up. I had never experienced that before. All I could ever remember feeling when I had refrained from communion in the past was a smug sense of superiority to everyone else, like I was a freethinker. I wondered why it was different now. When it was all over, there was no closing song and everyone left in awkward silence.

Once we were outside of the chapel in the lobby area, people gradually started talking again. I was following Maura toward the exit when we were stopped by Mr. and Mrs. Warren.

"Maura, Thomas, good to see you," Mr. Warren greeted, shaking my hand.

"What a surprise. I thought you two went to Blessed Sacrament," Mrs. Warren exclaimed, hugging Maura.

"Oh, we figured it would be packed there, it being Palm Sunday and all," Maura explained.

"How's the Beemer treating you?" I asked politely.

"Thomas," Mr. Warren patted me on the back, "I just want to thank you for the top-notch job you and your team did. I mean, if I had known, I would've been coming to your shop a long time ago."

"Oh, we're just happy we could help you out," I responded humbly.

"Well, you should know that I will be referring people to you," he shook my hand again.

"Thank you, that means a lot to us."

I meant it. It wasn't guaranteed business, but it was always nice to have a good reputation.

"So, have you started instructing at the center yet?"

"He starts with the youth this week," Maura informed.

"They are definitely in good hands," Mr. Warren complimented me again.

"Isn't Father Sean just the best?" Mrs. Warren commented, mostly to Maura.

"This was my first time seeing him preach," she said, sounding nonchalant.

"Oh, how nice."

Maura smiled, but I could tell she was done talking about it.

"Hey, you two," I turned to see Father Sean walking over to the four of us.

He shook my hand then leaned in and gave Maura a quick hug. She kept her arms loose and pulled away quickly. The Warrens didn't notice, but Maura had hugged me enough that I could tell she was being reserved.

"What a nice surprise," he commented, briefly smiling at her and then looking over at the Warrens.

"Maura and Thomas were just telling us that he's going to start instructing the kids this week."

"Great," Father Sean exclaimed. "I'll have to come by and check it out once you get things going."

He nodded along with the Warrens, who excused themselves to go talk to another older couple. Father Sean continued to stand there with us. This had to have been a record for the longest I'd ever stayed inside a church after mass was done.

"So, what'd you think?" he asked, looking at Maura.

"It was good," she said, keeping her answer brief.

He looked at her expectantly, wanting more feedback. She didn't say anything else.

"She's a hard woman to impress," Father Sean held his smile and looked over to me.

"What?" Maura was on the defensive. "I said it was good. What more do you want? A priest shouldn't be looking to us lowly parishioners for approval on his preaching. At least, Father Jack and Father Bernard never do."

The exchange was reminiscent of the first time I saw them together.

"I used your favorite poem in there," he pointed out proudly.

"A lot of people like that poem," she responded coolly.

She didn't say anything else. He finally gave up and turned to me.

"Thomas, it's really great to see you. This was your first time here for mass, right?"

I nodded.

"Well, I hope you liked it. Always good to see new faces as well as old ones," he glanced over at Maura and then shook my hand again. "I'll see you around."

He hugged Maura again. She still held back.

"I'm glad you were here for this one," he said quietly to her before his attention was directed elsewhere.

I turned to her. "Come on, let's go get some breakfast," I suggested.

She looked relieved and followed me out the door. We walked to the car in silence. I kept waiting for her to ask me what I'd thought of the mass, but for once, she wasn't in the mood to talk. When we got to her car, we discovered that the surrounding cars hadn't left much room for her to get out. She let out a sigh. I felt the urge to fix things for her.

"I can get you out," I said confidently, holding out my hands for the keys.

She looked at me with doubt.

"Trust me," I assured. "I'm a professional."

She handed over the keys. I maneuvered her car out within a minute without hitting or scratching anything. I had impressed even myself with my efficiency. She stepped up to the driver's side as I rolled down the window.

Somewhere in Between

"You think I'm going to give up driving now? It's not every day a guy gets to drive a fine piece of machinery like this," I said, sarcastically gesturing to her Honda Civic.

She sighed but didn't argue with me and joined me on the passenger's side. I started to drive.

"You know I kid, but I hate driving in the city with that Chevy," I said, referencing my father's boat of a truck. "So where are we going?"

"Do you know Blue Star?"

"Sounds good," I nodded. "You know, your alignment is off."

"Yeah, I figured. I ran up a curb a couple weeks ago," she said nonchalantly.

"Well, you should bring it in to get it fixed. If you wait too long, it's going to fuck up your tires." I suggested, wanting to help her out since she had helped me the night before by getting me to open up about my dad.

"I know," she sighed.

"Should I just call your dad and have him make the appointment for you?" I teased, finally getting her to smile.

"I'll look at the schedule when I go in tomorrow and text you some of the open times. I don't know if you heard Mr. Warren, but me and my guys do a top-notch job," I said.

She gave me the same unimpressed look she gave Father Sean. I was surprised she had yet to ask me what I'd thought of mass.

We sat down to breakfast and still she didn't bring it up.

Once we ordered, I had to say something. "I am shocked you haven't asked me anything about mass."

"I figured you'd bring it up if you wanted to talk about it," she shrugged.

"Hmm, interesting...some reverse psychology, I see."

"I'm pretty sure that's not reverse psychology," she corrected. "If I had told you not to talk about mass, that would have been reverse psychology."

"It's some kind of psychology." I stared at her, realizing this was an opportunity to get more information from her rather than revealing more about myself. "Why the Newman Center?"

"It's more laid back than Blessed Sacrament."

"Yeah, but your ex-lover priest friend is there. You yourself said you didn't like being around that soap opera when you didn't have to be."

"One, it's not a soap opera; two, let's just call him Sean; three, I felt" –she paused– "I felt you were more likely to hear something of relevance to you with Sean preaching instead of Father Jack."

"But you said you've never heard him preach," I challenged.

She looked unaffected. "I had a hunch."

I didn't comment either way whether the homily resonated with me or not.

"You didn't want to be there, did you?"

She shrugged. "I can think of other masses I would have preferred going to...but I guess it was good for me to get over it with and see him preside."

"So, what you're really saying is: I helped you. Wow, I feel so used...I mean, you're welcome," I said sarcastically.

I took a sip of my coffee.

"Are you the friend he talked to about his brother?" I asked, referencing the story from the homily.

She nodded. We were quiet for a moment.

"Well, it sounds like you made him into a better person," I said.

I knew what she was thinking; she made him a better person, and in the end, he left her because of it.

"You weren't crying because of him, were you?" I asked, thinking he clearly was not worth crying over.

"Crying?" she questioned, apparently forgetting that she had cried during mass. Suddenly she remembered. "Oh that," she exclaimed. "No, I just cry every time we read The Passion. I like Jesus. It's always sad when he dies," she said sincerely, and I couldn't help but smile.

She spoke like he was a person she knew, without going into a long, drawn out, awkward explanation about her Lord and Savior, Jesus Christ, which I appreciated.

"What?" she asked.

I shook my head.

"Nothing," I responded, knowing I couldn't sufficiently describe what I was thinking about her without sounding stupid.

I had never met anyone like her, and the way she saw things entertained and amused me but also left me continually curious. Before she could press me for an explanation, our food arrived. She grabbed her fork.

"You know, I highly recommend going to Easter mass. It has a happier ending than Palm Sunday."

"Yeah, but then you have to deal with all those Chreasters showing up and taking all the seats," I lamented ironically.

"Nah," she said, "the people who come back to church after being away tend to have the most interesting stories," she smiled at me. "Also," she added, "it's fun to watch them try to figure out when to stand and when to sit. Sometimes my dad and I keep a tally."

MAURA

I DROVE HOME AFTER BREAKFAST WITH THOMAS AND checked my phone to discover that I had a missed text and phone call from Ethan. He had been trying to figure out what mass I was going to. Honestly, I had expected him to want to go to mass together, so I'd avoided checking my phone until that afternoon. Thomas had never said specifically that he didn't like Ethan, but I got the sense that he wasn't the biggest fan, and I knew that any chance of Thomas tolerating mass would have been shot if Ethan had gone with us. I tried not to think too much about the effort I was putting into keeping them separate from one another.

I still felt awkward talking on the phone with Ethan, so I texted him.

`Sorry, I ended up going to 10am at the Newman Center.`

Quickly, I received a response.

`I'm sorry I haven't been around this weekend. Would it be possible to see you tonight?`

I was surprised he hadn't asked any follow up questions about going to mass at a church other than Blessed Sacrament. Once again, I told myself that maybe I was making everything into a bigger deal than it really was.

I texted back.

`Sure`

I had never been over to his apartment. Maybe this was a good idea. It would help me figure out how to define the relationship that I still didn't know how to define. Before he could pick a place to meet, I decided to put myself out there.

How about I come by your place around seven?

His response alone would tell me how serious he felt the relationship was.

Sounds good. See you then.

Okay, there I had it. No fancy dinner or planned date activity like going to a movie theatre or bowling. Just hanging out at his apartment. That was definitely a thing you did when you were in a relationship. Of course, that was exactly what I had done with Thomas last night...and despite my initial misgivings, it had been less awkward than any time I had ever spent with Ethan. I decided that the sole reason things were so easy with Thomas was because there were no possibilities with him. He was a friend and would never be anything more, thus taking all the pressure off trying to figure anything out.

When I was with Ethan, I was constantly trying to figure out whether I felt any chemistry, if he was interested in me, and if I had said anything that would offend or chase him away. It was becoming exhausting. I reminded myself that most relationships probably started with a little bit of stress about putting your best foot forward as you tried to get to know the person.

Since I had nothing else to do and was starting to feel anxious at the mere thought of seeing him, I decided I would make chocolate chip cookies. Not only would it give me something to do, but I also could bring them to Ethan as a nice girlfriend-like gesture. I didn't consider the reality that I would end up eating about a third of the dough in response to feeling anxious. This was both the benefit and the downside of living alone and having no one around to monitor me and my utter lack of self-control when it came to sweets.

I filled the remaining time by calling my parents. It probably wasn't the best idea to calm my nerves. It started off fine, hearing my mom share about the women's retreat she'd just gotten back from.

Then she asked about how I had spent my weekend. Before I could answer, she answered for me.

"I know you babysat for Michael and Colleen O'Hollaren on Friday. That's what Jackie said. How was that?"

"Good. Four boys is a lot. Colleen has her hands full, but they were fun."

"You know, Jackie shared that Thomas is going to start volunteering at the youth center and teaching the kids how to work on cars."

"Yep," I said, not offering more information.

"Well, how come you didn't tell me that?"

"I don't know. It hasn't come up."

"Well, you don't know how excited she is that he's taken an interest in community service. She's hoping it means he'll stick around. She said that you guys were running together on Sundays. How come you didn't tell me that?"

Because you would read into it and ask a million questions, I wanted to say.

"I've only run with him three or four times. I didn't think it was interesting enough to share."

"Hmm."

That was her way of telling me she thought I was lying, but it wasn't a big enough lie to challenge me on. I decided to use the only information I had to prove her wrong, even though I had been keeping it to myself for the past month because I didn't want her to get overly excited like she always did anytime I was dating someone new.

"So, I wanted to tell you that I've been seeing someone."

"Oh!" she exclaimed.

"But it's not super serious yet, so don't get too excited," I warned.

"What's his name? What does he do? Have you met his parents?"

I had successfully moved her off of talking about Thomas.

"His name is Ethan Linden; he works for Microsoft; he's a computer programmer. No, I haven't met his parents. I told you it wasn't serious."

"Well, when can we meet him?"

Obviously, my mother did not understand that I considered meeting parents to be a step for serious relationships.

"I don't know, not now."

"It's too bad Daddy and I aren't in town for Easter; we could have invited him to have dinner with us."

Fabulous idea, Mother, let's introduce him to you and Dad on a major holiday. No pressure there.

I had to accept that now that I had told her about Ethan, she would make it her mission to meet him as soon as possible.

"I'm sorry that we won't be here for Easter, honey," she went on. "I feel so guilty to be leaving you on a holiday." Luckily, she had moved on to worrying about me and how I would possibly function without her and my dad on Easter Sunday. "Did you call your Aunt Mary yet and tell her that you'll be going over to her house?"

"Uh, not yet, but I will."

And for the rest of the conversation, I managed to get her to focus on the cruise she and my dad were taking for their spring break that week.

That night, I drove over to Ethan's apartment building in East Lake. It wasn't surprising that he lived in a much nicer building than I did.

He buzzed me in and I made my way to the elevator, taking in all the contrasts from my building. For one, it had a lobby that made me feel like I was in a hotel. It had a couple of dark grey couches and green accent chairs with end tables and a coffee table. There were fresh flowers in vases displayed throughout the room. My building didn't have a lobby, just a beige hallway that led to the elevator. Clearly, this place was meant for grownups who could refrain from eating large quantities of cookie dough when they baked.

I got off on the fifth floor and found his door. I knocked quietly, feeling like anything louder would have disrupted someone else who lived in the building. Ethan answered the door looking uncharacteristically casual in his glasses, an untucked navy Oxford shirt and jeans.

"Hey, you found it all right. Sorry, it probably would have been more appropriate for me to come down and walk you up. But I've been trying to run this program and it keeps freezing," he explained.

"No need to apologize," I said, wondering if he was always going to feel the need to be on his most gentlemanly behavior and apologize when he didn't live up to the incredibly high bar he seemed to have set for himself.

"Do I need to take my shoes off?" I wasn't sure and thought if I just assumed and took off my shoes he would think I was weird.

"Sure, get comfortable, stay awhile."

He closed the door as I slipped off my shoes.

"Can I take your coat?" he asked, then noticed the plate of cookies in my hands.

"I made these for you. I know you gave up dessert for Lent, but it's Sunday, so enjoy," I said, referencing the Lent loophole that people could have whatever they gave up on Sundays.

"Oh, so you're one of those Catholics," he said with a grin, taking the plate and putting it down on the counter while I took off my coat.

"What?" I asked.

"You like to cheat during Lent."

"It's not cheating," I defended, having had this argument with people before. "You celebrate the Resurrection every Sunday, even during Lent, so it's like a mini Easter."

He gave me a doubtful look.

"You can even ask Father Jack; he would agree with me."

I knew Ethan was the type that would be won over by an argument simply by hearing the same information come out of a priest's mouth.

"I mean, it's fine, it's not like I made these from scratch just for you because I wanted to do something nice for you." I said, introducing him to my secret skill of administering guilt. I had perfected it from many years of interacting with my mother.

"Wow," he laughed. "That's pretty impressive. I haven't been put on a guilt trip like that since I last talked to my mother."

He grabbed my coat and hung it up for me.

"They look wonderful," he complimented. "I will be sure to bring them to work tomorrow and tell everyone my amazing girl-friend made them."

He wrapped his arms around me and kissed my forehead.

So there I had it. He said it without me having to ask. He considered me his girlfriend. And there he was, holding me and expressing more affection than he ever had before. Yet what registered more was that, despite the fact that I had said I made the cookies specifically for him and even referenced one rather conservative priest to support my claim that it was "okay" to have them, he still was not going to eat the damn cookies. This annoyed me, but not enough to stop him from holding me.

I looked up at him, hoping he would kiss me on the lips. He did, marginally redeeming himself, but once again, it was over just after it started. Ethan broke away and walked into his living room. I turned and followed him, surprised that I hadn't noticed the amazing view of Lake Union when I first walked in.

"Whoa," my mouth dropped open. Not only did he have a view of Lake Union, he had the entire Seattle skyline lit up through his window. I could have stared at it for hours. He knew exactly what had impressed me.

"It's pretty cool on New Year's and the Fourth of July."

He took a seat on the couch with his back to the window. I sat down next to him, kind of wishing I could sleep in his living room. I turned my attention away from the window and got my bearings in his apartment. It was immaculate for a guy's apartment, but it hadn't really been decorated. It looked kind of sparse. He did have a book-case full of books, a crucifix, and three framed pictures. I'd wait to ask about who the people in the frames were later, not wanting to come across as too nosy right out of the gate.

He took the opportunity to check his laptop that was open on the coffee table in front of him while I was looking around his living room. He let out a heavy sigh and typed something for a few moments before closing out of whatever program he was running.

"Well, that's not getting done tonight," he concluded, sounding depleted. He removed his glasses and rubbed his eyes.

"Is that what you did all weekend?" I nodded over at the laptop.

"That and mass," he responded and then let out a yawn. I thought about asking him to describe what exactly his work that weekend entailed, but decided it was probably that last thing he wanted to talk about if he was as tired as he looked. Honestly, I didn't have much desire to learn the specifics of what a computer programmer did...which was obviously something I needed to work on if this was going to be a long-term thing. Just not tonight.

"Should I go?" I asked seriously, not wanting to keep him up if he was exhausted.

"No, no, stay," he said, yawning again but putting his hand on mine. "You're the best part of my weekend."

I felt guilty because I didn't know if he was the best part of mine.

"So, why'd you go to the Newman Center for mass today?" he asked.

I tested the waters of how Ethan would respond to Thomas being my friend. "You remember Thomas O'Hollaren?"

Ethan nodded. "Yeah, the mechanic who's going to be helping with your voc-ed program," he verified.

I nodded.

"Yeah, well, he doesn't really go to mass, but he suggested going. He grew up going to Blessed Sacrament, and never really liked it, so I thought he would like Newman more since he knows Father Sean and had never been there before."

I was relieved when it sounded more innocent than I had worried it would. Then again, I didn't mention Thomas cooking me dinner and my spending the night at his house.

"Well, I guess you are just like Saint Monica," he said, referring to my confirmation saint. He was leaning back against the coach with his legs stretched out in front of him. I was turned toward him and scooted down so that my face was at the same level as his. I wanted to cease any further comparison of myself to a saint.

"How bad is your eyesight?" I asked randomly.

"Uh, not horrible, but obviously not the best," he said vaguely. "It's probably all the years of looking at a computer screen that's made them bad."

"I always wonder what it's like because I've never worn glasses," I explained. "Like, how far away can you see?"

"I couldn't read any of the titles on the books over there," he said, gesturing to the bookcase. "But I can see that there are books over there."

He looked over at me.

"I can see your face, but it's little hard to make out all the details," he reached over and touched my cheek. "Like your eyes. I can see them, but it's kind of hard to make out the color. Lucky for me, I've looked at them enough to know they're blue. Prettier than your average blue eyes because they have some shades of green on the outside," he described as he leaned in, keeping his hand on my cheek, letting his fingers touch my hair.

I closed my eyes and he kissed me. Finally, he let the kiss deepen, opening his mouth, which I mirrored. I didn't feel his tongue and stayed conservative on my end, but was relieved that it finally felt like a real kiss that lasted longer than two seconds. I wasn't in the most comfortable position, so I tried to figure out where and how I could move while still keeping the kiss going. I moved back, hoping he would stay attached. Unfortunately, he broke away. Maybe he thought it was my intention to break away. But it was definitely his decision to have ended that kiss. I sat up, trying to figure out how I could go back to kissing him without him thinking me too forward.

We sat there in silence, staring at one another, him running his hands through my hair. I melted anytime anyone I ever dated played with my hair. I leaned in and kissed him again and he kissed me back. I was still in an awkward, uncomfortable position on the couch, but based on last time, I knew I was going to have to hold it if I wanted to keep kissing him. It lasted longer than before and I felt my heart beat faster. It wasn't the best kiss I had ever had, because, well, we were still new to one another, but it wasn't horrible, and the excitement of kissing someone new after such a long period of not kissing anyone was more than enough for me to keep going. After all, the only way to get better at kissing each other was to practice, right?

I had impressively managed to maneuver myself from being on my side to having my back against the couch, making it a little less uncomfortable for me. However, Ethan, following my lips, was now the one having to hold the awkward position on his side. As we were kissing, I felt myself beginning to slide down the back of the couch. Before I ended up on my back, he abruptly pulled away and sat up.

"I'm sorry. We need to stop," he announced.

His declaration made me feel a little guilty, and I wondered whether I should apologize as well, even though I wasn't really sorry. I stayed silent and sat up.

"Maybe this was a bad idea," he reflected.

I feared I was about to get kicked out of his apartment.

I also worried because part of me didn't think it was that big of a deal. I tried to figure out whether I was objectifying him. I had to be fair and recognize that I still didn't really have an extensive list of qualities that I liked or loved about him. Currently, the list was that he was cute in a preppy way, had a good work ethic, and was Catholic...and volunteered in the summer at a Mexican orphanage. Perhaps that wasn't enough to be making out with him on a couch?

"Who are the people in the pictures?" I asked, changing the subject before he banished me for trying to lead him astray. Also, I thought maybe getting to know him more would make me feel less guilty for really just wanting to make out with him.

"Uh, that's my family on the top, my grandparents in the middle, and the one next to the crucifix is my Godchild, Javier, from the orphanage in Mexico. Well, one of my Godchildren – I'm the Godfather for three of my nephews back home."

"Do you make them offers they can't refuse?" I joked.

He raised an eyebrow at me, indicating he didn't get the reference.

"You know, from The Godfather...the movie," I explained.

"Haven't seen it."

"What?" Okay, so I thought Rainman was excusable; not everyone has time to sit around and watch a Tom Cruise movie from the

80s, but The Godfather? Even people who have never seen it usually get the reference from pop culture alone. I looked at him with obvious disbelief.

"I'm not a big fan of movies," he confessed.

"Do you dislike puppies and sunshine, too?" I exclaimed teasingly, and probably less tactfully than I should have.

"I don't know," he shrugged. "I just tend to get bored. I'd much rather read a book. Do you read?"

"Sometimes...when there's nothing on TV," I grinned, but unfortunately the statement was probably more true than false.

I always made it my New Year's resolution to read more, but it never came to fruition. I joked with Sydney that I was still recovering from the PTSD I developed from all the reading we had to do in grad school.

"Okay, so maybe I should read more," I admitted, still thinking it was weird that someone could not like movies at all.

"You should," he agreed readily.

"Here," he stood up and walked over to his bookshelf and grabbed a book, then turned back to me. "You should start with this. I think this is a great book."

He handed me The Dialogue of Saint Catherine of Siena. I had never read it, but knew it was written by Saint Catherine in the fourteenth century and it was an intense account of a conversation with God regarding spiritual exercises and philosophies.

"Unless you've already read it," he gave me the benefit of the doubt.

"Nope, only heard of it."

I was not super excited about the idea of reading it because, well, I just couldn't understand mortification as a form of holiness – especially given all the knowledge I had regarding self-harm behavior from a mental health perspective. Nonetheless, I kept that opinion to myself and reminded myself that Saint Catherine was about unity and helping the poor, and I was a fan of that.

"Does that mean you're going to watch a movie with me?"

"Maybe," he laughed. "After you finish that book."

I tried to tell myself that maybe it wasn't the worst thing that he was challenging me to step outside my comfort zone. He sat back down.

"So, I wanted to talk to you about my family," he said.

I looked at him and waited for him to begin, doubtful he was going to say anything similar to what Thomas had shared the previous night.

"I heard from my dad today, and my grandpa was diagnosed with cancer."

"I'm sorry to hear that," I said reflexively but also really meant it. He sighed.

"They aren't sure exactly what it all means, but they wanted me to come home for Easter. I know it's kind of short notice, but I was wondering if you would want to come with me? I'm going to leave Thursday morning."

I paused, thinking of how my mom and Ethan seemed to be on the same page regarding when a good time to meet his parents would be.

"Uh," I hesitated.

"I know you probably have something with your family, but I just thought it would be a good step to take."

His choice of words was less than romantic, which was probably a good thing because if he had been mushier, I would have had difficulty coming up with an excuse.

"I don't think I can get the time off to travel to Spokane," I lied.

I had an abundance of vacation time saved up. The truth was, I wasn't ready to meet his entire family.

"And I haven't seen my family in Olympia for a while. Plus, don't you think it might be a good time for you to be with just your family? I mean, I wouldn't want to be the random new person hanging out while you guys are dealing with family stuff."

"You're probably right," he didn't challenge me. "I guess, selfishly, I just wasn't looking forward to spending another weekend away from you."

"I'll be here when you get back," I said, wondering whether I was supposed to echo the sentiment.

I squeezed his hand and looked up, thinking that now would be a good time for him to kiss me, but I knew he wasn't going to kiss me again as long as we were on that couch.

We talked for a while longer. I got him to open up more about himself than I ever had before. I made him tell me stories about his time at Gonzaga, different things he did with his family growing up, why he kept going back to volunteer in Mexico every summer. The more he talked, the more it confirmed that Ethan was as good of a person as I anticipated him to be. When I saw his eyes looking more tired than before and realized it was after ten, I announced I would be going. I was sure to glance one more time out his window at the beautiful nighttime cityscape before I got up and collected my things.

He offered to walk me downstairs but I insisted that was silly and I preferred that he go to bed. He walked me to the door and my heart began to beat faster, knowing that I was going to get to kiss him again. I turned to him and said good night. I was met with a gentle, subdued kiss on the lips, followed by a kiss on the forehead before he said goodnight and opened the door.

As I walked out of the building and to my car, I thought of all other the relationships I had been in and how this was uncharted territory. I had never felt like I wanted more in the physical area of a relationship. I knew for certain that the guys I had dated in the past had felt like I was the one holding back too much. Perhaps this was karma for all the frustrations I had caused past boyfriends.

I wondered if I was so hung up on wanting more because I was getting older and it was getting too hard to wait until I was married. The idea didn't seem to fit because it wasn't like I was longing to have sex. I just wanted to experience that exciting part of a new relationship when you just can't stop kissing each other. Yes, I knew that would lead to potential challenges, because, well, the longer you kissed, the more likely it would turn into other things.

As I drove home, I couldn't help but think about when I'd dated Sean. He first kissed me at the end of our second date. It was after he dropped me off at this crappy student apartment where I lived with five other girls. He had given me a hug and walked away. Less than five seconds later there was a knock at the door. When I opened it to see him standing there, he quickly grabbed me and kissed me. It seemed like all he wanted to do was kiss me every time he saw me after that.

I still had the vivid memory of agreeing to watch one of Sean's favorite movies, Die Hard, at his apartment, because I had never seen it. I ended up still not really seeing it, because we were too busy making out. Throughout our relationship and all the making out we did, it never seemed like we were doing anything wrong or had anything to feel guilty about. One of us always managed to stop before things went too far.

There was the exception of the night of my twenty-first birthday, when I ended up on top of him and the technical term "outercourse" could have been used. Sean had been sound enough to stop it before either of us completed anything.

At the time, I may have felt bad about the incident. Mostly because Sean ended up feeling so guilty and apologized for mistreating me when I knew in my heart, in my uninhibited state, I had encouraged the whole thing. Still, I didn't feel like it was a very sinful thing to have happened. I mean, by that point we had said we loved one another and had started to talk about getting married. If you're really that interested in marrying someone and spending the rest of your lives together, shouldn't it be a little challenging to keep your hands off one another?

I pulled into my building's garage with several memories of kissing Sean floating around in my head and found myself in a place that I hadn't been in a long time. A place I had wanted to avoid ever going to again. I missed Sean. Well, I missed kissing him, at least. He was the best kisser I had ever dated. Probably because he'd been a little bit of a slut in his younger days, and I had gotten to enjoy the product of his years of practice. I told myself that it wasn't fair to compare Ethan to Sean, but I couldn't help longing for the past. Not because I wanted to be with Sean, but because I missed being in sync with someone when it came to all areas of a relationship; physical, spiritual, and emotional. Regardless of the disaster my relationship with Sean had turned into, there had truly been a fair amount of time when everything felt like it matched up and I had been content. As I went to bed, I hoped that I could shift myself to be more in line with where Ethan was at, because I knew it was very unlikely – and probably unreasonable – to expect him to align himself with where I was at.

THOMAS

I WALKED INTO THE SHOP TO START MY SHIFT. THE NIGHT before at our usual family dinner, I had told Michael I wanted to talk to him about something at work. I wondered if he would remember when I saw him that day. I was going to leave it entirely up to him. If he initiated the conversation, then I would take it as a sign that the conversation was supposed to happen. If not, then I would just continue doing what I was doing: pretending like I didn't have any questions about my dad and what he really thought of me.

I wasn't sure if I really wanted answers to any of my questions, but after last weekend and the pathetic extent I had gone to in order to avoid being alone in my parents' house, I knew it wasn't in my best interest to continue pretending like I didn't care.

It was busy, like Mondays often were, and I jumped into working with the rest of the crew who had been there since six. As it approached noon, I thought that maybe I would get away with not having to follow through on the talk. Then Michael walked up to me.

"Hey, I just finished up on a transmission; now's a good time to talk to me about whatever you needed to talk about."

I looked up from what I was doing.

"Well, I just started on this," I tried to find an excuse to delay the conversation.

"Alternator. Will can finish it," he assigned. "Besides, I was hoping you would take an early lunch and look through the book for this month. I have some questions about projections."

I realized I couldn't blow off a legitimate business concern, so I let Will step in. I wiped off my hands and followed Michael to the office.

Michael sat down at his desk to log on to the computer. He also had the account book out on the desk. Yes, the shop still archaically kept a history of all business done for the year in written form. At least we had it on the computer as well, but my dad had insisted on not abandoning the way his family had always kept records. I hoped one day I would convince Michael that there were ways we could back up the information without having to keep the written record. I didn't really see this happening anytime soon though.

"So," he began and I took a seat in front of his desk, "we actually increased our revenue this month compared to last month."

I nodded.

"And I was looking at the month before and that was up as well."

I scanned the book as he talked.

"With all this extra coming in, I thought it was only fair to ask if you needed or wanted any of it, since you're considerably underpaid right now."

"No, I'm good," I answered immediately.

"Tommy–" he began to reason.

"Seriously, Michael, we need to put it away and save it. We don't know what the rest of spring and summer will look like."

"Those are actually our busier months," he informed me.

"Well, the fall and winter then. I don't need it. I'd rather anything extra be there just in case, or we put it into buying something we need," I replied.

"Okay, well, I know it's still kind of soon, but things are looking better than I thought, like you said they were, so I just wanted to let you know."

Apparently, this was Michael's version of telling me I was right.

I nodded.

"So what did you want to talk about?" he asked.

"Oh, uh," I paused, reminding myself that I had promised to follow through if Michael brought it up. "Well, it's just, uh, Dad's desk," I started.

"Yeah, sorry about that. We do really need to clean that up," he admitted.

"It's just that I found the keys to the storage in there the other day like you told me, and–" I stopped, now thinking that the whole concern seemed stupid.

Undoubtedly, Michael was going to roll his eyes at me the minute I got the statement out. He had turned from the screen and was looking at me, waiting for me to finish my sentence.

"You know, it's nothing. I just, yeah, was wondering when we could maybe go through everything and get it organized," I lied.

"You found your stuff, didn't you?" he asked.

I froze. How did he know? I stared at him, unable to respond.

He leaned back in his chair. We continued to sit in silence; I didn't want to ask him for validation. Finally, Michael spoke.

"You know, ever since you were like, five, he would talk about you all the time. 'My boy, Tommy, he's so smart. You show him anything and he remembers it right away. He's gonna make a great mechanic.' And then," Michael paused, "and then you didn't want to be one. He couldn't understand how that was possible, for something to come so naturally to someone, when they don't even want to do it. I mean, the rest of us, we have to practice over and over, constantly refer to the manual, but you, Tommy, you always seemed to get it right away – ever since you were fifteen. Even now, after not picking up a wrench for how long? Four years?

"But that's how everything was for you," he shrugged, "baseball, school…for Christ's sake, I feel like you were constantly high from age fifteen to seventeen and you still had good enough grades to get into the University. You haven't used any of your business background since college, and you come here two months ago and automatically know all the fiscal and accounting shit that comes with running a business."

He looked up at the corner of the room and sighed. "Dad saw how good you were without even trying, and it drove him crazy that you could be that good and not care."

"I cared about painting," I countered quietly. It sounded so cheesy saying it aloud, like some horrible after-school special.

"He thought you cared more about upsetting him and proving him wrong than about the actual art."

I let the statement sink in and considered it. If my father had encouraged the art, I don't know how I would have responded. Thinking back, once I was in New York and had all the creative freedom I craved, I didn't produce anything of quality compared to the stuff I had done when I lived at home.

"That didn't mean he didn't think you were talented," Michael continued. "He just didn't see why being talented meant you had to run away."

I sat, staring down at Michael's desk, not wanting to make eye contact, knowing he was right and I had no defense for my past behavior. Michael, clearly done with sharing, concluded the moment.

"Look at it this way – if you were a real dumbass and a shitty mechanic, he wouldn't have cared what you decided to do with your life."

Another silence passed.

"I'll come in this Saturday and help you clean out the desk," he said.

I nodded and stood up, still unsure whether I should say anything. I walked to the door and grabbed the doorknob.

"Tommy," Michael stopped me. "He was just as stubborn as you. I'm sure if he could've gone back and done some things differently, he would have...he thought he had more time."

"Thanks," I said quietly and went back to the floor. I was going to be in my head for the rest of the day, counting everything I regretted and couldn't change.

———

I got to the youth center early on Wednesday to set up. It was my first day working with kids and I was nervous, but I would never have admitted it to anyone. Sydney came into the garage while I was setting up.

"Hey, Thomas," she greeted me. She was more dressed down than her usual vest and tie, wearing jeans and a black T-shirt. Her tattoos, which I hadn't been able to see fully before, were clearly displayed on her forearms. She was the complete opposite of who I expected Maura to be friends with.

"Hey." I continued scanning all the tools, mentally reviewing what I was going to cover for the first day. Memories of the first time my dad took me out to the garage at our home filled my head. I had been interested for the first five minutes and then quickly became bored. I worried whoever was joining me that day would have the same response.

"Not sure if anyone let you know, but either Maura or I will always be out here with you."

"I know. Without supervision, I might lead them astray." My response was sarcastic, but inside I was grateful that one of them would be there. I didn't know the first thing about homeless teen-agers and only had stereotypes and images of panhandlers to work off of.

"It's more about making sure they don't act like punks with you," she clarified. "Since this is all new for everyone, we've chosen six of our kids. Four of them are seventeen, the other two are eighteen and sixteen. We chose them based on stated interest, but also they have a history of consistently showing up for appointments, and well, they have a"–she paused, trying to choose the right words–"higher level of stability right now." She looked at me to see if I understood.

"So no meth addicts or schizophrenics," I summarized, taking a chance that I wouldn't offend her.

"Well, no one actively dealing with that right now, no," she said nonchalantly.

I knew I couldn't ask specifics about the histories of the teenagers I was about to work with. I tried my best to hold my poker face, but Sydney saw through me.

"Chances are, none of them are going to reveal anything big or heavy while they're out here with you in a group, and we'll be here if things start to go that way, so you really have nothing to worry about," she assured. "Any questions before I bring them out?"

I shook my head.

"You want to go by Thomas or Mr. O'Hollaren?"

I raised an eyebrow, never having thought of myself as 'Mr. O'Hollaren.'

"Thomas is fine."

"Kay, cool. I'm going to go get them and introduce you."

She started to turn around but then quickly turned back. "One last question."

I looked up.

"I couldn't really go over this in the training, because we are technically a Catholic organization, but you're cool with diversity in regards to, like, gay and transgender people, right?"

"Uh, sure," I wasn't sure if I was supposed to give a more passionate, articulate answer about human rights. I didn't have one.

"All right then," Sydney smiled and slapped me on the shoulder before she walked back into the main building. It would have been amusing to see Michael in the same situation that I was in now. I could see his puzzled face asking, 'What do you mean, he wants to be a girl?'

I didn't have anything else to set up. I couldn't stop fidgeting, double checking everything because I felt like an idiot just standing there waiting for everyone to come out. I liked Sydney all right, and felt confident in her skill level, but part of me wished it was Maura who was going to be there with me that day.

I was starting to notice that I felt better when I was with her. I was pretty sure she had that calming effect on everybody, given the line of work she had chosen to go into. Then again, she probably would have made me play get-to-know-you games with the kids, and that was something I was happily avoiding by having Sydney there instead.

Sydney walked out the back door of the building, followed by six teenagers. They ambled into the garage where the donated cars were parked. They looked like typical teenagers, a few of them with more piercings and tattoos than I would have expected at that age, but teenagers nonetheless. I surveyed the group and saw there were five boys and one girl. At least, I thought it was a girl. Sydney's question about my level of acceptance came to mind and I was left unsure. Not that it mattered. I just didn't want to fuck up and say the wrong thing.

"This is Thomas. He's going to be volunteering here once a week," Sydney introduced me. "Maura and I are going to be hanging out too when he's here. He is a volunteer so please give him your respect. How about we go around and say names," Sydney instructed.

She sounded a lot less firm than at the training I went to, but still gave off a vibe that she wasn't one to play games with. She motioned for the boy wearing a black hoodie and jeans to start. His dark hair was long and tied back.

"I'm Eric," he said simply.

"I'm Juan," the boy next to him said.

"Jesse," said the following boy.

"Justin," the largest boy, who was about the same height as me but at least a hundred pounds heavier, said in a low voice.

"Nicki," said the one who looked like a tomboy. I tried to not to make any assumptions.

"River," the shortest, youngest looking teenager finally said.

Sydney then turned to me, signaling for me to start.

"Has anybody ever worked on a car before?" I started.

Jesse, Juan, and Eric raised their hands. I asked them to share what they had worked on in the past. It was pretty standard; changing a tire, changing oil, putting in a battery. I then gave my disclaimer.

"Okay, so today's going to be kind of boring because I have to go over basics, but next week, we'll start ripping apart the car. First, safety...pretty much, as with most things in life, it comes down to 'don't be a dumbass,'" I quoted my dad.

I realized I had technically cussed and looked over at Sydney, who looked back at me, unaffected. "Just listen and ask questions," I said simply.

There was a silence. I had not realized how much talking I was going to have to do. Sydney had said these were teenagers who were interested in the subject, so why not turn it over to them?

"So," I started and took a step forward, lifting the hood of the Corolla, "did you guys have any questions about what any of this stuff is?" I worried for a moment that they would stay silent. Thankfully, Juan spoke up.

"Yeah, Eric wants to know where the engine is," Juan laughed.

"Shut up, Juan," Eric quickly responded.

"Well, I want to know where the engine is," Sydney prevented the situation from escalating by joining the group.

I pointed out the engine.

"Engines are more interesting when you pull them out," I explained. "We'll get there later."

"And what's that?" Sydney modeled for the group, pointing at another part of the car.

"That's the speed sensor. Any guesses what it does?" I asked dryly.

No one answered.

"Seriously, guys this is your chance to test me and make sure they didn't bring in a random guy who had some coveralls lying around. I mean, Sydney looks nice and all, but do we really trust her judgement when it comes to mechanics?"

"More so than Maura's," Juan quipped to the group.

"Well, I would agree with you there," I responded. "Then again, I'm her mechanic, so...awkward..." my voice trailed off.

Sydney laughed, which seemed to get the group to relax.

"What's that?" Nicki asked in a quiet voice pointing at the Mass Air Flow Sensor and Intake Air Temperature Sensor. I went on to identify and then explain what both things did.

Eventually they started quizzing and testing me more. When someone asked me about the radiator, I was able to tell them the story of when my brother was seventeen and got his hand stuck in the car for an hour while he was changing a radiator hose. Michael hated that story. I loved it because it involved him wearing a friendship bracelet that a girl had made for him. They continued to ask more questions about how the parts and tools worked.

Before I knew it, Sydney announced that the two hours were up. The group said their goodbyes and returned to the main building. I closed the hood and put the tools back, then pulled down the garage door, wondering if I needed to check-in with someone before I left. I turned around to see Maura walking out towards me. As always, she was smiling.

"You just had your first day," she declared excitedly. "How did it go? Sydney said it went great."

"It was okay. I don't think I permanently damaged anybody."

"Well, that usually happens the second week," she teased. She locked up the garage and turned back to me. "So," she smiled wider, "Did you like it?"

She had enough zeal for the both of us.

"It was fine," I said evenly, looking down at my shoes and then back at her. She had her arms crossed and was obviously looking for more expression from me.

"What?" I asked.

She shrugged. "I'm Thomas, I'm really cool, I don't get excited about anything," she said in a gruff mocking tone.

"Yep, that's exactly what I sound like, spot on," I said flatly.

"Well, it doesn't matter if you're excited or not. The group is, and that's all that matters," she said.

"Pollyanna strikes again."

I wanted to tell her about all the things that Michael had told me about my dad and all the things it had led me to think about. It felt strange to want to share that with her, because I usually never wanted to share anything about relationships with anyone.

"You're wearing your fancy boots," I observed, changing the subject.

She gave me a playful glare, assuming I was teasing her.

"I'm starving, do you want to go grab something to eat?"

"I'll have to take a rain check," she said. "I'm getting dinner with Ethan before we go to mass."

I nodded, hoping I didn't look disappointed.

"You're welcome to come to mass tonight if you want," she invited, knowing it was a long shot.

"Thanks, but, I think I'll take a rain check, too," I declined.

She stood there for a moment, waiting to see if I would say anything else. Maybe she expected a joke about Ethan.

"So," she said, "I guess I will see you next week then."

"Yep," I nodded. "See you then."

I walked to my truck as she headed back inside the main building. I knew if I told her I really needed to talk, she would make time for me, possibly even cancel on Ethan. However, when I considered actually telling her that I needed to talk, it seemed pretty selfish, and I was currently making more of an effort to do less of that.

MAURA

WEDNESDAY BROUGHT ANOTHER CHURCH-RELATED date with Ethan. Personally, I thought it was a little overkill to go to mass Wednesday night right before Triduum. I mean, it's not like I hated mass, but I found that going any more than three times in one week was a little redundant. Yeah, I had room to grow in my holiness, but at least I was able to confirm at a young age that I wasn't called to be a nun.

We ended up going out to the bar for a drink with everyone else after mass. This was our first social event with the young adult group as an official couple. Jessica was particularly interested in everything Ethan had to say about the traditions of Triduum. I especially loved it when she exclaimed that he would make a wonderful priest. Kind of a tactless thing to say to a guy when he was sitting next to his girlfriend, but my past probably made me sensitive to stuff like that. Not one to be above pettiness, I wrapped my hand around Ethan's arm and eventually held his hand, ensuring it was in Jessica's line of vision.

At the end of the night, Ethan and I stood at my door, talking about his plans for the weekend and when we would see each other again. We decided on Monday night. I took it as a good sign that he wanted to see me as soon as he got back. But I felt strange when he kept saying that he was going to miss me and I didn't really feel like a weekend away from him was all that much to pine over.

I didn't say this to him and just told him I would miss him too, because that seemed like what I was supposed to do. I invited him in, but he declined, saying that he didn't think it was a good idea. I wondered if he would ever think it was a good idea. He did grant me a nice, long kiss goodbye. I thought about inviting him in again, but figured I was probably already walking a thin line of him thinking I was more of a harlot than he had bargained for when he'd first asked me out.

By Thursday I still hadn't called my aunt, which I realized was somewhat rude because she liked to have everything planned, especially large family meals. The lack of a final headcount was probably maddening to her. I thought about what Easter would be like: driving down to Olympia by myself and seeing a large portion of my extended family, who I loved and enjoyed, but knew the conversation would revolve around whether I was dating anyone, predictably followed by encouragement that I would find "the one" someday. I wasn't in the mood for it, which was odd given the whole situation with Ethan. Shouldn't I be excited to tell them all about him? Maybe I just didn't want to jinx it.

By lunchtime I had decided that I wasn't going to go to Olympia, despite what I had told Ethan about wanting to see my family. I called my aunt and gave my apologies, using the excuse of having to catch up on work, which was not a total lie. I did have a lot of case notes to catch up on, just not a whole weekend's worth. I had never spent a holiday alone and thought maybe it was a growing experience that I had missed out on.

*Good job being independent, Maura! It's not like sitting alone at Easter Mass, completely surrounded by families, is going to make you lonely or self conscious at all...*I mentally started to second guess myself.

Okay, calm down. This is an opportunity to be alone with God – something Ethan probably expects you to be decent at if you ever want things to get serious with him.

I went to Holy Thursday Mass and Good Friday Service, and bawled like a baby, as I normally do. I sat in the back, away from the other young adults, and tried to truly embrace being a solitary mass goer. Okay, so I might have still been a little miffed at Jessica. I chose to believe I was challenging myself to grow in spirituality and not being petty again.

I considered going to Easter Vigil on Saturday night because there was less likely to be a plethora of families there. An actual sigh came out when I thought about the three-hour service. So instead I turned on Netflix, and after two episodes of Breaking Bad, knew I wasn't going anywhere that night.

Yes, clearly this was the call to holiness I had been searching for that weekend. Obviously, I didn't feel that guilty about my entertainment choices, because the Saint Catherine book that Ethan had lent me sat on the coffee table, unopened, all night.

I woke up on Easter Sunday, tired from binge watching.

Maybe I should go to the Newman Center instead of Blessed Sacrament? There'll be more single people there...but unfortunately that includes Sean. Ugh. Okay, Blessed Sacrament and all the families it is.

I dragged myself out of bed and threw on a floral lavender sundress. I grabbed a light blue cardigan because the dress was strapless, and even I wasn't that much of a rebel when it came to church attire. I kept my hair simple with a fishtail braid; something easy, but which gives the impression that effort was put forth.

I got there early to find, as I'd hoped, my favorite spot in the church was still open; on the left, in the middle set of pews. I liked it because it sat right next to a devotion to Saint Jude. I had loved that statue ever since we started going to Blessed Sacrament. I hadn't made the connection until a few years back that Saint Jude, as he was depicted, kind of looked like my grandpa when he was younger, and that was probably why I had been fond of it. As I got older, I had decided it was a good saint to have a devotion to since he was the patron saint of lost causes and dire circumstances, and I had encountered a few of those situations in my line of work. I took my seat and sat in silence by myself as everyone else filtered in.

On a busy day like Easter Sunday, I am not the best at praying before mass. Okay, so, I'm not good at praying before most masses. I tend to observe everyone arriving and have an inner commentary going in my head about the things I wonder about them. I decided to try harder that day and ended up bowing my head down and staring at my hands.

I began with the old standby of thanking God for all the things in my life and apologizing for the areas where I fell short. I prayed for the kids and people I worked with, for my parents' safe return, Ethan's safe return, his grandpa's health...and when I got through my laundry list of things, my brain stopped. My mind went blank, in a good way. It was the most relaxed I'd felt all week.

Then all of the sudden he popped into my head. Thomas. And there went the clarity. Did he pop into my head because I felt the need to pray for him? I had been praying for him and his family off and on since the funeral. Rather than obsess over why he popped into my head, I threw a quick prayer in there for him, too. Frankly, God and I knew Thomas needed all the prayers he could get.

It gradually became busier as more and more people entered the church. I finally looked up at the people, deciding I had made enough progress for that day on my pre-mass reverence. The moment I looked up, I saw the O'Hollarens walking into the church. Michael and his family led the group, followed by Margaret and her family, and then Jackie walked in with Thomas.

My eyes followed him, completely surprised that he was there, wondering what had made him decide to come with his family to church that morning. They filed into one of the few available pews left toward the front of the church. Thomas stood on the outside, waiting to sit while Margaret and Colleen determined how to divide up the kids. I saw him start to scan the church. I immediately switched my attention to the altar, not wanting him to catch me staring at him and his family.

There was quite a bit of time left before mass started, but I willed myself not look over in the direction of the O'Hollarens. I don't know why I felt the need to avoid them. Maybe because I knew it would be obvious that I was there by myself and part of me felt like that might look pathetic to Thomas...not that there was a reason to care what he thought. I was thankful when mass finally started and I had something else to focus on.

At the end of the service, I made my way to the side exit, bypassing the crowd that was gathering out front. I stepped out the door and walked briskly down the path that led to the parking lot when I heard Thomas call my name. I turned to see him hurrying out the door and across the lawn to where I stood on the sidewalk.

"You were gonna run off without saying hi?"

"Hi, happy Easter," I said smiling, trying to act natural. "I'm surprised to see you here."

I could see the rest of the O'Hollarens gradually making their way out of the church. The children immediately started running around and chasing one another while the adults talked with a few other parishioners.

"Someone told me this mass was happier than Palm Sunday," he referenced with a grin. I gave him a look of doubt, knowing that wasn't the reason.

"That, and my mom said she'd really like it if I went with her."

"Aw, what a good son. And you wore a tie."

"I know, something about Jesus resurrecting himself makes you want to step up your game. I see you feel the same way. I forgot you knew how to wear dresses," he motioned to my outfit.

Most guys would have just told me I looked nice. Not Thomas.

He looked around. "So, are your parents here? I was hoping I could finally meet my stalker in person," he joked about my mother.

"No, they are actually on a cruise in Mexico right now."

"You're alone today?" he concluded.

"Uh, technically, I guess,"

"Well, we can't have that." He stood with his hands in his pockets, looking as relaxed as I wish I could have been in that moment.

"No, really it's fine," I started to turn down the invitation I was anticipating.

He ignored me and turned back to see his mom walking towards him. "Mom," he called, "Maura just told me she has no one to spend Easter with because her parents are out of town."

"Well, Tommy, I hope you invited her over," she answered immediately.

"I was going to, but it looks like she was about to turn me down," he told on me, maintaining eye contact to gage my reaction.

"Oh nonsense, Maura, you must come over and have dinner with us. I just wouldn't be able to stand the thought of you alone on Easter."

An older couple called over to Jackie and caught her attention. "Tommy, you make sure she says yes. Don't take no for an answer," she said with friendly firmness as she walked away.

Thomas turned back to me. "That Jackie O'Hollaren is a force to be reckoned with. And what kind of son would I be if I didn't follow my widowed mother's orders?"

I sighed, knowing I didn't have any excuse.

"What time do I need to be there?"

"We're eating at two. Rumor has it there's an Easter egg hunt afterwards, but Hunter could just be full of shit."

Thomas was the only person I knew who would feel completely comfortable cursing as he stood outside of the church where he'd just gone to Easter mass.

"Okay, I will see you at two."

"Great, looking forward to it. We like to do what we can for the lonely and downtrodden," he teased as I walked away, but I didn't give him the satisfaction of a reaction.

THOMAS

I CHANGED OUT OF MY DRESS SHIRT AND TIE AS SOON AS we got home from breakfast. Knowing my mom would still like me to look somewhat presentable at dinner, I put on the one short sleeved polo I owned. In the past, I would have considered a small gesture like this a great inconvenience, but now I couldn't recall the exact justification I would have had for feeling that way.

I think I had thought if I was being forced to endure a whole meal with people I found completely uninteresting, the least they could do was let me wear whatever I wanted. And then there was the one year I got high before Thanksgiving, partly because I thought it would make stuffing my face more enjoyable, but mostly because I wanted to piss off my dad. I had succeeded, and then ended up getting kicked out of the house for a good five hours. I still remembered how hard it made my mother cry. It all seemed so stupid now.

I found my mom in the kitchen prepping the lamb to go into the oven. I offered to help but she turned me down. She was clearly waiting for my sister and Colleen to get there. I could cook well enough, but my mom tended to reinforce traditional gender roles when it came to cooking for holidays. Knowing she still wanted company, I sat down.

"It was so nice to have you come to mass with us this morning," she said without looking up. "Did you enjoy it?" she asked hopefully.

"I enjoyed that you enjoyed it." I was truthful before taking a sip of the coffee I had poured myself.

She sighed. "Well, that's better than nothing."

We sat there silently for a moment.

"What made you decide to come?"

I shrugged. "I knew it would make you happy. It's not a hard thing to do."

She gave me a doubtful look.

"What? I'm being serious.

"After over ten years of pleading for you to come to mass with me, suddenly you're okay with it?"

"Maybe I'm trying to be a better son," I attempted to give her a simple explanation.

"You're sure this doesn't have anything to do with Maura McCormick?" she looked up from the potatoes she was now peeling.

"What?" I laughed. "No, it does not have anything to do with her."

She put her hands up, claiming innocence. "I'm just saying, you seemed to run up to her pretty quickly after mass, and this is the first girl to my knowledge that you've ever invited over for dinner, let alone Easter dinner. I was wondering if she might be special," my mom hinted.

"Mom, she's just a friend," I said. "She's not really my type."

"Well, I wouldn't know what your type is, since you never bring anyone around," she guilted.

"Maybe I haven't met anybody good enough to introduce to you yet," I attempted flattery to put an end to the conversation. Maybe it had worked, because she was quiet for a moment.

"So, if Maura's not your type, then who is?"

"Mom," I sighed, but smiled at her second attempt to get information.

"I'm just saying, I know a lot of people who have daughters around your age, and I imagine it gets pretty lonely living with an old woman like me."

I stood up and moved around the counter to hug her.

"Are you kidding? A momma's boy like me? I am living the dream right now."

Never one to turn down a hug from any of her children or grandchildren, my mom let me hug her, but gently swatted my shoulder for my sarcasm when she broke away. She went back to peeling potatoes.

"Well, I don't know what it is, Thomas, but there has been something different about you lately."

"Different?"

"The Tommy I remember would have been out 'till God knows when last night, and probably still in bed right now."

"I guess I've mellowed in my old age." I joked even though I knew what she was getting at.

"You seem happier. I find myself feeling so grateful that you don't look as miserable as before, and then I start to wonder if it's because…"

I knew where she was going because her voice cracked. I reached out and touched her shoulder to stop her from asking if I was happier because my dad was no longer there.

"No, no, it's not because of that," I denied immediately.

I decided now as was as good as time as any to finally be humble. It was the least I could do now.

"I hated New York. I don't know why I thought I had to leave home. Dad was right…I wish I wouldn't have been so stubborn and come home sooner."

Unfortunately, my words didn't keep her from crying.

"You know it wasn't all you. He was so stubborn too. And I was so angry at him for refusing to talk to you after you left," she admitted.

She wiped her tears away and then went to wash her hands, almost as if it would signify to her mind that she was done crying. Then she looked at me.

"You know, he surprised me last Christmas, saying we were going to go visit you this summer. I couldn't believe it."

I couldn't either and I wasn't able to mask my surprise. I could see my reaction registering in her eyes.

"Your father loved you, Tommy. He didn't always know the best way to show it. I know he wanted to make things right," she said simply, sounding like she had gone over it in her head several times before.

She touched my cheek. All I could do was nod. She took her hand down from my face to hold my hand. I realized how much I had put her through, having to deal with the conflict all those years.

Then something came out of my mouth that had not come out in years, at least not with the amount of meaning it had in that moment. "I'm sorry." I said, looking her in the eyes.

She broke down in tears, triggered by my rare apology. I didn't need to say anything else. My mom knew exactly everything I was apologizing for; the years of putting her in the middle, the years of being unappreciative, the years of not listening to anyone else, the years of being selfish. She hugged me and gradually her crying slowed. She backed away to look at me. She didn't say anything; just gently patted my cheek before taking her apron to wipe away her tears. Then she turned back to the potatoes.

I didn't know how to move on from a moment like that, particularly because I hadn't had very many of them in my life. That might have been the first. Thankfully, Margaret and her family came busting through the door. Two-year-old Sophie raced into the kitchen holding a basket, jumping up and down, repeatedly saying what sounded like "eggs" and "Easter." Margaret and Chris followed, carrying their youngest, Elizabeth.

"Sophie, not yet," Margaret reminded her oldest calmly. "After we eat. Did you say hi to Grandma and Uncle Tommy?"

My mom bent down and received her hug and kiss from Sophie. I followed after her, and I couldn't help but think how only three months ago, I'd barely known the names of Margaret's children and was a complete stranger to them. Now Sophie knew my name and willingly hugged me. I'd never really considered myself someone who cared one way or another about small children, but lately, I loved to make my nieces and nephews laugh and rile them up – much to their parents' dismay.

"Can you get them set up in the family room?" Margaret asked Chris, walking over to the drawer and pulling out an apron.

Within minutes, the chaos of Michael's boys burst into the room, Hunter of course leading the charge. The boys didn't even stop in the kitchen, but went right through to the family room, knowing that was where all the toys were. Michael and Colleen arrived close behind. Colleen went into the kitchen after hugging me and everyone else hello. Michael said hi but was quickly distracted by the sound of a child crying, which sounded like Gabriel.

"Hunter! I told you not to sit on him!" Michael rushed into the family room.

I moved to the outside of the kitchen, but remained at the counter with my coffee, enjoying the fact that I was the uncle and not responsible for watching anybody.

"So," my mother started as Margaret tended to a pot on the stove and Colleen began chopping vegetables, "did Tommy tell you he invited a girl today?"

Margaret's head immediately shot up from the pasta sauce she was stirring and looked at me.

"No, he didn't!" she exclaimed. "Tommy, are you dating someone?"

"No, I'm not dating anyone, and I didn't invite her. Mom invited her when she found out her family was out of town," I clarified, looking at my mom, expecting her to come clean.

"I may have extended the offer," she admitted, "but I feel like it was your idea," she argued calmly.

"Well. Who is she?" Margaret asked with great interest.

"Maura McCormick, Laura McCormick's daughter," my mother informed before I got a chance.

A smile crept up on my sister's face and she started to nod.

"It's not like that," I defended unsuccessfully.

"Is that why you came by and helped her babysit last Friday?" Colleen happily gave my sister more information, conveniently leaving out that fact that it had been Michael's idea.

"I don't know, Tommy, it's not like you bring many friends who are women around," Margaret pointed out.

"Exactly, I don't bring any women around, so–"

"So, this one must be special," Margaret sing-songed.

I looked over at my mother to see that she was thoroughly enjoying what she had started.

"He says she's not his type," she interjected effortlessly, quickly checking the pasta sauce.

"Oh, honestly, Tommy, what does that even mean?" Margaret asked.

"It means that you all need to accept that we're not in the old country and we're not marrying people off anymore."

"I don't know, Tommy, I think we could get a couple of goats for you, maybe even a mule," Margaret winked.

I was regretting my decision to invite Maura now. In the past I would have anticipated this reaction from my family and not invited her. Hell, in the past I wouldn't even have been at mass. But there was something in me that knew that Maura didn't want to be alone today. Why I was willing to overlook the goading from my family for her sake was beyond me.

Luckily, I knew Maura and I would never date each other. Unfortunately, she was exactly the type of person my mother and sister wanted me to end up with. I knew they would get their hopes up by the end of the day, no matter how many times I warned them not to. Suddenly, I remembered that Maura was dating someone else.

"You know, actually, I believe she's dating someone," I announced.

Margaret inspected my face, always the best at identifying when I was lying.

"Then why isn't she with his family today?"

"I don't know. Maybe we can ask her – after we find out if she comes from good breeding stock, of course. Or we could just act normal. Unless mom's making capozzelli; then you can win her over by insisting that she eat the eyeballs," I joked, getting an eyeroll from Margaret.

Thankfully, the three of them eventually moved on to other topics and I was able to enjoy the rest of my coffee with the sound of the kids playing in the background. No one else heard the knock at the door when Maura arrived, which was good because I'm sure it would have been met with a lot of needless excitement. There would be more than enough of that after Maura left. I got up to answer the door without anyone noticing.

She was standing there in the same purple and white dress she'd worn to church. Her hair was down and wavy now, and she was holding flowers and a bottle of wine.

"Hi," she stepped inside. "I didn't know what to bring, so I went with this."

I closed the door and took the items from her, noticing that the dress underneath her cardigan was strapless. It wasn't revealing, but I started to wonder what she looked like in the dress with the sweater off. Naturally, I had established when I first met her that she was attractive, but it had been a long time since I had caught myself eyeing her in that way. I blamed my sister and mother's encouragement for my brain even going there.

"Aren't you the teacher's pet?" I quipped. "I thought we were working on not making the rest of us look bad?"

"I guess I'm a lost cause," she sighed.

Since Maura was somewhat acquainted with everyone through her parents, it wasn't as tedious as I imagined it would've been if I'd brought a complete stranger over. When we sat down to dinner, I was impressed by how effortless Maura made dining with acquaintances look. She was an amazing conversationalist, knowing exactly what questions to ask to get people to share about themselves, but she didn't come off as nosey, just friendly. At one point, she pulled me into the conversation. She was talking about the voc-ed program that we were starting and then humorously described our trip to the auto parts store. Her retelling of it even made Michael smile and I briefly forget how upset I'd been when it had occurred.

That's when it happened.

In that moment, while we were sitting around the table with my family, I looked over at her as she talked, and I felt it.

It was like we were a couple.

It was what I had seen depicted throughout the years with my parents and even with my siblings and their spouses. Not large romantic gestures, but sitting together and telling other people about mundane things that you had done that led to something funny or interesting.

I wanted to stay in that moment, acting that part, because for some reason it felt fulfilling. Not the best feeling I had ever had with a woman, but still contentment.

I caught my mom looking at me, and knew she was reading me. Being the stubborn soul that I am, I didn't want her thinking she could further her matchmaker plans, so I casually stood up and went to the bathroom to reset.

When I came out, they were serving dessert. My mom went to pour Colleen champagne, which we traditionally had with dessert on Easter. Colleen attempted to nonchalantly turn it down, but in my family, you can't casually turn down alcohol unless you give it up for Lent or are a recovering alcoholic. My mom gave Colleen a predictable look of confusion, which Michael interrupted before it could turn into a look of dawning comprehension.

"Actually," Michael began, raising his voice for the room to hear, "I guess this is as good a time as any since you all have your glasses." He reached out and held Colleen's hand. "There's going to be another O'Hollaren."

The room erupted in excitement. My mother enveloped Colleen in a hug. I looked over and saw Maura sitting by herself, where I had abandoned her. That didn't keep her from looking genuinely happy for my brother and Colleen.

"Well, that's why you gave up alcohol for Lent!" My mom exclaimed wiping away happy tears. "I'm sorry, I'm just so emotional today," she laughed. "When is the due date?"

"December twenty seventh," Colleen said.

"Oh, another Christmas baby, just like Tommy," my mom exclaimed, looking over at me.

I smiled but I was thoroughly shocked that Colleen and Michael didn't appear the least bit panicked that they were going to have five kids before the year was finished. And I couldn't even commit to sitting next to a woman through a whole dinner without feeling overwhelmed.

"We are the best presents...just like Jesus," I said smartly, bringing myself out of my shock as I moved back to my seat next to Maura.

"Personally, I would've been happier if you'd been a girl," Margaret said.

"I think that's the same thing Mary said when Jesus was born."

"Jesus was supposed to be a girl?" Hunter asked.

"Yep, that's why his middle name is Christina," I falsely informed.

Margaret gave me a stern look and I smiled.

We finished dessert and, much to the grandchildren's dismay, cleared the table before prepping for the egg hunt. Maura offered to clean dishes and of course her help was declined by my mother. Maura then turned to me, as everyone had moved into the kitchen or the family room.

"Well, I think I'm going to head out."

"You don't want to stay for the egg hunt? It's the most exciting part. I have money on Hunter ending up in timeout at least three times," I said, making her smile.

"That's okay. It'll be good for you guys to have some family time without a guest hanging around."

"You know we pretty much do this every week, but without the good china," I pointed out, wondering why I was trying to convince her to stay when earlier I'd felt the need to physically distance myself.

"I should get home and check in with Ethan." she reminded me of the boyfriend I had momentarily forgotten.

"And what is Ethan up to today? I thought Easter was like the prom for you people."

I earned a slight glare from her, but I still thought I was clever.

"He's in Spokane with his family."

246

"He wasn't ready to show you off? It must be the strapless dress," I teased, wanting her to know that I'd noticed her dress.

She folded her arms.

"For your information, he invited me and I turned him down. I was the one not ready to meet his family," she said proudly.

"And yet here you are, hanging out with all of mine," I pointed out, thinking it was funny.

"I know," she said as if she had already considered this. "Which is probably why I need to go and call him. Wouldn't want anybody getting jealous of you."

Her tone was sarcastic, but I started to realize there was a possibility that that could happen.

"Well, I gotta say, I'm impressed with how you can just walk into a family and fit right in. I'm pretty sure when I go back in, they're going to ask if they can trade me in for you."

"What can I say? I'm a people person. But I think at the end of the day, your family's pretty fond of you," she assured.

"Come on, I'll walk you out," I offered.

We stopped at her car.

"You know, I recall sending you a text earlier this week about bringing this thing in to get the alignment fixed. But it's the weirdest thing, I never got an answer."

"I know," she sighed. "It's just that work's been busy, and I didn't want to coordinate getting out there on a work day and then having to take the bus back and then picking the car up," she made her excuses.

"Maura, a car is a responsibility, not a right," I quoted my dad in a serious tone. "Ownership is about care, not neglect."

She rolled her eyes.

"Seriously, you're gonna fuck up your tires. It's going to drive me crazy if you don't get it fixed."

It was a pet peeve of all O'Hollaren men when people put off car maintenance. I remember right before I moved to New York, Margaret had run down her tires more than she should have, and when she finally brought the car in to get new tires, my dad refused to give her the car back for three days.

"Okay," she sighed.

She pulled out her phone, presumably to look for the appointment times I had sent her. "Those times are probably all filled now," I told her.

She put her phone down and looked at me expectantly.

"Tell you what; the shop's closed tomorrow. I'll pick up the car from your work, get it aligned, and bring it back to you."

"Your shop's closed tomorrow?"

"Yeah. It's Easter Monday," I said obviously, like she didn't know. "Our business is Catholic-owned. Has been for over sixty years, Maura, geez." I sighed heavily like I had no patience for her.

"Then who's going to work on it with you?"

"It'll take a little longer, but a car like this I can do by myself."

"And that's what you want to do on your day off?" she asked with disbelief.

"Well it's not like you left me a choice, driving all around town running up on curbs."

She still looked at me skeptically.

"What else am I going to do? My running buddy is at work."

"Okay," she agreed, still a little hesitant. "I start work at eight," she said, and then stared at me.

"What?" I asked, wanting her to stop trying to figure me out, mostly because, at the moment, I couldn't figure myself out. Hadn't been able to all day, for that matter.

"It just seems like you're kind of making the rest of us slackers look bad right now," she quoted me.

"Maybe I just really like to realign Honda Civics. It's a fetish," I joked.

She stopped staring at me and seemed to accept it as a simple act of kindness.

"Well, thank you, and thanks for inviting me. Please give my thanks to your mom."

"Sure, sure, no problem. I'm glad we were able to save you from crying into a TV dinner while watching reruns of Seinfeld."

For the first time, I could tell she didn't know if she should hug me or not. I took a chance and went in to hug her first. I kept it brief, not wanting it to feel as natural to me as it was now starting to become.

"Have a good night. I'll see you tomorrow."

"Night," she said quietly before getting into her car and driving away.

MAURA

IT WAS A LITTLE BEFORE FIVE WHEN I GOT HOME. Luckily, Ethan was under the impression that I was in Olympia with my family, so he probably wouldn't consider it weird that he hadn't heard from me yet. I changed out of my dress and into my pajamas because what else would somebody want to do after being in a dress all day?

I looked at my phone and thought how texting had been both the greatest and worst invention. It had become such a crutch for me. I now only associated talking on the phone with work and my parents, and as a result, I felt like phone calls with anyone else required an incredible amount of effort, even with someone I considered my boyfriend.

I copped out and used stupid traditional gender roles as an excuse. A lady never calls a gentleman first. It was important to make him do the work. Thus, it justified that a text was acceptable in this situation. Yes, it was handling a first-world problem like this that made me an amazing social worker when kids came to me not knowing where they were going to sleep at night.

I pulled up our last conversation and typed.

Happy Easter! Hope you had a good day with your family. Look forward to seeing you tomorrow.

I determined emojis to be too immature and figured Ethan wouldn't take them as humorously as I would intend them. The thought of throwing in a random panda or koala bear with a car and a star made me laugh to myself. It didn't take much to amuse me.

I put my phone down. Once again, I saw the Saint Catherine book staring me in the face. Great. He's probably going to ask if I've started it and want to know what I thought about it.

Gee, Ethan, all four hundred pages weren't dreadfully boring and dry at all. I can't believe people have been wasting their time with Harry Potter when they could've been reading this!

It felt like when you have to get homework done on a Sunday night and you just want the weekend to keep going...which was why I had always done all my homework on a Friday afternoon when I could. But that proactive attitude didn't seem to hold true for the Saint Catherine book.

Ethan was doing the right thing by challenging me to be a holier, better person and I should be appreciative, right? I gave myself an incentive and poured a glass of wine to accompany me as I sat down to start my assignment. I made it through thirty very dense pages. I was so proud of myself, I poured another glass of wine. I didn't read anything exceptionally challenging or unsettling. It was all things I had contemplated before, related to suffering leading to Christ and the importance of total devotion to him.

I didn't know what I would share with Ethan if he asked my thoughts on it. What could I say? Being spiritual is hard and sometimes – well really, a lot of the time – I failed at it? I had never been a super prayerful person, but I found redemption in being able to consider acts of service a form of prayer. Ethan would probably expect a more intellectual review. Unfortunately, I didn't have one. I was tempted to search for the Cliffs Notes version.

Lord knows some holy person somewhere thought it was a good idea to upload that shit to the internet. Oh, shit.

I had just called reader notes on a book by a doctor of the church 'shit'...on Easter. Good thing God loved me unconditionally...and was the only one who had access to my thoughts.

I looked at the clock and noticed it was well after eight and I had not yet heard from Ethan. I checked my phone to make sure I hadn't missed anything. There was nothing. I thought it was odd, but was also relieved that I wasn't going to have to tell him where I'd spent Easter. Maybe I should've gone to Spokane with Ethan. I would have spent more time with him and probably felt surer about everything... maybe.

What was looming over me was that I knew that Ethan had some definite opinions about life and I wondered what would happen when he discovered that I didn't necessarily hold the same perspective on things. We seemed to agree on the big things, but sometimes that wasn't enough for people. Frankly, it confused me that he was as interested in me as he claimed to be, because lately I had developed a bit of a reputation within the young adult group for being a little too liberal for their liking.

Why our potentially different perspectives had not come up yet, I didn't know. Okay, that was a lie. I knew exactly why. It was because I had kept my mouth shut when opportunities to share a differing opinion presented themselves. I saw how Ethan looked at me, and selfishly I wanted him to keep looking at me that way. I had a sense that some of my beliefs and habits would eventually disappoint him. I didn't think there was anything ultimately wrong with how I viewed the world, but it seemed that if I ever wanted to marry a Catholic man, I was going to have to change. I tried to reframe it and tell myself that changing was another word for growing.

With this in mind, I picked up the book to begin reading again, which mostly led to me staring at the same page for twenty minutes. I decided I had had enough growth for one night and turned on the TV, deciding I would give Ethan another hour to call before I went to bed. I laughed when a rerun of Seinfeld came on the screen.

***

Ethan never called or texted, which was weird. As I lay in bed, I theorized all the possible reasons why he didn't respond. Maybe something happened to his phone, like he lost it or forgot his charger. That seemed too irresponsible for Ethan though. Maybe his family celebrated Easter in a strange way where they took a vow of silence. I'd never heard of anybody doing that but maybe they were pre-Vatican II people like Mel Gibson...but not being allowed to talk on Easter isn't a pre-Vatican II thing...yeah, that would just be weird. But was it possible?

I held back from getting my phone to look up "do people celebrate Easter in silence?" Finally, a reason that seemed the most plausible popped into my head. Perhaps going away had given Ethan the opportunity to reflect and he'd realized he didn't like me as much as he thought. In my experience, the first sign of a guy telling you it was over was usually not calling when he said he would. The more I considered this possibility, the more my brain took it as fact. I congratulated myself for not becoming too invested.

The next morning, I drove into work to find Thomas standing casually next to his truck. I was still caught off guard by how nice he'd been over the past two days, but my neurosis had been too focused on Ethan to spend much time on wondering why he was being so kind.

"Good morning," he greeted. "I see you're the type who likes to clock in at the very last minute. As an employer, I'm not sure how I feel about that," he pretended to evaluate me, even though his zip up hoodie made him look less professional than me.

"Bitch, I'm salary."

"Wow, sassy in the morning, even at work, on a Monday. I had thought that was just a weekend thing."

He held out his hand for my key.

"Here, you can take the keys to this beast in case you have an emergency and have to go feed some old people soup or something," he said, exchanging my key for the key to his truck. "Just don't run up on any curbs."

"I doubt I'll be going anywhere," I informed him.

"I should be back by noon." He pushed off of the truck and went over to my car.

"Please tell me you left your iPod in here and I get to listen to Maura's Dysfunctional Top 40 Mix. I'm really in the mood for some Ace of Base."

"No, I chose NPR today."

"Nerd," he teased before getting in and driving away.

I welcomed the start of the work day because staying busy would keep my mind off of Ethan. Also, I had been highly productive on Saturday and was all caught up on case notes and reports, so I could finally focus on projects that I had putting on the back burner.

Ten o'clock arrived quickly, its presence announced by the arrival of Ashland. She was wearing leggings and an oversized blouse with, of course, flip flops. She took off her messenger bag and ran her fingers through her smooth, dark hair.

"So I'm back," she announced, like we should've thanked her for returning.

Sydney looked up from her work and nodded coolly. I looked up and smiled.

"Welcome back," I exclaimed more eagerly than I needed to. I couldn't help it. When I sensed someone didn't like me and I couldn't figure out why, I always overcompensated by being too friendly. If I just knew why Ashland didn't care for me, I could let it go and find petty reasons to not like her back. You know, just like any good Christian.

"How was spring break?" I inquired cheerily.

"Oh my God, it was so relaxing," she sighed dramatically. "We went camping on the coast for like, four days. Sydney, the hikes were amazing. You have to see the pictures I took."

Ashland scrolled on her phone to pull up the pictures from her amazing hike and walked over to show Sydney.

"Oh cool," Sydney looked up. "Is this near Ocean Shores? It looks familiar. I think I've hiked out there before."

"Yeah, about twenty minutes out. It only rained, like, one day. We couldn't believe it. So great."

Ashland pulled the phone back and was now staring at her own pictures. I accepted that she wouldn't show me without me asking to see them. I rationalized that this was because she knew that Sydney was really into hiking and I didn't share the hobby. I was pleased with myself when I refrained from asking to see the pictures and instead went back to finalizing a needs assessment for one of the teenagers.

"So," Ashland sat down in the small corner designated for her, "anything exciting happen while I was gone?"

I decided to keep working and let Sydney answer. A few moments passed and Sydney realized I had deferred to her.

"Uh, not really," she paused to think over the past two weeks. "We had two new intakes. We're supposed to have some new undergrad volunteers start this week. I think we are going to put two of them in art group with you, but they'll just be participating along with the teens."

"Cool," she said pulling out her laptop. "Anything new with either of my kids?" she asked, referring to the two teenagers she was acting as case manager for under Sydney's supervision.

"Some stuff came up with Rhianna's mom while you were gone. Read over the notes and let me know if you have questions. She has court next Thursday," Sydney filled her in. "River started the auto-mechanic training last Wednesday. He seemed to like it; you'll probably want to check in with him about it."

"Is that with the good looking dark guy who was in here before I left?" Ashland asked. Clearly, she was highly concerned about what was going on with Rhianna.

"We're trying to call him Thomas," Sydney responded without looking up from her computer.

"I know you wouldn't notice Sydney," Ashland started matter-of-factly, "but between him and that priest, there's been a lot of eye candy walking around here. Then again, it could just be the deprivation from grad school talking," she over-shared. "What day is he going to be here?" She pulled her hair up and effortlessly put it in a sloppy bun – the kind that looked ironically perfect.

I was now wishing we had scheduled Thomas to come on Tuesdays or Thursdays when Ashland wasn't here.

"Wednesdays," Sydney answered. "But you might be lucky and see him this afternoon when he comes back with Maura's car," Sydney said, revealing that she had talked to Thomas in the parking lot that morning.

"Look at Maura, soliciting favors from the volunteer," Ashland joked.

"Ashland, you know that would violate the Code of Ethics," Sydney began, "which we know our dear Maura would never do. Clearly, Thomas is more than just a volunteer to her," she kept her tone even, almost expressionless.

"Oh, Maura," Ashland exclaimed. "Are you dating him? He doesn't look like anyone who would date you at all."

Why did Ashland feel so comfortable posing relationship questions to me? I'd had a lot more boundaries with Ann when I'd been an intern. I could only blame myself and my pathetic attempts to be overly nice to her instead of acting more like an authority figure... and Sydney for encouraging the question.

"He's a family friend. My family takes our cars to his shop." I held back from providing more information.

Ashland seemed uninterested in my answer and switched her focus to reading emails that she had been included in while she was away.

I continued my productive morning despite the addition of Ashland. After meeting with one of our drug counselors about a couple of the kids I worked with, I got a text from Thomas telling me that he was in the parking lot so I went outside to meet him. He was standing by my car, holding a familiar paper sack from Dick's Burgers, a Seattle favorite. My mouth started to water.

"Here you go," he handed the key back to me. "Hungry? I brought lunch."

"Why'd you bring me lunch?" I returned the key to his truck.

He shrugged, walking over to his truck to unlock the tailgate.

"The idea of getting to talk about that one time we shared Dick's amused me too much to pass up."

He hopped up on the tailgate. I continued to stand back. He patted the door, signaling for me to sit next to him. My stomach was growling at the hope he had brought a Deluxe.

"Well, what kind did you bring me?"

"Obviously a Deluxe," he answered and I was sold, regardless of how weird I thought it was that he'd brought me lunch.

I sat down next to him and he handed me the burger. I took my first bite, savoring it, trying to remember the last time I'd gone to Dick's. Most likely I'd been drunk at the time. I let out a contented sigh.

"Should I give you some privacy with that thing?" he laughed.

I ignored him.

"How much do I owe you?"

"For the two-dollar burger? I'm not that cheap."

"No, for the car."

"On the house," he responded simply, eating his fries.

"Come on," I argued, not liking the idea of him working on my car for free.

"Seriously, there were no parts involved. It was just labor, and we weren't even open today, so it's not like it took away business. One of the many benefits of knowing me," he said proudly. "Oh, and I went ahead and rotated your tires."

I stared at him like I had when I knew there was a reason he was trying to get me to spend the night at his house.

"What?"

"What's up with you?"

"You're not the only one who's allowed to do nice things."

"But why are you doing nice things for me?"

His leg was swinging as it dangled over the tailgate, almost as if he was nervous. He sighed.

"I don't know," he paused. "I guess...I just...like doing things for a friend?"

"Is that a question?" I laughed at the way he sounded uncertain.

He sighed. "Not everyone's got a master's degree in feelings, okay?" he teased. "Look, I don't really do the friend thing. I don't think I've ever had a friend...who I could talk with..." He trailed off, hoping that I would just accept that as an answer.

I stared at him, waiting for more information.

He laughed nervously and looked down at the ground. "…And I just…appreciate having someone to talk to…so thank you."

He looked up. His eyes examined mine and it looked like he wanted to say more, but when he didn't I decided to make light of the situation.

"Should we make each other bracelets to commemorate this occasion?"

"Whoa, hold up, I never said I wanted a serious commitment like that or anything," he joked.

"Fair enough. Anyway, I wouldn't want Sydney to get jealous."

"You're the one supervising my amazing work with the children this week?" he changed the subject.

I tried my best not to analyze the suspicion that he had held back from something more.

"Yep. It's my turn to make sure you don't inflict any serious damage. Do you know what you'll be doing?"

"Well, I don't want to give away too much, but first I was going to have everyone sit in a circle and share what car part they're most like and why. Then I was going to tie it into this big, meaningful metaphor about how the car needs all the parts to work, just like how in life all of us have to work together for us to get to where we're going."

He maintained a straight face throughout his bullshit answer. I smiled and shook my head.

"What?" his face finally broke in a smile. "Isn't that the type of shit you social workers like to tell people?" he laughed. "I'm being totally serious." He stared at me intently, like he was taking record of my eyes – I mean, I think he was because by now I knew the exact mixture of green and gold his eyes were.

"Really? And what car part are you most like?" I challenged. Our exchange was gravitating toward flirting – the fluttering in my gut was telling me so. My eyes refused to break contact with his.

"Uh," he paused to think of another bullshit answer. "Clearly I'm a piston."

"Oh, wow, a piston, huh?" I sarcastically marveled.

"Well, yeah." He inched closer to me with his eyes locked on mine and quietly said, "Without a piston, the car doesn't move forward. I have a way of making things progress."

He shifted his gaze briefly to my lips and then back to my eyes. My knees went weak and my brain started firing.

Holy shit. He's going to kiss me. I thought. Then I immediately started second-guessing.

Wait. No. Does he want to kiss me? What the hell is going on?

And then my unfailing awkwardness was triggered. I let out a guffaw, unable to maintain any semblance of composure, let alone the intense stare he had initiated.

I was now laughing at him.

"You're laughing, but I was also going to have them make collages of their spirit car part." he continued to entertain me with his dry tone. He shook his head. "It is so like a catalytic converter to not be open to artistic expression."

He kept me laughing. I felt myself relax – he had to have been messing with me this whole time. How embarrassing would it have been if I had actually leaned in?

"Glad my ideas are so amusing to you."

"Sorry," I apologized between chuckles.

"No, no; don't be," he said as I quieted down. "You have a nice laugh." He wasn't looking at me anymore. "I like it."

There was a silence as the sincerity of his tone sunk in. He looked up at me. The perplexing nature of the whole situation resurfaced in my mind. Being around him felt comfortable, but I knew it was supposed to be because...because...

Ethan.

There he was, walking toward us.

I felt my smile disappear. Immediately, I stood up.

Thomas looked over to see what had made me stand.

"Hey," I exclaimed with a smile, trying to sound excited, but knowing there was a hint of confusion in my tone. "What are you doing here?"

I felt like it was a legitimate question.

"I came back early, hoping I could take you to lunch," Ethan explained, keeping a good five feet away from us.

Despite wearing jeans with his red jacket and a Gonzaga t-shirt underneath, Ethan still gave off a vibe of formality. I held back from hugging him. But maybe I should have. Maybe not hugging him made me look like I had been caught doing something wrong.

"Oh, I just ate," I said, hoping I sounded disappointed. "And I have to get back to work in about fifteen minutes."

"I see," he sighed. Then finally he looked over at Thomas.

"We've met before," Ethan announced, holding out his hand. "Thomas, right?"

Thomas wiped his hand on his jeans before shaking Ethan's hand. "Yeah, good to see you again," he said cordially.

Ugh, this is awkward. I thought. *Is this awkward? Maybe I'm the only one who finds it awkward. Just because no one is talking, that doesn't mean it's awkward, right? Just because I totally thought Thomas was going to kiss me less than a minute ago, that doesn't mean I cheated and got caught, right? Is Ethan wondering why Thomas is here? Should I explain it? It's not like we're doing anything wrong. Like he said, he's just helping out a friend. We're friends. Why is Ethan still standing so far away? Why is nobody saying anything?*

Luckily, before I could start spewing any of this nervous babble out loud, Ethan finally spoke.

"So, Maura tells me you're volunteering here and teaching the kids how to work on cars?"

"Yep," Thomas said simply, grabbing the fast food bag filled with paper wrappers.

He stood up and locked the tailgate. He didn't offer anything else. Why was Thomas making this so difficult on Ethan, who was being perfectly polite?

"Well, that's really cool," Ethan commended.

Thomas nodded and then turned to me.

"I think I'm going to head over to the garage and get some things ready for Wednesday," he announced.

"Sydney can unlock it for you," I said.

He nodded and made his way toward the main building. I turned to Ethan, wondering what his reaction was going to be now that we were alone. I was surprised to see him smiling at me.

"So, am I going to get a hug?" He held out his arms.

I walked over and embraced him and he kissed my forehead. He continued to hold me, which felt nice. Slowly, I felt my guilt melt away.

"I probably should have texted this morning to let you know I wanted to take you lunch, but it was early and I wanted to surprise you. I thought it would be a good way to make up for not calling or texting you yesterday."

He pulled away to look at my face but kept his hands resting on my arms. His face turned serious when he looked into my eyes. "I'm really sorry about that. We were at my sister's in the country, and there was no reception out there, so I didn't even get your message until after eleven."

I shrugged. Now that I knew the reason for his lack of response, it seemed like a silly thing to get upset about. Especially since I had already prepared myself for him breaking up with me. That was probably why my brain had overanalyzed the whole interaction with Thomas; I was trying to make myself feel better in anticipation of Ethan breaking up with me.

"Don't worry about it. I figured you were busy," I said breezily.

Thank God that man will never know what goes on inside my head.

"Well, thank you for understanding." He stared at me as if there was something more.

"What?" I asked.

"Nothing," he smiled. "I just missed you. Can I still see you tonight?"

I nodded.

"Okay, I'll bring you dinner around six. I'll let you get back to work. Have a good day."

He leaned in and kissed me quickly on the lips before walking back to his car. I ordered myself to go back to the office and stay clear of the garage for the rest of the afternoon. My brain didn't need any extra interactions with Thomas to overanalyze.

———

As promised, Ethan showed up at my apartment that night with dinner. It was the first time he had actually stepped inside. I was a little self-conscious about my apartment after seeing his upscale place with the amazing view, but he was polite enough not to make any comparisons out loud. I stopped myself from showing off my fabulous view of the grocery store parking lot across the street – the obvious contrast would have been funny, but I think the joke would have been lost on him. My brain started to spiral while I got out plates.

You don't know how to make your boyfriend laugh. That's weird. You should know how to do that if he's ready to introduce you to his family.

Ethan served up the Italian take-out he had brought while I silently argued with myself.

That's a stupid standard, Maura. Shut up and eat your food.

I took a large bite of pasta in the most ladylike way I could muster. Ethan did have good taste when it came to restaurants... and wasn't food more necessary to survival than laughter? Food and shelter were at the base of Maslow's hierarchy of need – you couldn't say that about humor. And we were having a very nice conversation without any laughter at all.

That's right. Laughing with someone is not the sign of a mature relationship. Sitting together and eating twenty dollar pasta while you listen to him share about his grandpa having cancer is...not that you need his grandpa to have cancer in order to have a substantial relationship.

"So, how was your Easter with your family down in Olympia?" he asked just as I put a meatball in my mouth.

I started to chew, allowing myself time to contemplate the reper-cussions of telling the truth or lying. Lying would only to lead to more trouble and also validate that I had done something wrong.

"Actually," I opened with a casual tone, "I didn't end up going to Olympia. I stayed here."

He gave me a look of curiosity.

"Really?" He looked down at his ravioli. "I thought you had been missing them?"

I nodded, remembering that was what I had told him to get out of meeting his family.

"You know, I do, I just ended up having all this work to catch up on and the thought of spending all of Sunday in Olympia really started to stress me out. I just decided to stay here."

"So you spent the day alone?" he asked with genuine sympathy.

I paused. Integrity won out.

"No, I actually ended up having dinner with the O'Hollarens."

I took a drink of water and looked away, hoping Ethan's response would be, 'Oh that's nice. Do you want dessert?'

His silence forced me to look across the table at him.

"So, Thomas' family?"

"Mmmhmm," I nodded and toyed with the pasta on my plate, failing to look nonchalant. Maybe using simple sounds instead of full words would help.

"Maura?'

"Hmm?"

"Exactly how good of friends are you with Thomas?"

"Oh, not that good."

"So how often do you hang out with him?"

"Well, he's been at my work a few times since the program started...and we've gone on a couple runs together." *And the one night I spent at his house comforting him about all of his unprocessed rela-tionship issues with his dead father. No biggie.*

"And you go to mass together and spend holidays together," he added. "Oh, and of course, weekday lunches in your work park-ing lot, which you looked to be thoroughly enjoying today until I showed up." He finally called me out for what I had suspected he'd observed that afternoon.

"Well, he only recently moved back to Seattle after his dad died in January. He didn't really know anybody, so we started hanging out occasionally. Why? Is that a problem?" I asked innocently, trying to turn the tables. Were we about to have our first fight?

"No," he said evenly. "I would never tell you who you can and can't hang out with." He was too smart for my deflection. "Although, I don't really think men and women can be close friends when they're dating other people."

He waited to see if I would argue with him.

"After his dad died, I just felt like he probably needed someone to talk to," I said honestly.

"And you're probably right, and I don't doubt that you have the noblest of intentions," he assured. "But Maura, you have to understand, men think differently than women."

When I didn't respond, he continued with his unintentional patronizing. "Now, I know you think you're just doing the right thing by being friendly – and even concerned by his unfortunate loss – but you have to trust me when I tell you that a lot of guys, especially a guy like that, are looking to take any advantage when it comes to a girl like you, and it's very easy for them to misread your friendliness as an invitation to accept their advances."

My first instinct was to brush off Ethan's lecture as ludicrous, but Thomas' expression and tone of voice from that afternoon replayed in my head. Guilt settled firmly into my gut as I acknowledged that I had probably encouraged the attention.

"Obviously you're going to see him at work, and by all means if you want to invite him to come to young adult things to meet more people that's great, but–"

"You would prefer that I not spend as much time with him alone," I finished his sentence.

My tone was level and I wasn't feeling any heightened emotion. I knew my friendship with Thomas was not a life-long one that needed to be preserved at the cost of one day getting married to someone like Ethan. But after what Thomas had shared with me that afternoon, I felt a pang of remorse that I was able to be so detached at the prospect of pulling back from our friendship.

"What I'm saying is," Ethan paused, trying to find the right words to clarify. "It's very simple, Maura: do you see this ending in marriage, or not?" he asked matter-of-factly.

He was right to be so blunt about it. Really, this is what I had been praying and hoping for for two years – to find a guy who was willing to seriously commit and not use vocational discernment as an excuse for not wanting to settle down. I had no right to sit here and be picky because he didn't laugh at my jokes or kiss me enough.

"Look, I'm not asking you to marry me right now," he clarified. "But if you already know that you don't want to marry me, I need to know now. I'm twenty-nine. I don't want to waste any more time. And neither should you. I need to know if you are in this with me."

Admittedly, his confidence was appealing. I was speechless, which is kind of a difficult reaction to get from me. Inside, my heart was screaming for a sign from God. If this really was the man I was supposed to marry, He could give me some sort of message that I was on the right path.

But when Ethan continued to look at me expectantly and no angel appeared or trumpet sounded, I relied on logic. Ethan embodied all the characteristics I had envisioned in my potential spouse. It was stupid to let my insecurities about not being devout enough for him get in the way of something – I mean some*one* – I had always wanted. I was letting my desire to help Thomas get in the way of what I truly needed, and Ethan was right to call me on it.

"Maura?"

My train of thought had left him hanging.

I blinked up into his eyes. They were steady and predictable.

How nice it will be to finally know how the story ends, I thought as I held his gaze.

"Yes," I said, doing my best to mirror the steadfastness he presented. "Yes, I see this ending in marriage."

A smile spread across his face as he reached across the table and intertwined his hands with mine.

"You have no idea how happy I am to hear you say that," he said.

I smiled, proud like a kid who chose homework over TV.

"I feel really good knowing that there won't be any more distractions getting in the way of where we are heading," he concluded.

I nodded back at Ethan and put my friendship with Thomas behind me. While caring for lost causes like him seemed to be a specialty of mine, I was not going to let that tendency sabotage my chance to marry a man I truly believed I could be happy with... eventually.